The
HIDDEN RIVER

The
HIDDEN RIVER

STORM JAMESON

HARPER & BROTHERS PUBLISHERS
NEW YORK

Library of Congress catalog card number: 54-12186

For
CARL AND CAROL BRANDT
the true parents of this book
with love and respect

The
HIDDEN RIVER

CHAPTER I

I SHALL LEAVE THE HOUSE TOMORROW morning."

Jean Monnerie had no need to turn his head to look at the speaker, to see the expression, of refusal, of implacability, hardening her face. But he turned. It was, he knew well, useless to plead, but he pleaded—with a half-smiling gentleness. As always, anger struck years off this woman's age; her narrow upright back appeared suppler, her throat rounder, the delicacy of her face less sharp.

"I see no reason why you should go away, Cousin Marie. I wish you'd think again."

"No." The light voice and the quick light movement of a hand were final. "No, I prefer to go."

Monnerie turned back to his window. There were four windows in this room: one faced west, the other three due south, opening like doors directly on the rough lawn which sloped gently to the Loire. All, except the west window, were shuttered against the strong July heat: through this single opening the rays piercing a green sun blind filled the room with a subdued light, half-watery shadow. Standing with one shoulder outside, he could see between willows as straight and supple as Cousin Marie's back a long sandbank and beyond it a second, narrower and paler: like a tress of blond hair, the river twisted round them.

"You haven't forgotten that Adam Hartley will be here this evening?"

"Ah," she cried, exasperated, "nowadays we can't even keep our shames to ourselves. Some wretched outsider must force himself in, staring and interfering."

"You wanted to see him," he reminded her.

"Yes, I know. If only he would have the kindness to leave again at once. But he won't, he'll be hanging about for days."

Monnerie lifted his hand. "When I tell him what has happened he'll offer to go away. . . . I shan't let him, it would be absurd."

"Do as you like, Jean." She reached the door so quickly, moving as suddenly as a girl, that he could only watch her go. Over her shoulder she said, with a gleam of amusement, "I've never met a civilised foreigner, just as I have never known a stupid Frenchman, but I'm convinced that both animals exist."

Jean Monnerie was smiling. You were never sure with her: at her unhappiest she might fly off into mockery or laugh at herself, as if something in her, forgetting that it ought to have aged, could not help mocking the old.

Alone, he gave a moment's thought to the man he was expecting. This is not the first time, he thought. But the first had been very different. . . . With two of his small group he had waited in the thicker darkness of the pines at the edge of the field for the aeroplane promised, after two failures, for tonight. An hour passed, two hours, three. The summer night was only his listening. Very soon now the protective darkness would start to fray out at the edges, becoming opaque, dissolving, thinning to a fine mist drawn rapidly into the treacherous sky. Between one breath and the next, his ear picked up that vibration of the air which precedes the sound of the engine, then the sound, coming nearer, circling, veering off: across the black sky and inside Monnerie's skull a pen traced ominously tense lines. The plane circled once more and went off; he started to limp across the fields towards where he supposed its passenger had been dropped. When—in the kitchen of the little schoolhouse—he saw Hartley for the first time clearly, he almost laughed. If ever, he said to himself, I saw "the English captain" of any and every war, in any century, here he is. The long jaw and pointed chin—an oddly sorrowful line, contradicted by the long straight aggressive nose and fine mouth—the flatness and delicacy of the cheekbones, the pale grey eyes, formed exactly the type as Monnerie, reading history as a schoolboy, had imagined it. When he knew Hartley better he discovered that the type is less simple than his fixed idea of it, but the image of "the English captain" persisted. . . .

He turned as the door opened. The girl who came in, wearing a workman's faded blue cotton trousers, rolled to the knee, and a thin blouse, had the nervous step and energy of a graceful young animal. Her long sunburned legs were as delicate as a crane's; a fine nearly invisible down had the same effect as bloom on the skin of grapes.

Monnerie's face changed. "Ah, Elizabeth. I was just coming to find you."

Elizabeth smiled at him. She had a wide charmingly firm mouth, and her smile showed strong white teeth, splendid teeth. "I'm not lost."

"Has Cousin Marie warned you that she's going away tomorrow?"

"Yes, she told me. She's sent for old Madame Bonet to bring her rheumatism and her red wig here to keep an eye on us. It's ridiculous. Why need she go?"

"I can't argue with her about it. But just now it's an infernal nuisance."

The girl made one of her quick gestures. "When will he be here?"

"Uncle Daniel? The day after tomorrow—probably very late in the evening. That's all they say in the letter."

She frowned, hesitated, and said,

"I meant Captain Hartley."

"Oh, any minute." The amused glance he turned on her hid an impulse to take her in his arms. "Aren't you going to change before he comes?"

"No, I'm not." She threw herself into an armchair in the attitude Cousin Marie detested and always scolded, one leg across the other: a wing of her magnificent hair, dark and springing, fell over her cheek. "Why should I take trouble for him? Must I?"

He answered placidly, "You must do as you like. For my money you look very fine as you are. But since you always do wear a dress in the evening . . ."

The girl tapped her foot impatiently. "You want your friend to find us very respectable. Why?"

Monnerie shook his head. "No. But I warn you—you'll be told what Cousin Marie thinks of you, even in front of a guest."

He crossed the room and leaned over the back of her chair, taking her face between his hands and tilting it gently back. Without awkwardness or haste, she slipped from his hold, and stood up, smiling.

"Dear Jean, of course I'm going to dress. I'm not a savage, I don't mean to disgrace you." With the back of a hand she lifted the weight of hair off her neck. "I'm so hot. Can't we open the shutters now? It's after five, and there's no air at all in this room."

Without waiting for his answer, she ran to the nearest window and flung it open. Light rushed into the room: Monnerie closed his eyes for a second, opening them again at once to watch her. When he was tired, the whole expression of his face came from his heavy eyelids and from the fold of irony at their outer edge—an irony without bitterness, smiling, indulgent.

Elizabeth went on talking lightly over her shoulder.

"Why I'm so hot is because Cousin Marie sent me to the station to make certain of the time of her train tomorrow."

. . . Useless to try to telephone: the stationmaster was stone deaf, and refused to allow anyone else to lay a finger on the telephone in his office. A question of prestige. That the village station was cut off from the rest of the country disturbed no one. What is time for but to spend? . . . "I called at the garage on my way back and asked when they were going to have the car mended. Maurice said that he's remaking the engine, and then, if we fit four new wheels to her and a new body, we shall have a respectable car, with decent morals."

Jean laughed. "A couple of wheels, perhaps. For her new body she must wait for the resurrection, like the rest of us."

"That's exactly what I told Maurice," she said absently. She looked at his face with what might have been a shadow of remorse, and something of the frankness and curiosity of a child. "Jean—you're tired. Does your leg hurt?"

"No."

"Then what it it?" she asked, frowning. "No, I can guess. Cousin Marie has been making one of her superb scenes."

Monnerie brushed this away. "No. And she has some right to her scenes, don't forget." He spoke without impatience, with amused indifference.

The girl said fiercely, "She has no right to add to your burdens, you have enough . . . you're working yourself to death." She went on more lightly, but with a certain defiance, "Captain Hartley will think it very strange if she goes away the moment he comes."

Jean smiled. "You don't remember him—if you believe he'll think about it at all."

"Oh, yes, I do! I remember him very clearly." Turning away, she looked with clear disapproval at the roses in a bowl, and began to pull them about, her back to Monnerie. "He'll have forgotten me, of course. I was much younger—and he had more important things on his mind. . . . I've altered a great deal."

No, not a great deal, he thought. You're still—he tried to find the word—not set. Unpredictable. At one minute a self-willed healthily restless child, in the next, without the least effort, a sensible but not tiresomely sensible young woman, surprisingly beautiful and, with her air of living in a friendly world, charming. It is not the same thing.

"I don't remember you as you were six years ago. I don't even remember you as you were yesterday or this morning; when you come into the room you send all the others flying." She did not answer. He went over to her and took her a little roughly in his arms. "But in fact you're still—in spite of everything that has happened in the last six years—a little girl. You stiffen yourself like one when I take hold of you."

She lifted her hand and touched his face. "I'm sorry. I don't mean to, I don't want to. I'm an idiot."

Monnerie half closed his eyes. "I love you beyond any words."

Smiling at him she said, "Dear Jean—and I love you, you know."

His hands on her shoulders, he held her away from him. "Perhaps," he said calmly. "Since you tell me, I believe you—but you make it difficult. Why—if you really mean what you say—did you want to wait a year before marrying? It's—let's say absurd, but there are harsher things I could call it. Are you afraid of me? Tell me—what are you afraid of?" The glance he gave her under his heavy eyelids was ironically frank. "If something about me—" he hesitated briefly— "bores you, tell me. I can't, you know, make love to a schoolgirl." He took his hands from her and said gently, "Why not treat me as if I were a friend, the friend that—living cut off here—you haven't got—and tell me the real reason why you put our marriage off?"

She was still smiling. "I don't know."

"Is that true?"

"I know one thing," she said impulsively. "I'm behaving

badly. Wait just another month—no, two months—
September."

"September," Monnerie repeated. His voice had an in-
flection of mockery: but it was not the girl he was mocking.
"I'm satisfied with that. But are you sure this time? Be sure."

"I am." A look of stubborn candour came over her face.
"I'll do my best, Jean. I promise. We'll be happy—as we
are now."

"You shall be happy," he said, with difficulty. "This isn't
happiness—it isn't even the beginning."

For less than a moment he had the weight of her body
against his own: his hands moved from her shoulders to
the slight hollow between the bone of her thigh and the
knee. She drew back.

"I think—yes, I'm sure I hear a car." ·

He lifted his head, listening. "Yes."

He released her and went out, walking with the long rapid
stride which almost got the better of his limp.

Alone, the girl stood still. The colour that had rushed
into her cheeks when she heard the car disappeared, leaving
her pale. She lifted her head, her forehead wrinkled by the
effort she was making to seem calm. Her body had become
rigid; an expression at once childish and driven hardened
her face into a look of fear—but there was something else in
it besides fear: a strange half-smiling excitement. Catching
sight of herself in one of the two cloudy blackened mirrors
facing the windows she looked hurriedly away. "No, I'm
an idiot, a fright," she said aloud. "Nothing is going to
happen, nothing. What could possibly happen?" She stretched
her arms out and, hearing steps and voices, Jean's and
another, in the hall, sprang through a window into the
garden and out of sight.

CHAPTER 2

W HEN, IN THE EARLY MORNING, HE DROVE
his car off the night ferry, Adam Hartley felt everything
an exile feels on his way home—without the exile's secret
fear of disappointment. This was his first visit since 1944—
five years. Five years too many, he thought, with a crazy
excitement. It did not show in his face. He had always been
reluctant to give himself away; what now, at thirty-two,
was a comfortable habit, had begun as the defense of an intelligent child against the mockery of his domineering mother.
She loved him, and he knew it, as jealously as she felt everything, but she could not keep her tongue off him. She had
died when he was fourteen. Separated, as long as he could
remember, from his father, she did what she could to make
her son as savagely unsociable as herself. That she had not
succeeded was a triumph of nature—his or that of the
father she persisted in teaching him to be ashamed of—
over art. His father was a north-country industrialist, and
in her least guarded rages she would tell the boy: I married
into the gutter. Or: I married a dull fool. In fact, as during
the one week he spent with his father the boy discovered,
she had married a man of wide experience, cultivated, indifferent, and concealing, under the Yorkshireman's placid
and stubborn air, the eccentricity and freakishly violent
temper of the north.

His mother came of an old moderately distinguished
family. To punish herself for the failure of her marriage,

8

she cut herself off from it completely. She lived, and forced
on her son, a life without family or friends. As a child he
was overgrown and clumsy, which gave her her chances,
rarely missed, to make cruel fun of him, and though he had
learned to ride well, to fence, to dance, he still thought of
himself as awkward. For much the same reasons he under-
estimated his intelligence, which was considerable. He
became used from childhood to dismiss his successes as
accidental and to take responsibility only for failures. These
for the most part happened entirely in himself, and in the
light of a judgment severer than any his mother had turned
on him. His friends knew an active hard-working competent man, who in a few years had turned a stiff-jointed
old firm of agricultural engineers into a modern and lively
one. He was respected, his advice asked, envied a little.
He enjoyed his life. He liked a great many people: he
liked women easily—he was not an anchorite. Was it his
pleasure in living and working hard that kept him from
marrying one of them? Or a mistrust so deep that he
scarcely knew it existed? He never thought about it.

He would have been astonished, vexed, if he had been
told that more than one unfriendly person had detected in
him under, a long way under, his air of simplicity and
friendliness, a possibly inherited habit of contempt. And
in the end of indifference. . . .

With every mile he drove into France his happiness grew
until it became an immense liberation. A man just out of
prison, he thought, must feel exactly this when he begins his
first night of freedom. Heaven knows there is nothing
beautiful about this part of northern France, nothing to
induce ecstasy, yet here he was, looking at everything with
an infatuated smile, feeling alive as he had not felt for years.
He was so happy that he began to be sceptical, and tried to
prick the bubble by reflecting on it. . . . Why the devil
am I always happy in France? I don't particularly like the
French, politically they stink, their intellectuals take a pride

in being dangerously ignorant about other countries, and while it's true that a good Frenchman, whether he happens to be a baker or a distinguished scholar, is the best of men, a miracle of goodness, a lay saint, in almost all the others, from your narrowly bred aristocrat, your most subtle intellectual, to your Paris-born concierge, there exists a grasping suspicious peasant—they caught it from the Romans, who made a more lasting mark on them than on us. And yet—yet what? The truth is that they are the most human of all civilised peoples, the most firmly seated in their own nature. Something, some warmth from the Mediterranean, mother of civilisation, penetrates as far as the Loire and even north of it. Even where I am now. . . . He glanced joyously into the courtyard, filthy, oozing filth, of an ugly farm. In the now blinding sun an old woman in a black dress crossed it, bent double under the weight of two pails; behind her, a skinny barefoot child, dragging a pitchfork longer than herself. . . . The oldest of the family and the youngest, Hartley thought. And both will work with this patience until the last moment. *O bonne France invincible,* and all that. But those two are nearly animals. . . . He had lost the thread: groping for it, he thought: No, no, the truth is that we have yearned for France ever since we were thrown out. If the French don't yearn for us—and they don't—so much the worse for us both. No redemption for our old whore of a Europe short of Anglo-French union, the two loyalties, the two kinds of courage and humour indissolubly married and the house set finally in order.

Impossible, in this heat, to think. With relief, he dropped it, and gave himself up to the pleasure of letting the sun feel through his shirt for his bones, dissolving in them the acids of an English winter. He was beginning to feel hungry.

It was after twelve o'clock. He had reached another village—like the last, nameless, and dusty and unlovely: a deserted street between flat scrofulous houses, shuttered against the heat. A yard or two ahead he saw a small café

Café Central—centre of what, my God?—as dirty and unat-tractive as every other place. He decided to risk it, and pulled up. Inside, a long low room with a bar counter at one end and a few trestle tables. Only one was occupied, by five workmen who must eat here every day. While he hesitated, feeling that he was an intruder, a substantial dignified woman came from the kitchen and greeted him civilly. He asked her if he might have an omelette.

"But why not?"

In less than ten minutes he had it, and salad and a carafe of thin red wine. It was all admirable. And fed more than his bodily hunger. He ate and drank France—a communion meal, a benediction. While he ate he was turning over in his head the phrases he would use to thank the woman for her excellent omelette. But before he finished eating she walked rapidly past him, shopping bag on her arm, and he was left with his friendliness on his hands. Her husband had come out of the kitchen and was behind the bar: he looked a sick man, he was tall, dark, with a fine forehead and sunken cheeks—except that his eyes were as clear as a child's he might have been any distinguished French writer. Impulsively, after he had paid the young girl who served him, Hartley walked the length of the room and held his hand across the counter.

"Goodbye, and thank you very much," he said warmly.

For less than a second the Frenchman stared curiously at the big strongly built foreigner, noting his long jaw and innocent-seeming eyes; then, with a surprised pleasure, shook his hand, setting down the tumbler he had been polishing, and came round the bar to walk to the door with this friendly customer.

"Ah, you drive a French car," he exclaimed, looking at the shabby Citroen.

"From before the war," answered Hartley.

"Yes, I can see that. But—you know what they say—the best stock from an old pot. It's a good engine."

"None better," Hartley said gaily. "Goodbye."
"Goodbye, goodbye. A happy journey."

Towards eight that evening he reached the town of V——,
where he meant to stay the night. Narrow streets were giving
up the day's heat, heavy with the smells drawn out of
gutters and low dark rooms, crossed here and there by the
sharper scent of chopped herbs. In the middle of the town
a big unpaved square, the earth baked iron-hard, had drawn
round itself houses which had nothing in common except
age and their air of haggard decency. One of them was
the hotel. To his surprise every room was taken except an
attic he reached out of breath: the stairs were almost per-
pendicular. It was dark, airless, clean—that is, every day
for centuries the dust had been polished hard into the bare
boards. The proprietress, an elderly woman, was taciturn
and unfriendly, but his happiness was proof against any
snubbing. He washed off a little of his sweat in a basinful
of cold water, ate an excellent dinner of mullet and veal,
then went out and sat at one of two small iron tables taking
up most of the narrow pavement outside the hotel. It was
nearly dusk, the square and the streets entering it were
empty; the old buildings leaned their heads together sleepily.

He sat with his back to an open door which led by a short
passage to the room, little larger than a cupboard, where
Mme. Bouscat kept a hostile eye on servants and clients
alike. She was in there now, talking in a voice as harsh as
a rusty key—harsh and strangely cajoling. Hartley began
to listen. Suddenly she raised it, and he heard,

"My poor Germaine, I swear to you that you are not to
blame. What has happened is iniquitous, shameful, cruel.
You must, you certainly must appeal, and if there is any
justice left in this world you'll be cleared. Don't worry."

What Germaine said he could not hear, her words were
distorted by tears and a querulous dragging exhaustion.

"But, my poor old Germaine, don't I tell you that it is

not your fault! Not even I could have mastered Angélique, she breeds of her father, and the Pilons are all good-for-nothings. If you had thrashed her when she was a child—but you were too Christian and soft." The tenderness vanished from her ugly voice. "I'll tell you something else. Never, never again, so long as I have a breath in my body, shall that woman or her sister or any of hers set foot in this house. Never, Germaine, never."

The waiter, a young man, had come out with Hartley's coffee and brandy: he set them down and stood listening. At this moment, as if she had just noticed it was open, Mme. Bouscat slammed the door of her room. Hartley looked at the waiter.

"What was it all about?"

The man hesitated. He gave way to his sense that the Englishman was a decent and sympathetic character. "It's quite a story," he said softly. "Our patronne's sister, who is a widow, has a daughter, a young tart"—the word he used was *drôlesse*—"born it, if you ask me. You should have seen her when she was only eight or nine, waving her bottom. She ran away at sixteen and went to Dreux. The next year—it was '41—she took up with a German in the Gestapo, and as if that wasn't enough, she got a lad she'd known all her life arrested and packed off to a camp. He died there. Naturally, after the war, she was sentenced to death, but the sentence was changed to life imprisonment. And now the poor lad's mother has been suing widow Pilon for damages for her son's death, because, says she, if the girl had been brought up decently, she wouldn't have taken to bad ways. Therefore, her mother is responsible. D'you see?"

"Good God——" Hartley began.

"What's more," the man interrupted with a joyously youthful smile, "yesterday the court agreed with her. Her daughter's morals have cost Madame Germaine Pilon nine hundred thousand francs in damages and costs. How's that for justice?"

Hartley was too shocked to be tactful. All these years after the war, to find a hatred still bitter enough to strike at the wretched girl's mother. "Justice? It's entirely unjust," he retorted. "Punish the criminal if you like—why not? But why torment her mother?"

The waiter made a gesture half soothing, half amused.

"Oh, as to that—if your dog attacks a child you are responsible. All the more so if you let loose on the world a daughter who turns out to be rotten and denounces people to the Gestapo. Besides, it cost the lad's mother more to rear him than she'll collect in damages. She's still out of pocket . . . Do you need anything more? Another brandy?"

Hartley shook his head. He sat for a time in the growing darkness, trying to recover his feeling of contentment and ease. We come here, he thought, we drive through these villages and little towns and look admiringly at these old strong shabby houses, without having the faintest idea what goes on behind the shutters, or what poisons are still working. . . . For the first time it struck him that there was something secretive and unyielding in the very look of the town, with its gutter-like streets and yellow peeling walls.

Swallowing the last drops of his brandy, he got up and went inside. As he passed Mme. Bouscat's door he heard her voice murmuring on and on, with its strange rasping tenderness, as if she were trying to get a child to sleep.

In his brass bed with its very old thin mattress, he fell instantly asleep.

He was wakened by voices and the sharp tapping outside of—was it hammers? Glancing at his watch he saw that it was not yet four o'clock. To see through the window squeezed into the few inches of wall below the steep roof, he had to crouch on the floor. All over the square stalls were going up for a market. He watched a child run out of the hotel yard with a jug of water and pour it carefully in four places, enough water to soften the earth so that his father could drive home his poles. A young woman flaunting cotton petticoats and a wide hat staggered under bales of calico between her cart and a stall already set up. In the clear light without sun Hartley could see the swell of muscles in her neck and arms, and the child's anklebones sticking through his dark skin.

He went back to bed, and in spite of the noise and the powerful excitement springing at him from the market, slept. Four hours later, when he was drinking his coffee at the table on the pavement, the whole square throbbed and chattered like a circus. In the hot sun, women's skirts, voices, cries of excited children, and the smell of ripe fruit and dust, blended and flew apart again, like the opening and shutting of a bright fan. Every face, from the child being cuffed for fingering a peach to the decrepit old boy nursing a white rabbit as large as a terrier, gave out the same flash of gaiety, nervous energy, greed, fervour—and, yes, enjoyment. They worked with a fearful single-mindedness, as children play. One thing struck Hartley. The silent rather sinister square of the night before had vanished, whisked off by the score of hands working to fling together this enchanting pandemonium. All his disturbance and discomfort when he sat here alone now seemed ridiculous, needless.

Mme. Bouscat, too, when he paid his bill, was calm and less hostile. Her amiability might be only a matter of business, but he responded eagerly. Too eagerly. She despised him. . . . There was no sign of Germaine.

Strolling about the market, he bought cheese, bread, peaches, a bottle of wine, and set off. About noon he stopped in the shade of a little wood to eat. The wine was stronger than he had expected; his head swam and his eyelids felt leaden. Lying down under the trees, he slept. He woke sober, with an empty head. He could hear a curious sound, like the humming of a small dynamo. He walked through the trees, away from the road, and came on a child, a boy, crouching low over a reedy pool; he had launched a paper boat and was poking it with a stick and humming loudly. Glancing at Hartley through eyelashes like the neck feathers of a fledgling blackbird, he said with an adult politeness, "These are private tests. Please leave at once!" Hartley took himself off.

The road now ran perfectly straight, down, up, down again, up, without a hint of a curve, mile after mile. There were trees on both sides, immense poplars, pines, acacias, walnuts, their shadows curled tightly round their feet; the road was a strip of white-hot light, blinding, dusty, with only now and then a breath, a sharp scent like the smell of raspberries, from the pines. That child and his boat, Hartley thought: it could have been me, except . . . He saw the thin ice-cold beck behind his mother's house on the northeast coast; it ran fast and swept all his boats to their death in a whirlpool between rocks. The August sun fell on his neck, but his fingers playing under the water were stiff and purple with cold. I couldn't have been happier, he thought— or more alone. . . . Since no one ever visted the house where his mother nursed her violent temper and her resentment against his absent father, no friends, no other child, the only human beings of his own age he saw were the village children: he could only stare, he was not allowed to speak to one of them. This solitude lasted until he was eleven, when he was sent away to school. . . . Is that, he wondered, why I have always been happiest alone?

Oh, nonsense, nonsense, he thought; I'm happiest when I can sit at a café table in the sun and watch people living with every part of their bodies and every throb of blood in their veins. Like this morning in V——. Abruptly he remembered the *drôlesse* and her crime—and the bitterness and hatred still working in the obscure prudent little town. But now he felt that his indignation had been naïve. What

would you expect of a community of peasants and trades-
men, but that they should run a debit account against the
sinner for years, and insist on being paid? Wouldn't it be
exactly the same in England? Of course it would, he told
himself drily. Exactly the same. Wouldn't common men and
women in any country be affected by four years of breathing
the same air with an invader who was also a sadistic brute?
. . . With his mania for exactitude, he corrected himself:
an invader whose mass included an unduly high proportion
of bestial human beings. . . .

When the war began, and he joined a local regiment, he
was twenty-two, and mortifyingly innocent. Even Dunkirk
did not teach him very much. A series of chances—except
that nothing is chance—and his uncommonly fluent French,
landed him for a time in Special Intelligence: from then,
from the first day of his first mission in occupied France,
he grew up. Enough at least to accept that resistance to a
tyrant involves more than courage. Some of the resisters
had the luck never to be asked for anything more than a
heroism praise cannot reach. But others, no less pure in
heart or clear in spirit, were forced to things which sickened
them and could be done only with strict disgust. Hartley
himself was driven to forbid an attempt to rescue a young
man, almost a boy, who had helped him loyally, knowing
quite well that he was sentencing him to be tortured. The
occupiers used a perverse, an unbelievable cruelty, with what
seemed nature. (It may be necessary, if you are occupying
a neighbor's house against his will, to keep a shrewd eye on
his movements, but need you torture him?) Could it be
helped that mistrust, cruelty, violence, lying, had to become the second nature of a dedicated resister? Hartley
learned that anything is possible. And that things which
are not humanly permissible have in some circumstances to be
permitted. No one who learns this lesson remains innocent.
If France stood in his mind for ease and a consoling warmth,

there was in it as well a bruised place which was just as much France. And just as deeply.

And, with everything else, he had come back to pay a debt.

As he drew near the Loire the excitement he was suppressing seemed likely to burst his veins. With an instinct to delay the moment of supreme pleasure, he drove slowly. But at last Saumur came in sight—the first houses and the first bridge, the island with its war-shattered streets, the second bridge. At its summer lowest, a few yards across of grey-green water, the river divided and divided again round its sandbanks. He walked with a heavily beating heart into the hotel and asked,

"Can you give me a bedroom looking on the Loire?"

The clerk hesitated, running a plump finger down her ledger.

"Yes, I have one," she said placidly.

He thanked her with the feeling that he had escaped a disaster.

Later, about half-past nine, he stood leaning on the stone parapet of the river, his back to a street and a square as noisy as any in France, hearing nothing except the faint sigh when the water brushed against the stones, and the voices of young men playing with a dog on the embankment below him. A few men were fishing, intent and rigid, silhouetted against the slowly darkening air. The sun had gone down: a bronzed smoky haze lay along the western horizon of the Loire, and bars of copper and dark amber were stretched just below the clear surface. Strangest of all, the arches of the bridge were completed, exactly completed, by their black velvety shadows, so that from where Hartley was standing he could look straight through this rectangle of stone and shadow to watch the flawlessly smooth water beyond the bridge fading from bronze to luminous grey. In the finely clouded sky trembled a crescent moon and a few modest stars. Bats flitted about the arches.

How alien, how senseless, had become his memories of hatred and bitterness. But what had roused them? Only the *drôlesse*, safely in prison. He glanced over his shoulder at the strolling chattering summer evening crowd, rather staid, certainly—Saumur is a staid town—but gay. . . . No, no, he thought, it's over, they've turned their backs on it, thank God.

For a few minutes longer he leaned against the parapet, letting his happiness flow quietly through him. Then he went in to bed.

The next morning when he looked from his window there was not a soul in sight—yes, one, a child crossing the bridge—not a vehicle of any sort. He remembered now that, still asleep, he had heard church bells: it was Sunday, that Sunday morning silence in France, through which, as through the colours on an obscure canvas, appear suddenly and vaguely the outlines of a much older, simpler and more traditional painting, placed there a century earlier by another hand. Under an immense pure sky the river, lying awake and perfectly still in the centre of its wide bed, gave back that light of the Loire valley which is never the same from one hour to the next, and unlike every other in the world for clarity and strength.

Monnerie was not expecting him before afternoon. He drove, dawdling, along that valley which seems all grace, all fineness, all measure—why did Stendhal despise it?—yet knows, in the stones of its old streets and the roots of its trees, everything about violence and treachery. The same joyous light had caressed victim and assassin as today fell over the lichenous slate roofs of old houses, the colour of a dry leaf, over willows plunging their roots into the sands of the Loire, over patient fishermen, over the doors of troglodyte houses burrowed in the chalky cliff.

He reached the house before six. On his one visit, in 1943, he had arrived at night and left at night, so that he saw it now for the first time. It was smaller than he had thought, a small manor house, strong and in a shabby way elegant, set back from the river on rising ground. From the road he drove into a courtyard: on one side a brown-roofed gallery sheltered carts and waggons, through an arch in the opposite wall he caught sight of a kitchen garden laid out with geometric strictness, espaliers of fruit, box-hedges.

For no reason at all, as he stopped his car, he felt a pang of dismay. Perhaps, he thought, it was a mistake to come. . . . His memories of Jean Monnerie were curiously sharp, almost physical. In the first place, Monnerie had been competent— an enormous relief to Hartley, who had suffered from the catastrophic enthusiasm of his first resisters. Often bitter-tongued, sometimes brutal, unquestionably honest, incorruptible, unsparing of himself, Monnerie dominated his group as much by his manner as by his greater experience and intelligence. Even to his voice. Monotonous, either biting or resonant, it gave off—very much as a wild animal gives off its peculiar smell—something puzzling and insinuating, which at first was disturbing but very quickly imposed itself, on Hartley as much as on the others. . . . It might all, he thought coldly, be an illusion created by the circumstances—of tension and danger. He hoped it was not. If he were going to discover that his friend was a small village landowner with a habit of giving orders, he would be absurdly disappointed.

He saw Monnerie coming towards him from the doorway, quickly.

CHAPTER 3

"YOU HAVEN'T CHANGED!"

"It's only six years," retorted Monnerie, "what did you expect? Come in."

The heavy body, still supple, hard generous mouth, involuntarily mocking glance, were familiar. And the voice . . . How old is he now? Hartley wondered. Thirty-nine? . . . He had been surprised when he first knew Monnerie to learn how comparatively young he was. He had seemed years older. Because of its animal perfection, his body must have been mature at any age, and always under his control—as was his quick mind. There was a trace of envy in Hartley's liking for the other man, but the liking was warm.

"What sort of a journey have you had? You must have a drink. Just a minute."

He went away, leaving Hartley to stare round a room he had not seen before. It had the modest splendour of panelled walls, thick sculptured beams, and old very heavy long-polished furniture. Better than these, beyond the dry grass of the lawn it had an immense reach of the Loire. At this hour the light seemed to be filled with an infinitely fine yellow pollen, living, translucent, warm. He was looking at it when Monnerie came back with bottles and wine glasses.

"Your health, my dear Adam," he said gaily, "I'm very glad you're here. We owed you something better in the way of hospitality than you got last time you were in this house."

21

"You weren't here then," said Hartley. "But you won't, let me tell you, be able to do more for me than your family did in '43."

Lifting his eyebrows, Monnerie looked at him with tart amusement. "What? All of it? In '43 this wasn't the safest house an Englishman could be in."

Hartley caught an accent of bitterness, or was it exasperation? "I was looked after very well. . . . I suppose Madame Regnier is here? How is she?"

With the same accent,

"Quite well. She's here at the moment—for the moment. She's going away tomorrow morning."

"Oh, is she? Lucky for me I didn't miss her. Half my reason for coming was to see her. The other——" He hesitated. This is hardly, he thought sharply, the moment.

Monnerie was looking at him with a lively curiosity. "The other . . .?"

Hartley gave way to temptation. The question on the end of his tongue had filled, obsessed, one corner of his mind for nearly six years.

"Did you find out—are you any nearer finding out who it was denounced Robert in '43?" He was conscious of a scandalous abruptness—in bad taste. He added hurriedly, "I made enquiries myself after the Liberation; I put our own people on to it, and at one moment I thought I'd got my hand on something. But the line went dead—like every other. I was never able to find out anything. Not a damned thing."

Monnerie had a trick of lowering his head and staring, from widely opened and prominent eyes, with penetrating irony. "Why did you bother about it?"

"Bother . . . ?"

Monnerie moved his hands. "What—if you had discovered the man—or woman—it could have been a woman—what did you propose to do? Hand him over—in your turn?"

Hartley did not answer. He was at once disconcerted and—why not admit it?—humiliated. Humiliated by finding

Monnerie against him. Disconcerted, profoundly, because—
unbelievable as no doubt it would be to Monnerie—he had
not, in thinking about it, gone beyond the moment when
he put his hands on the guilty man. If he had ideas of
vengeance it was of a personal vengeance, in his own hands.

"Probably not," he said at last. "I don't know. In any
case that can wait."

"You're an extraordinary fellow," Monnerie said. He
smiled.

"Not in the least!" He added slowly, "Your attitude—your
detachment—indifference—whatever you like—seems to me
a good deal more extraordinary."

Monnerie lifted his eyebrows over an inexpensive stare.
"After all—it's over. Past help."

Startled, almost shocked, Hartley said, "For one thing—
I've never been able to shake off the idea that I may have
been responsible. Or half responsible. I wanted—you can
imagine—to clear that up."

He was giving away no more than one of his motives.
The rest concerned only himself.

"Absurd!"

"Not at all. The day I saw Robert for the last time I
saw and talked to several other people. I may quite well have
dropped the wrong thing to the wrong man—who knows?"

"I know it's improbable—too improbable to be worth
thinking about, even for a moment. Forget it."

"Can you?"

The unconscious arrogance of his tone amused Monnerie.
"No." He paused. "But I haven't tried to find out who betrayed Robert," he said quietly.

"Why not?"

Monnerie shrugged his shoulders. "I'm not a politician."

"I'm sorry," Hartley said drily. "I don't understand."

"Of course not. It's hardly likely you would understand
that all you're still thinking of as treachery, heroism,
justice—and the rest of it"—he smiled slightly—"has become

part of the usual political gamble—same cards, same tricks, same men; the same furious chase after jobs, the same squalid rivalries between ministers, between generals, the same backstairs intrigues, the same corruption and assassinations, the same running abscess of eloquence—in politics, in literature—poisoning the country. . . . And even the first days—even the justice of the Liberation . . ." his smile became openly malicious—"I should hate to destroy your innocence by telling you too much. No, really, my dear Adam, I've had enough even of justice. I've turned my back. I do what I can to make one village—and my own few hectares of land —as decent, good-tempered and fruitful as possible. If everybody would do as much. . . ."

No, after all, he has changed, Adam said to himself. Merely politeness required that he should drop the thing at once. He felt a violent reluctance. Something in him rebelled against this—this abandonment of Robert Regnier, dead. A second, and nearly as unforgivable betrayal. . . . He was too honest not to admit that this was not all he felt: as well, there was his hatred of being defeated by a problem.

"My innocence, as you call it, understands why you want to turn your back. But why on Robert? He had nothing to do with politics. It's a personal matter. . . . No, I don't understand you. And in any case, you're wrong. You might have turned your back in 1940. You didn't. Then why now? Why now?"

"How sure you are that what *you* feel is right," Monnerie said, with a smile. "I can't help envying you."

"Well, forgive me," Adam said coolly, "I daresay you're wise. . . . It's strange—we've never, never once, seen things from the same side, yet we were able to act together without a hitch. This is the first time . . ."

"You're disappointed."

"No," Hartley lied.

"Yes. . . . Let me fill your glass." Turning to set the

bottle on the tray, he went on in a carelessly brusque voice, "I'm afraid you may find Madame Regnier rather upset."

"You mean she would rather not see me?" said Hartley. "I'm not surprised. I'll take myself off at once. I noticed a very decent-looking inn as I came through your village, I can put up there for a night——"

Monnerie cut him short. "It has nothing to do with you." He hesitated and said, "How much do you know about Cousin Marie?"

"Not a great deal."

"She's impulsive and quick-tempered—not at all easy. We're devoted to her—and she to us. She came here, with Robert, when I was twelve—after my mother and father had been killed in a car accident. François—my brother— was only a year old: he never called her anything but Mamma. I suppose she must have been about thirty; she had been a widow for two or three years. Now and then, for a split second, I can see her as she was then. She was extremely beautiful, a thinly made young woman, alive with a sort of mockery that never hurt—she was passionately gentle." He laughed. "She moved so quickly that for a long time my brother believed she flew up and down stairs."

"As I remember her in '43 she was still rather beautiful," Hartley said.

"Not as when she was young. She was enchanting then."

Hartley frowned. "Robert was her only child, wasn't he?"

"Yes. He was six when she brought him here. She used to speak of us as 'my three children.'" Monnerie had been smiling. His face changed abruptly; in a heavier voice he said, "But I ought to tell you what the trouble is——"

He stopped as the door opened behind them. Hartley turned, setting his glass down so hurriedly that he spilled part of the wine on the floor, and mopped at it uselessly before straightening himself to speak to Mme. Regnier. She was laughing at him.

"Please don't ruin your handkerchief, Captain Hartley, nothing can damage these floors. How are you? Are you very tired?"

"No, not at all," he said, adding ingenuously, "After all, I'm in France." Yes, he thought, she must have been beautiful. And still is. But it was a forbidding beauty, as if the slackness and softness of age were being kept at bay by a never-relaxed will: every angle was sharp, and on each sunken temple the yellowing skin looked as though it had been bruised. He felt sure it was will: he did not suspect her of vanity.

Cousin Marie's eyes gleamed. "Ah, I had forgotten how sentimental you are about us."

"Am I?" He looked at her with a friendly smile. "I have every reason to be grateful to France—to you especially."

"I don't want and I don't deserve your thanks," she said very drily. "You exaggerate. Anything I did for you was not meant for you personally. It was for the work you were doing. That was important. I had too few chances to help that."

Hartley was amused. How offensive and immodest of me to draw attention to myself, he thought. "At any rate, you'll allow me to thank you for letting me come here now."

She dismissed this with a quick movement of her hand. She had seated herself with her back to the windows. Pointing at a chair, she said peremptorily,

"Bring that in front of me where I can look at you. . . . Yes, I wanted to see you." In a slower thinner voice, she went on, "It was a month after you were here that my son was caught. You were the last friend who saw him alive. Tell me about it."

Although he had prepared for this moment Hartley felt himself growing hot. He wanted to tell her everything, but without hurting her; and she had made him feel clumsy.

"We were in Paris together—I was there only for two nights. I had to talk to a man who couldn't be seen except

in Paris, and I arranged to see Robert the same day—but
in the early morning." He saw himself leaving the room in
the rue de l'Abbé de l'épée where he had spent the night,
and walking down to the *quai* facing Notre Dame. There was
a thin white mist over the Seine. The cathedral seemed not
so much to be anchored on the opposite bank as riding
the blanched windless air above it. High over head the sky
promised warmth, promised—if it were not lying—a day
when nothing could go wrong. There were only workmen
in the streets. Impossible under this sky to remember that
Paris was a city occupied by the barbarians.

"Captain Hartley, I'm waiting," said Mme. Regnier.

"Forgive me—I'm sorry," he stammered. "I met Robert,
we had coffee and a glass of some sort of red wine, very
acid, in a workman's café. I got from him some details I
needed, about the man I was going to see. We decided
whereabouts in Orléans to meet next day, and the time—
six in the evening. Then Robert went off, and I—" he
broke off: she had no wish to hear about him. "Well—next
evening I waited for him in Orléans, at the place we'd
arranged—a café at the corner of the Quai Barentin and
some street or other, I forget the name. . . ." But he
remembered the trees on both sides of the *quai,* and sitting
looking between their light branches at the Loire—and the
growing sense in him of failure and disaster, everything
gone, empty—except for the crazy leap of his heart when a
quick dark young man walking a few yards away looked for
an instant like Robert. He could almost feel in his knees
the effort it had cost him to get up, pretend to hesitate, and
saunter off. Certain parts of his walk through Orléans to the
railway station were vague, others still nightmarishly clear:
he had crossed a small square with trees, then he was in
the noisy Place du Martroi, staring blindly as he passed it
at a hideous statue of Joan of Arc; after that, a long street
crowded with people—some of their faces scored in his
brain, the face of the young man drinking pernod at a table

on the pavement, the dangerous bestial face of an old woman. . . . "I waited for him until I was forced to leave." He gripped his hands. "The worst—as always—was that there was nothing I could do except warn two or three people."

"Of course not," Mme. Regnier said coldly. "What could you do? What could anyone have done?" She threw her head back. A cord leaped to the surface under the skin of her throat. "He came here after seeing you in Paris, you know—and spent that night here. The next day he went off to Orléans. And he was arrested that evening—probably on his way to you. . . . Tell me one thing, please. Did he—when he left you that morning in Paris, did he seem . . . unhappy?"

"No," Hartley said with energy, "far from it." He frowned, trying to find words to pass on to her his last sight of Robert Regnier, smiling, handsome, dazzlingly young, as if his body did not contain one single tired or worn-out cell. . . . If he could have found words for it he could as easily have explained the real, the profound reason why he had tried, with such absurd persistence, to find out who had betrayed him. What he had loved—this word at least was accurate— in Robert Regnier were all the qualities he felt lacking in himself: the spontaneity, the grace and energy of mind and spirit. Every time he remembered that this energy had been crushed out, brutally, he felt the same corrosive anger, the same pity: something in him contracted, like the hands of the dead contracting in the earth. . . . "You remember how he walked—with long steps," he said at last: "he went off like that, very gay, lifting his hand."

The lids fell for a moment over Mme. Regnier's eyes. "What was the last thing he said to you?"

"Something about this house . . . that we'd come here together after the war, and fish."

"He adored it," she said slowly. "And they took him, and

tortured him in a small basement—no window—they must have had the electric light on. When I think of it——"

Jean Monnerie interrupted her. "You shouldn't. It's not good."

She turned on him with a smiling anger. "Good—good? Yes, I know. You think it's absurd to tear away the silence stifling us, we ought to tread on it and press it down, press it over Robert's eyes, and hands. And on all the others. Torture is indecent—so don't look at it, shut your eyes, don't listen to their cries. Don't see . . . ah! It oughtn't to have happened, it was an aberration, a tiny flaw in our age of reason—and the polite, the sensible thing now is to forget it and go to sleep. No, I tell you. No one must sleep." She stopped, and said in a gentler voice, "I couldn't be so unkind to him."

Hartley looked away. He was desperately sorry for her, but he reflected that Jean, if he had to stand much of this, was unlucky. The lines from Monnerie's strongly arched nose and between his eyebrows had deepened in the last minute; he was listening with a heavy look of disapproval and tenderness. He said quietly,

"Robert isn't those last days. He's everything else you remember about him—his good looks, his courage."

"Yes, his courage," exclaimed Hartley. "Almost certainly I owe my life to the fact that he held his tongue. I came here to say that to you."

Mme. Regnier stood up. "He saved everyone but himself." She moved towards the door, stopped sharply and, turning her smooth head to look at Jean, said fiercely, "And you expect me to risk touching the fingers that touched others— in a chain of hands stretching back—and back—until they become the hands pressing the life out of my son. How ridiculous of you!"

She went out.

CHAPTER 4

THERE WAS A MOMENT'S SILENCE. HARTLEY kept his mouth shut because for all his pity he could not stop the thought jumping into his mind that she had no right to suffer in public. He looked stealthily at Monnerie—and felt that however horribly disturbed he was this man never ceased to judge: he pitied but he judged, coldly.

Monnerie caught his glance: if he smiled, it was less a smile than a flicker of his heavy eyelids. "I'll tell you all about it in a minute. But give me your glass." He filled it and his own. "Thank God for a wine you can go on drinking."

"I couldn't go on drinking this," said Hartley. He held his glass against the light; they were drinking a pale red wine, young and deceitful; it had traces of a salty roughness, and was stronger than he had thought. "I'm a little drunk, I think. It's very good. Is it yours?"

"It is. But it's not the best—I'm going to give you that later, at dinner."

"Then for heaven's sake don't give me any more now!"

Monnerie laughed at him. "Nonsense, you'll be sober again in ten minutes. What's more, our wines really clear your brain. Even when you can't walk straight you'll find you're thinking twice as well." He emptied his own glass and set it down. For a minute he prowled about the room, with the movements of a powerful animal pushing his way through undergrowth. At the moment he shared to the full his cousin's resentment. Why need he let a stranger, even a man he liked, into a family scandal?

He stood still in front of Hartley and spoke in a half-rueful half-ironical voice.

"Adam, you remember that my uncle was living in the house when you spent those five nights here in '43?"

With the feeling that something unpleasant was coming, Hartley said, "I didn't see him."

"Did you realise that he was very friendly with the German commander in Tours, General Otto Kettler?"

"Not at the time."

"But you heard later?"

How like them, Adam thought, to want to insist on it after all these years. And as if it mattered.

"Yes."

"They shared a passion for the seventeenth century, fishing, and very good burgundy," said Monnerie drily. "In short, completely above the battle."

Adam glanced at him. "Isn't it possible?"

"Not in our age of unreason—must we go on calling it reason? And not in this house. . . . My poor cousin likes to believe that Daniel is a monster and not, as he is, a common specimen."

If he had been completely sober, Hartley would have waited, with an air of attentive interest—perfectly real, so far as it went—for what might be coming. Since he was not sober, he laughed and said,

"Damned if I know what good we do ourselves by picking out traitors and brutes as the real representatives of humanity in our time. I don't mean you—we all do it. I used to read serious novels, I've given them up, I can't stand any more of these portentously self-centred types committing adultery or sodomy or treachery in the greatest possible gloom and unhappiness. They're all such frightful bores." Pulling himself up he said remorsely, "I beg your pardon for talking nonsense. . . . What were you going to tell me about your uncle?"

"Did you know that in 1945 a tribunal sentenced him to five years imprisonment as a collaborator and an unworthy citizen—oh, and the other things?"

The last trace of Adam's lightheadedness disappeared. He touched Monnerie's arm by way of apology.

"No, I didn't know."

"Ah, you only heard about the celebrated traitors. There were a great many others. By no means all of them were punished. In some ways my uncle was unlucky. There was no real vice in him, his only crime was his close friendship with Kettler. The truth is he wasn't interested in the war, he thought of it as a supreme idiocy and irrelevance. He'd known Kettler before the war, when he went to Germany— you know, as a boy he lived in Berlin with his mother and his stepfather, who was a diplomat. He spoke German. I don't think it ever crossed his mind that in inviting a German general to this house he was offending against certain elementary decencies. In fact, he believed the exact opposite. He believed he was the one civilised, decent, intelligent member of the family—the really sensible human being. The rest of us were tiresome and destructive. Barbarians. What he looked forward to was the day when he could draw on the money he has in New York and Stockholm, and spend his winters in Italy."

Impossible to tell whether he were serious or mocking. Adam asked.

"Well?"

Monnerie began walking about the room again. "He has always had a weak heart—it kept him out of the first war. Prison has done it no good. In fact, he's said to be dying, and they're letting him off his fifth year." He hesitated and said curtly, "He'll be home—here—the day after tomorrow."

"I'll clear off tomorrow, of course," Adam said.

Monnerie laid a hand on his shoulder for a second. "No

don't—if you can bear to stay." In a different voice, warm, lively, he went on, "You must see my brother. He went into Tours this morning, and he's not likely to get back until after dinner."

"Surely you'd rather I went?" He was ashamed of his feeling of annoyance. Why must they have an uncle dying this week?

"Oh, if Cousin Marie hadn't been going I'd have let you leave." Monnerie's eyelids twitched. "With her at home we shouldn't be comfortable. She's—implacable."

"It's very natural."

"Yes. . . ."

Glancing at Hartley's face, at his stubborn forehead and the pale eyes which seemed clear but were curiously impenetrable and opaque, like a bird's, Monnerie gave up any idea of trying to explain Cousin Marie to him. How do you explain to an Englishman that hatred can be a religion—and justice a pitiless and terrifying innocence? Cousin Marie, he thought sharply, has precisely this unmanageable innocence. No reasonable arguments bite on it. Always, it has always driven her to see, see passionately, only the victims—the child beaten by a brute of a father, the wrinkled finger-ends of old women. All the tired and voiceless humble—and now the tortured. She will never turn her eyes away for the sake of comfort. Not even for the sake of peace. She is one of that race of innocents willing to destroy a nation to save one sickly child.

"I don't," he said, "share her passion for keeping alive uncomfortable truths. But I don't argue with her. How could I? And in her own way she's right. It's unkind to the dead to forget how they died. In whose sordid hands. But—the poor old devil is dying himself. Surely we can keep up appearances for the few weeks or months he may last!"

"He's really as ill as that?"

"Too ill to walk upstairs. Tomorrow we're going to turn the library into a bedroom. That room through there——"

he jerked his head towards a door in the wall behind him.
"He can indulge his passion for the seventeenth century by
stretching an arm out of bed to the shelves." He passed his
hand over his face. "It will be easier with you here. All these
absurd violences of ours don't touch you. . . . You must feel
it was unfair not to put you off—but we only heard last
night."

Adam asked abruptly.

"Why are your people so ready to hate each other?"

"Oh, it goes back a good deal farther than the Occupation," Monnerie said. "It's an old bitterness and hatred.
Take care your people never learn it."

"Can you afford these violences?"

"No, of course not." Monnerie laughed. When he laughed it
was like a boy, with none of the cynicism and mockery he
gave away when he smiled. "Are you naive enough to believe
that the war ended in '45? It paused then—when the Russians
were halted at Berlin. I am just as sure it will start up again
as I am of tomorrow's sun. And we shall be defeated again.
We——" he pointed a long finger at himself. "I know nothing about your chances. . . . It will be a much worse defeat—
the same senseless destruction of all valuable and lovely things,
the same savagery, defilement, thoughtless killing, as when
an earlier horde of barbarians fell on a Roman villa. And the
same people, millions of them, who could have done something, some small thing, to resist the Germans and didn't, will
do their best to efface themselves again. In the hope of sur-
viving. As they survive now—and talk about their rights
as citizens of a country they did nothing to rescue from the
Gestapo. Impossible to blame them—they are what they are,
modestly reasonable cowards. *They* won the war. Robert lost
it."

The depths of bitterness he had caught a glimpse of horrified Adam.

"But you would fight again?"

"Of course." He had been leaning against the table, speaking with an energy which seemed jerked from him by nervous rage. Abruptly, lifting his arms, he let it drop with them, and looked blandly at Adam.

"You'll stay?"

"Very well. If I'm in the way you can tell me to leave."

"Good. . . ." He walked towards the door of the library. "I must move my papers and account books out of there before we turn it over to Uncle Daniel. A confounded nuisance." A thought struck him; he stopped, and turned round. "Do you remember seeing Elizabeth when you were here?"

"Miss Gueswiller?" Adam said. "Yes, of course."

It was scarcely true. Frowning, he tried to recall something definite about her. A little to his surprise an image dislodged itself from some obscure corner. . . . He had been standing, his back to the door of the attic, trying to look through the skylight. All he could see was a sky of unfathomable blue, across which floated a bird—surely a seagull? The heavy wooden sneck of the door lifted, he turned, expecting Mme. Regnier again. A girl came in. She was young, and moved with a quick half-dancing step. . . . The memory went to pieces here. Wasn't she thin and sunburned, with a smile always on the point of breaking through her young gravity? Much less clearly he recalled that she had long very thin legs and ankles, and a habit of appearing before him one day brushed and clean, and the next in washed-out cotton shorts, her hair in her eyes.

"Surely she was very young? A nice little tomboy?"

"She was eighteen," Monnerie said. He smiled imperceptibly. "You didn't know she was engaged to Robert?"

"I don't think so. . . . Why should they tell me?"

"They were engaged when she was seventeen, and were going to marry at the end of the war. When you were here she still had a father living near Strasbourg. He sent her to us at the beginning of the war—she's a very distant cousin—third, fourth, tenth—of Cousin Marie's. She wasn't quite fifteen. Just before the end of the war her father died, and she stayed here. She hasn't any other family."

Adam noticed that when he began talking about the girl his face changed; it became less heavy and his glance less guarded and inquisitorial; he looked younger—even a little uncertain.

"After Robert was killed she worked as a messenger for my group here. Before then I wouldn't let her risk it. Cowardly—but you know, I couldn't face it. And then Robert's death—and I had to let her. She turned out to be extremely good—kept what fears she had to herself— and very careful and intelligent. I don't mind telling you, she was my worst nightmare . . . when one knew that the women they caught weren't spared anything. . . . In fact, sometimes I believed that they tortured men simply because it was part of the routine, and women because it was exciting." He stopped abruptly.

"My God, and you let her risk it," Adam said. He was angry—and irritably conscious that his anger was naïve and ridiculous.

Looking into his face, Monnerie said softly, "No one had any right to keep anything back."

He smiled. Adam thought unexpectedly: It's only in very old, civilised, and long-living families that you get these smiles—childish, and in the same breath worldly. And radiantly malicious, gentle, self-confident.

"I don't know why not," he said stubbornly.

"You know perfectly well."

Adam shook his head. "I don't approve of the courage it takes to risk letting a young woman fall into the hands of unpleasant brutes."

Monnerie said calmly, "You may not approve, but you would have done exactly the same. . . . When what's at stake is so important that nothing is more important—from the moment you realise that evil exists—and that some men —faithful husbands who sleep comfortably with their wives, scrupulous lawyers, surgeons who can do the most delicate operations—have deliberately chosen to serve it. . . . And these men are the enemies of France and of a French child's right to grow up in freedom, self-respect, love. . . . Then no risks are too horrible. Even the risk you take of sending girls like Elizabeth to——" he shrugged his shoulders— "to what a number of young women—English, some of them —had to take."

"No, I couldn't have done it," Adam said.

Monnerie burst out laughing. "You won't know until you have to try," he said lightly. "Wait until it happens to you. Lucky pigheaded Englishman."

CHAPTER 5

H<small>E</small> WENT AWAY INTO THE LIBRARY, AND Adam heard him pulling out one drawer after another in exasperated haste. The door from the hall opened. He turned. The young woman who came in, seeing him alone, hesitated a moment, then came towards him with the light step he remembered.

He felt the same physical shock that certain sounds gave him—the lowest notes of a cello, a bugle heard at night. . . . In the moment needed for her to cross the room she took complete possession of him—or he of her, was it? His mind closed round her with compulsive force, like a fist.

He realised that he was standing still, letting her move towards him. Mechanically, he held his hand out.

"How are you?" he asked. "You've probably forgotten me —it's a long time."

"But you haven't changed at all; you still have the grip of a bear," she answered gravely.

He dropped her hand, "I'm frightfully sorry."

She smiled for the first time. "Why? I like it."

Monnerie came back, his arms full of books and papers. He dropped them on the table and looked, smiling finely, from the girl to Adam.

"Would you have known her, or were you expecting the nice little tomboy? There's every chance you'll get that to-morrow." He ran his glance over her white dress, from the smooth brown column of her neck to her short feet in high-heeled slippers. It was an admiring glance, and at the same time, perhaps unconsciously, possessive, appraising. He came across to her and rested his hand on her shoulder. His voice gave him away shamelessly. "You look very beautiful, my darling."

Adam thought: So that's where we are. . . . He had a ridiculous impulse to turn and go away. Impossible, he thought dully, it's impossible. . . . It was not possible that he had come on the woman who could have satisfied him, mind and body, only to lose her in the some moment. He felt the emptiness of complete disaster. Nothing to be done.

The girl shook off Monnerie's hand. Moving quickly and easily to the other side of the table, she put a finger on the untidy heap of papers.

"Why are you moving all these now?"

"Because," Monnerie said, "I must get to the bottom of this ridiculous quarrel between old Fargue and his son-in-law before I talk to them tomorrow. Damn them for a pair of fools—it will take me half the night."

"No, it's absurd," she said angrily. She turned to Adam with a gesture so vehement that he was surprised: it struck him as exaggerated—even, in some way, false.

"What is the matter?" he asked.

"The matter is that Jean works too hard. As if he hadn't enough to do here—the vines were in a terrible state after the war—he let them elect him mayor. Did you know that? And what with the deportations, and the quarrels—if we had all been deported it would have saved a lot of resentment and bitterness! . . . He works like a dog, and for no thanks."

"You're talking nonsense," Monnerie said gently, "I do it to please myself."

"That's not true," she said, with another flash of rage, "you do it to satisfy your pride, your atrocious pride."

He looked at her with as much mockery as love. "I daresay you're right."

"No, I'm wrong," she cried. "You do it because these idiots get on your nerves with their troubles. I don't mind, but you do too much of it. . . . Can't you—when Uncle Daniel is here—can't you take a few days off?"

"There's no need," he said, with indifference.

"I wish . . ." She turned away, pressing her lips together.

Adam had recovered a measure of self-control. I shall find some excuse or other for leaving tomorrow morning, he thought. He was seized by derision for himself. What had happened to him was absurd; his anguish was absurd. A rudimentary vanity in him said: But so long as no one knows or guesses. . . .

"What do you wish?" he asked.

"Oh——" she lifted her thin arms—"I wish we were living in a barge, with no worries and no possessions—nothing but a pot of geraniums. We should be much happier." She looked at him with a smile. To his astonishment he saw that her lips were unsteady, as though she were just going to cry—perhaps to laugh. "Tell me about the place you live in. Is it like this?"

"Good God no," he answered. "Not in the least. I live near York."

"Well?"

He shrugged his shoulders. "If it were in France it would be charming, there would be at least two admirable restaurants of the class Monsieur Michelin decorates with one or even two stars. It would also be shabby, with streets of handsome dilapidated houses, and the smell of rotting vegetables, new bread, bad drains. . . ." Why the devil, he wondered briefly, has this country never been able to achieve either an efficient government, or a decent system of drains. . . . "As it is, it's clean, tidy, solid, the Minister is superb, the food quite barbarous, a pall of what may only be damp but is probably dullness hangs over the place, it's morally cold and outwardly respectable and—yes, cold, cold, cold. The people are the

salt of the earth. And you would find them extremely boring."

"How can you possibly know that?" she said, smiling.

"Because they don't——" he hesitated—"they don't give
themselves. Except when there's serious trouble. Yes, in
trouble they're fine."

He was surprised to discover his sudden unshakable
belief in the salt of the English. They can be dull, he thought,
complacent, tortuous-minded—in the north, worse than that.
. . . He reflected for a moment, with hatred and admiration,
on that peculiarly northern glance, appraising and (as they
say themselves) taking you down a peg—shrewd, mistrustful,
sneering, ungenerous. And yet. . . . No, by God, they are the
salt, he thought again.

"They know better how to die than how to live decently."

The girl had listened attentively, head bent. She was like
a child taking in a story less with its ears than with its whole
active body. "It sounds wonderful. I should like it."

"My darling child," Jean said in an indulgent tone, "you'd
be bored to tears."

She interrupted him to say lightly, "I'm not your child,"
and turned and went out of the room.

Jean watched her go without speaking. As the door shut he
moved quickly to the tray of wine bottles. "One more glass
and I'll take you up to your room. Not an attic this time."

"Thanks."

In the last few minutes the light, as if it had been brought
into the room by the Loire, had carried up the walls a clear
rippling brightness, like the vaguely kind smile on an old face.

"Come outside and look," Monnerie said.

A few yards beyond the windows, to one side, the ground
rose to form a small knoll: standing on it, you looked far
up the Loire uncoiling into the distance, its only movement
the ceaseless twitching of its bronze and gold skin, to the
point, invisible, where the Cher would join it. Sandbanks,
poplars, willows, meadows, glittered in a greenish light;

even the shadows were formed from a more opaque light. . . .
Adam felt at once on edge and appeased: a great many contradictory feelings ran together in him, and confused Elizabeth, the wine he had drunk, and this gay sensual valley in an extraordinary excitement. At this moment he did not know whether he would have the moral courage to go away tomorrow: half of him wanted nothing except to stay here and look at her—look, and suffer uselessly, like a fool, he thought; the other half would have given an ear to rush away at once.

"You haven't seen the front of the house," said Jean.

Obediently, he turned to look at it. He saw a quite simple grey building, with mullioned windows and a narrow octagonal tower which must enclose the staircase; below its pointed roof, filling the pediment of the dormer window, he could make out a nearly effaced coat of arms. Massive outbuildings running back at an angle to the house gave it rather the air of a substantial farm.

"Yes, it's handsome," he murmured. Hardly conscious that it was irrelevant, he said, "She's not a child, you know."

The inquisitive glance Monnerie gave him turned rapidly to one of amusement.

"You're perfectly right—I annoy her when I treat her as if she were. She's not a child, and not in the least naïve. The fact remains that she's both young and old for her age."

"How old is she?" He found it difficult to talk about her.

"Twenty-four. . . . The war, the Occupation—and living isolated here, among dull neighbours, not even a girl of her own age to try her wits on—and her experience, such as it was, of the resistance, taught her how unimportant any single life is, taught her self-control, and the sort of confidence other young women draw from having always been happy—and yet kept her ignorant. She missed all the ordinary experiences of a girl and a young woman. . . . She's far from being the only French girl of her age who missed her girlhood."

"But she was going to be married."

Monnerie shrugged one shoulder. "Ah, yes—and it was like all these too youthful love affairs—half idyllic, and half two vigorous well-brought-up children playing with each other. For Elizabeth, at any rate. Perhaps not for Robert, but . . . He was a believing Christian, did you know that? It surprises you? . . . In any case, it ended too quickly to touch her very deeply—sensually——" he had spoken the last words in a rapid undertone, as if talking to himself. In a harder voice, he added, "Possibly I'm too old, too disfigured."

He laid his finger absently on the scar running from cheekbone to jaw across his left cheek. In May 1940 he had been severely wounded, his face cut open and a leg so thoroughly smashed that the surgeons had trouble in saving it.

Adam said sharply, "Oh, nonsense."

"There are moments when I doubt whether I have any right to burden a young woman with—my tiredness—my pre-occupations . . ."

He was, Adam realised, repeating an argument he had had with himself a great many times. . . . And has always, he thought ironically, settled it in his own favour. But why not? . . . With the pleasure it gives a man suffering from toothache to drive a sharp point into his jaw, he said drily.

"You're talking like a fool. You're not going to be tired for the rest of your life. You'll recover. God knows why, shot up as you were, you ever went into the resistance."

A curious expression crossed Jean's face; it became smooth, arrogant, reserved. "No, that was nothing. The really exhausting thing was having to fight against the temptation to capitulate. I mean, the temptation to be reasonable."

It was true. During those first months, resistance had looked, even to him, neither splendid, nor useful, nor brave, nor tragic. It was only absurd. Infinitely more rational to make terms, to submit, to go quietly to sleep, sham dead and let the Occupation roll over him. Over the country. Absurd, and an instinct. When he was five years old and learning to ride he fell off his horse, and his father forced him, bruised and in tears as he was, to ride home. Very soon he understood why. . . .

"Perhaps if the occupiers themselves hadn't been such clumsy fools, if they'd refrained from torturing and killing —if there had been no dead resisters to call up others—the whole thing might have collapsed in discouragement and boredom. I don't know."

"Do you believe that?" Adam asked.

"No. No, there's always something left." He went on with a sudden gaiety. "When you get down to the level of being only a little animal, half dead of fear—which clever people imagine is the truth about us—then something revolts. And says: Why, you poor little beast, you're free. Even if you have only an hour left before they finish you off, you have time, all the time in the world, to decide what you want to do. Choose! . . . There's no point in choosing to fight. It's perfectly obvious you're spun. And nothing to keep faith with outside yourself—nor, for that matter, inside. Nevertheless, you decide to go on making a fool of yourself. For no reason. That's all."

He laughed. And if I've become immovable and narrow, he thought, a small landowner and vine-grower who thinks of nothing except passing his land on in somewhat better order than he got it, isn't it my God time for that now . . . ?

"I could never live anywhere but here," he said lightly.

Adam looked at the river again. It had changed; a breeze from the west was combing the surface into sharp-pointed ripples.

"The wind's getting up a little."

Jean put his head back to listen. "It will blow harder before dark. . . . Come along, I'll take you to your room."

CHAPTER 6

By THE TIME HE HAD UNPACKED AND washed, Hartley realised that Jean was telling the truth about the wines of the Loire; his mild drunkenness, the feeling of cloudy exaltation, blew away between one minute and the next. The inside of his skull felt as though an icy wind had swept it. For some time he stood in the window, trying to come to terms with his sense of defeat and failure. In the forbidding coldness and lucidity of his mind, a desert of contradictory illusions lay exposed to him. Picking up one after another, he ran his finger along the edge, a little surprised by the appearance and stinging rawness of the cut. There was the illusion that he knew himself, that among the several ways he had taken to justify himself as a human being—and get rid of the self-mistrust planted in him with his very first memories—none would involve him seriously with any woman. Without ever putting it into words he had believed that a man is only what he *does*, what he decides to do, and that sleeping with a woman is less an act of decision than a need, like any other need. He detested the idea of depending on any one creature. Perhaps he even felt an involuntary impatience with an instinct which made light of will and self-possession. Certainly he had been content with his freedom. And now this . . . this intolerable *coup de foudre*, dissolving in the space of a minute his self-satisfaction and turning to ridicule his energy, his will, his common sense.

Why to me, why should it happen to me? he asked himself, stupefied. For an instant he saw the girl with hallucinating clearness, seeing details he had not, or not consciously, noticed at the time: the turn of her head on its strong neck, a movement of her hand, the small arched nose. . . . For the whole of my life, he thought. With no sense of the meaning of the words, or that they had meaning—they were jerked from him like drops of water flung up by a stone—he repeated aloud, "The whole of my life."

His own voice gave him a saving shock. You fool, he said to himself, you singular fool.

No one watching him during these minutes would have guessed at the disturbance in his mind, and in the nerves of his chest, which seemed to have been dragged together roughly in a knot cutting off his breath. After a time, he managed to control them, and his mind as well. A feeling of emptiness invaded him. I have nothing and I am nothing, he thought calmly. He no longer felt disgraced or foolish: he had finished with that. A gambler who has just lost more than he can ever pay would understand the feeling: there is nothing to be done, the ruin is complete, final —at the same time, unadmitted, a flicker of new life, a confused half-formed energy, starts up on some obscure level of —of what?

He roused himself to look at his watch. It was eight o'clock. When he went downstairs, an old servant, wrinkled and smiling toothlessly, was carrying into the stone-floored dining-room a great dish of hard-boiled eggs in sauce; she had already placed on the table tureens, equally large, of tomato salad and very young broad beans. This was the first course. It was followed by young roast duck, and that by veal so cooked that it dissolved aromatically on the tongue. Then came a fine crumbling cheese, then raspberries, wild strawberries, nectarines, apricots. The wines were again Monnerie's own, a dry still Vouvray, robust in spite of its youth, and a fragrant red wine, smoother than the one they had been drinking before dinner, with the same deceptive lightness—light enough at any rate to fly to Adam's head. He let them go on filling his glass with it, only too willing to escape into the harmless intoxication it offered. Halfway through the meal he had reached a happy state of separation from himself. He was able to make use of his detached self. It talked freely and easily, and he listened to it with satisfaction.

He asked Mme. Regnier whether the cook were the old servant he had seen.

"Heavens, no," she answered, "I do the cooking myself."

"Cousin Marie," said Jean, "starts work in the morning at five, and is usually still up at midnight. She keeps my books, oversees the kitchen garden and the fruit trees, buys any food we don't grow ourselves—and as you've seen, cooks it like an archangel."

"I cook as I was taught," Mme. Regnier said drily. "There are plenty of houses where Captain Hartley would eat better."

"That I don't believe," he exclaimed. "In England a meal like this would have been uncommon before the war. And now, of course . . ." he shrugged.

Cousin Marie did not try to keep the contempt out of her voice. "I've always been told that Englishwomen are clumsy grudging cooks."

"I don't think it's a question of clumsiness," he answered. "They don't care to waste the time on it. How many hours do you spend preparing a dinner?"

She lifted her eyebrows, fine black half-hoops which gave her face its accent of gaiety. "What a question! Rarely more than five or six hours—and not a minute thrown away."

"Don't you," he persisted, "consider that very hard work?"

"Of course!" She moved her hands, smiling. "But I like it, it is my life."

"This is still a country of mediaeval craftsmen," Jean said, with a faint smile. "I don't know for how much longer. Perhaps not very long. . . . Perhaps we're due for a revolt of women."

"God forbid!" she cried.

The meal at an end, she did not allow the two men to sit at the table, but packed them off to the drawingroom. All the windows except one had been closed, but not shuttered, and the curtains had not been drawn: as a sail fills and swells, the room had filled with the dusk entering it from outside.

"Don't light up yet," exclaimed Adam.

He leaned against a window. For the moment, the branches of the poplars had turned to a dark moss and the willows to piles of cindery ash heaped along a river bristling with waves, steel-grey, angular, tossing perpetually from crest to crest a feather of light. He was looking into a vaporous blue plain, but when he turned to glance through the single window facing west there was still one sorrowful red gash in the heavy clouds. Through this window, open, came the melancholy noise made by a frog, and the thin cries of the swifts. The trees dissolved, slowly, into the dark air.

The old woman, old Amélie, brought in the coffee. Behind her, carrying a bottle of brandy and the swollen glasses for it, was a young man. In an amused voice he said,

"But you're all in the dark!"

He set the tray down and lit every light. Blinking at him, Adam saw a dark-haired young man, slender, rather small; he had a white thin face and dark eyes so brilliant that they gave his whole graceful body an air of energy and vivacity.

But I've seen him before, he thought, surprised. Where? Where can it have been?

"Ah, François!" cried Jean. "Have you had dinner?"

"Yes, in town. But I could do with coffee." He looked smilingly at Hartley. "Is this——?"

"Yes, of course it is. Adam, this is my brother—I talked to you about him."

Adam shook hands with him. "He told me so much," he said, staring, "that when you came in I almost thought I knew you."

The young man had an engaging smile, a later and merrier copy of his brother's. "How bored you must have been! But if you stay here you'll soon realise that the Monneries take an indecent pride in each other."

Jean Monnerie smiled.

"Did you," Adam asked him, "show me a photograph of your brother at some time?"

"I didn't carry such things," said Jean drily.

"No, of course not. I'm a fool—your Vouvray—I'm a little drunk."

He frowned, struggling to pin down the moment in which François's face had seemed completely familiar, a face recognised; and the recognition too sharp to be only the torn-off fragment of a dream suddenly dislodged and rising to the surface. It's a very French face, he thought. That must be it. . . .

"I suppose we look alike," François said gaily. "A family likeness."

Adam glanced from his face to Jean's. "I don't think I ever saw two brothers so completely different."

"All the same," Jean said, "the other day in Tours a stranger took us for father and son."

"You know why that is," retorted François, "it's because you still have an idea that I'm the brat you have to do everything for—hold his hand when he walks, see he doesn't fall, and mop him up when he does."

"Nonsense," said his brother gently, "I think of you as the future. I'm played out and lame. It's up to you to turn the Monneries into a force again, you———"

He was interrupted. Elizabeth put her head into the room to say in a brusque voice,

"Jean, old Arnoux is asking for you on the telephone. Shall I tell him it's too late, you're not at everyone's beck and call at all hours of the day and night? It's only a quarrel he's been having with a farmer. Let me tell him to wait until tomorrow."

Jean hesitated. "No, no, I'll come," he said.

He went out. Still groping in his memory for the resemblance hiding from him somewhere in the fog of the past, Adam asked,

"How many years between you and your brother?"

"Twelve. Only twelve. Between twelve years and as many weeks, or between sixteen years and four, it's a stretch. It's not such a stretch now, but he doesn't believe that."

"No. When you've always felt abnormally responsible for someone. . . . At the time I knew him during the war he was continually anxious about you. Proud of you, too, of course. You were running your underground printing press, in Paris, and he always had that on his mind."

"My . . . ?" François turned, as if he had been tapped on the shoulder. "Oh, yes, yes," he said in a light voice, "the famous press."

"I wish you'd tell me about it," said Adam politely. "I've always been curious to know how those clandestine presses worked."

"Oh, some time—I'll talk to you about it some time," the young man said nonchalantly. He waved his hand, dismissing the whole thing, and went on pacing quickly and restlessly about the room. Adam noticed his hands and feet, of an almost feminine delicacy.

"I'm afraid I've come at an awkward time," he said.

François stood still. "You mean poor old Uncle Daniel . . . I suppose," he went on, with his charming smile, "as an Englishman you think we're making a quite unnecessary fuss."

"How can I judge?" Adam frowned. "All that strikes me is that—to a man like your uncle, cultivated, intelligent, worldly—it would seem perfectly possible to keep up a human relationship with a German of the same age and with the same pre-Nazi world behind him. I don't suppose it ever entered his head that he was doing anything treacherous. . . . Forgive me if I'm making you angry."

"But you're quite right! Of course you're right," François cried. "There they were, the two old things, two civilised old gentlemen, enjoying the same writers, French writers at that, talking the same language—it would have been insane, ridiculous, for them to cut each other dead merely because they'd both been run down by the same tank. If you know what I mean!"

His eyes sparkled with a protesting gaiety. Adam was charmed by him. Come, he thought, if the younger generation is all as reasonable and generous. . . .

"Did you ever see this German general who was your uncle's friend?" he asked.

"Kettler? Oh, yes, a nice old boy—friendly, amusing. I liked him——" He broke off, turning his head swiftly, as the door opened.

Mme. Regnier came in with Jean.

"Adam, I'm sorry," said Jean, "we must move your car. There was shade where you left it this evening, but before you get up tomorrow the courtyard will be a furnace, every inch except under the gallery. We can put it in there with the carts. Do you mind?"

Adam followed him out of the room. The door had barely closed on them before Cousin Marie said sharply,

"Now that he knows what's happening, why doesn't he take himself off?"

François looked at her with an affectionate smile. "It doesn't seem terrible or important to him. How could it? He's an outsider."

"An outsider! The English are all but Germans. They feel like Germans, they prefer Germans, they have gross German habits. You have only to look at them!"

"But, my darling, one of their habits is fighting the Germans," François said gently.

The quietness and finality of a stone came over Cousin Marie's fine aquiline face. "Only because they're driven to it—and only in order to embrace them afterwards. . . .

No, no, *no.* . . . And it annoys me to leave him here with no one to look after him properly."

"Old Amélie will manage."

"She cooks idiotically, she has no wits, no delicacy!"

"Well, stay then," François said laughing.

She lifted a small hand, clenching it. "François, you know better than that. You know I can't. To be forced to look at Daniel—and every time I looked to see him smiling, smiling, at the brutes who killed Robert. No, no, I couldn't. Daniel is unforgivable, a coarse egoist, a traitor. . . ."

"Yes, he is all that," the young man said softly. He put his arm round her shoulders, laying his cheek against her head. "I know, I know . . . poor Mamma, poor love. Yes, I do know."

Cousin Marie abandoned herself for a moment to his warmth and youth. A smile softened her face, but when she closed her eyes it became that fugitive smile on the faces of the very old: the two large swelling mounds of her eyelids seemed fixed. The young man looked at them, and looked away; his hand continued to stroke her forehead.

"Oh, Babba, what should I do without you?" she said under her breath.

"That's better," he said gently, almost merrily. "I hate you to call me François, as if I were grown up."

Opening her eyes, she stepped back to look at him with a teasing affection. "But I always call you Babba, I've been doing it now for twenty-five years—it's absurd and I really must give it up."

"No, don't," he said laughing.

She sighed. "I never shall. But all the same, you know, you are grown up. And thank God for it. You must take Robert's place in this house—in the country—and do everything he would have done."

"You know I can't do that," he said, "I'm not half the chap he was. But I'll do my poor best. To please you, Mamma."

"No, not to please me," she began, with energy: stopped, and went on in a lighter voice. "Yes, yes, a little to please me—but more because you can't help it, you're not tired, and you're intelligent, you'll do better than just help us here, Jean and I. You must begin to make a name for yourself. It's time."

Jean Monnerie came in. Without even glancing to see whether Hartley were following him, she said,

"Need your friend stay here after tomorrow? He has seen us again and we him. Now surely he can take himself off!"

"That's enough, my dear," Jean said quietly.

Adam appeared in the doorway. Though she didn't care whether he had heard her or not, she made a careless attempt to seem friendly.

"Captain Hartley, I'm sorry I'm leaving tomorrow morning—but I can't possibly stay here. I won't live under the same roof as a traitor." Her eyes glittered with malice. "That's something you can't be expected to understand."

No one, reflected Adam, is able to be so cheerfully and unconsciously rude as a Frenchwoman—or man—when the chance is too good to miss. "I can understand why you are unhappy," he said.

"Nevertheless—you think I'm hysterical, or more vindictive than I need be." Hartley did not answer at once. She smiled and said, "You can speak frankly. I'm not a girl."

"But I have no opinion," he protested. "So far as I'm concerned Monsieur Monnerie is only an old gentleman—a man who lived in the past and could hardly be expected to——"

She cut him smilingly short. "To have the normal feelings of a man whose country has been invaded and one of his own family murdered. . . . So you think that decency is a question of age?"

"No, not quite that——" Her mockery was beginning to irritate him. "A little imagination . . . two men who have been friends for years, two civilised old gentlemen—" he turned to François—"as you were saying just now——"

Cousin Marie moved her head with the quickness of a little snake. "What can you have said to him, Babba?"

François looked at once penitent and bewildered. "I really don't know," he murmured. "Perhaps Captain Hartley didn't quite understand something I said." The glance he gave Hartley was one of complicity and appeal.

"You said, I think, that your uncle and his German general spoke French together," Adam said smoothly.

"As a child I was taught that even the devil learns French," Cousin Marie cried. She broke off, to stare at Jean. "What is it? What's the matter?"

For the last minute Jean Monnerie had been standing, his head lowered, a frown drawing the flesh between his eyebrows into heavy folds. Without answering, he moved quickly towards the door. It opened before he reached it. Old Amélie opened it and stood aside, one hand pulling at the brown loose skin of her throat: her mouth hung open, but she said nothing. Behind her, moving with extreme slowness, were two hospital orderlies in uniform, acting as crutches for an old gentleman whose head and shoulders rose well above theirs.

Adam stared at him with sharp curiosity. Daniel Monnerie might have passed anywhere in England as a country gentleman, owner of an excellent library he sometimes sat in after dinner, a book open before him, his head gradually sinking over it as his eyes closed. The illusion was helped by his tweed jacket and riding breeches, both of which, surely, had been made for him at some time in London. They hung round him in deep folds. He must, thought Adam, have lost more than half his weight: he must, too, have been very handsome— the lines of his emaciated face were strong and good. He held himself—with what was obviously a fearful effort—very upright.

Cousin Marie made a faint sound between a cry and a gasp. Horror at his looks, or only the shock of seeing him?

Turning his head towards her, Daniel Monnerie held his hand out.

"Marie," he said, "I've come home."

She stepped back quickly, ignoring his hand, and went out of the room. He gazed after her with suavely raised eyebrows.

"Dear me. Do I look so repulsive?" he murmured. "I didn't know."

CHAPTER 7

"D on't do that," Daniel said.

Jean had closed the west window and was pulling across it the inner shutter of grey oak, its edge, where generations of hands had fingered it, rubbed to the smoothness of silk. He was shutting out the dusk, the thin dark tissue formed of separate threads of light reflected from every leaf, thrown back from every grain of sand in the river, and drifting from the overcast sky. He turned, his hand on the hasp of the shutter, to look at his uncle. They had made up a bed for him on the couch; he was sitting propped against a heap of pillows, seeming, in his fine linen nightshirt, still more emaciated, and exaggeratedly long: one half of his face was in shadow, the other, with a sunken eye socket and a cavity beneath the wide cheekbones which might have made the sculptor's fist, had a primitive harshness and simplicity. His hands lay folded together on the blanket. They were like Jean's, long, fine, nervous. Or no, thought Jean, they are like mine will be when I'm dying, if I die old.

"You'll have moths in, and mosquitoes, if I don't close the window. I'll leave the shutter open."

"Oh, very well," Daniel muttered.

Without seeing them, he had behind his eyes the whole wide plain, and the Loire, wonderfully and smoothly curving and recurving, blond, sinuous—a river of sand as well as a pure surface which accepted and gave back all those images of tree and stone he had amused himself by evoking in prison.

"Tomorrow we'll arrange your bedroom in there for you," Jean said. He glanced towards the library. "We thought we'd give these two rooms over to you. You can sleep in there and, when you feel like it, sit here."

"Yes, I see," Daniel said. A flicker of irony stirred in the burned-out eyepits. "Well, it's a pleasanter isolation than a cell."

Jean said nothing.

"I should like to see Marie," Daniel said.

"She won't see you," Jean said quietly, "she's going away tomorrow morning to avoid it."

"Really? I'd forgotten her love of gestures."

Angered in spite of himself, Jean said, "Have you forgotten as well everything about Robert?"

"No," Daniel said. His voice and his manner rebuked a puerile incivility. "But to leave the house—isn't that excessive? Before—when Otto Kettler came here to have dinner with me, she used to shut herself in her room. Wouldn't that be a crushing enough comment now, on my existence in the house?"

Jean had recovered his good temper. "At that time she wasn't able to go away. Your German friends were in possession of the country."

"Don't be absurd," said his uncle drily. "I had *a* German friend, not more than one. Some of them—perhaps a great many—are uneducated brutes. Kettler was a scholar and a gentleman."

Is it any use arguing with him? Jean thought. More out of courtesy than for any other reason, he said,

"You would only have to take a series of steps back from this cultured old gentleman, to reach his less cultured countrymen, the chemists, the respectable civil servants initialling the necessary minutes, the industrious sanitary officials, ordering, creating, working the gas chambers in which women

and their children were reduced to a pile of soiled torn suffocated bodies."

Daniel gave him a glance of almost pitying curiosity. "I've
never understood you. You're how old?—nearly forty; you're
not stupid—no Monnerie is—yet you seem to me positively
adolescent. In prison I used to think that it might be possible
to talk to you. You might have learned something. But I
come back and find you still cherishing the same myths, left
over from the time when a German statesman could decide,
for his own reasons of state, to make war on a French emperor
—the wars of ambitious individuals. And all the rest of the
absurd charming *mystique* blown together by writers and
other scoundrels to cover up the bodies of dead peasants and
dead young men. Hasn't it ever occurred to you, even once,
that something else is happening now that we have mob wars,
and whole nations rushing to put themselves under the rule
of a powerful brute, a Hitler, a Stalin? The barbarians are
almost on you, my dear, and you go on repeating the same
gestures, rehearsing the same quarrels. Like ghosts. When
I listen to you I feel I'm the last survivor from an era of
sensible human beings. Positively a specimen!"

Jean had moved nearer the couch. As he looked down at
the incredibly thin exhausted body, the skeletal face, he felt
something so like tenderness that he was surprised.

"Yes—you're so intelligent," he said gently. "And when
I was a boy and a young man you always gave me such wise
advice. And you were so kind. What's missing in you? Passion? Faith?"

"Neither," said his uncle ironically. "Only the habit of
patriotic lies."

That's true, Jean thought. With something of a shock he
realised that he had gone a long way towards agreeing with
his uncle. But only with his intellect. With the rest of his
mind, or his spirit—call it what the devil you choose—he
rejected him completely.

"Don't you even believe that men—that Frenchmen, since

we're both French—have ways of thinking and feeling in common—a meaning, their own, growing very slowly in the same way as a tree grows, which they force into words? The word child, for instance, or the word tomorrow or casserole or freedom or decency. A meaning worth saving even when to save it you have to kill?"

A look of amusement altered Daniel Monnerie's face as much—as little—as a stone is changed by the light.

"I believe you're talking abysmal nonsense, murderous nonsense," he said coldly, "and I believe that I'm being punished because I'm a rational creature, and behaved like one."

Why, Jean wondered, do I want to force open this poor shell? Why smash it to let in what is after all only *my* light? I ought to leave him alone. . . . Although he was grieved and a little ashamed, he could not hold himself back.

"No. You're punished—cut out—as heartless. What did you suppose Cousin Marie felt while you were entertaining a countryman of the people who broke her son's body and put out one of his eyes? You pretended to be fond of her."

To his astonishment, almost dismay, he caught on the ruined old face the look you would expect in the eyes of a man coming suddenly out of an anaesthetic to find himself on the operating table, and the surgeon's knife moving in him.

"How can you know—how can you be sure of such things?"

"Secrets of that sort are rarely kept," Jean said calmly. "Robert was tortured . . . for hours . . . there's no chance that it's not true."

Under his breath Daniel said, "No. I don't believe it."

Jean stared. "So you do have doubts?"

There was a brief silence. Daniel seemed to make an effort of some sort, to be calling on a reserve of contempt and pride which fairly easily brought an uncharitable smile to his bleached lips.

"My dear boy, what have I lost in losing the approval of a self-dramatising woman? Dear Marie—she should have been an actress. Not to speak of the approval of our local heroes! I was very unlucky in being tried so soon after the Liberation . . . yes, yes, even I had looked forward to being liberated. . . . Nowadays, I believe, the courts are more lenient with people of our class."

"Why are you trying to provoke me?" asked Jean, smiling.

"Am I?" A younger and very charming Daniel Monnerie seized his chance. "Perhaps, you know, my dear, after four years of loneliness—may you never know such loneliness! —I'm hoping to be taken back as a human being."

It was an appeal. Jean felt grief, pity, an implacable distrust. He shook his head.

"No."

"Ah, you're incorruptible," his uncle said lightly, after a moment. "I must look elsewhere for company."

"You can certainly find it—in Paris, in Biarritz. . . ."

"I'm too weak to get there," said Daniel, simply. "I'm afraid I shall have to spend my last few months or weeks with people who disapprove of me. A pity. Unless—" he put his head on one side, with an ingenuous slyness—"unless I can corrupt the younger members of the family."

"François?" murmured Jean. "You won't find him any more—accessible."

A note between mischief and irony came into Daniel's voice. "Now—I wonder how you know that? François is young enough to be my grandson, and a virtue, you know, often skips a generation!"

Jean moved towards the door. It was a few minutes after ten. He wanted to see Cousin Marie, and to make sure that Hartley had not been left to amuse himself. A thought struck him. He turned back.

"There's just one thing. I'd like you to feel sure—if it interests you at all—that I never believed you were a traitor. Never at any time. I knew perfectly well that all you wanted was to spare yourself anxiety and difficulties in the new order of things. Your mistake was—you believed it was going to be a German new order."

As he said it, he felt a shock of uncertainty. Suppose, he thought, looking at Daniel, at the long fine bones of his face and still delicate skin, suppose this man had been required to choose, crudely, between losing his money and descending to active treason? What would he have done? . . . He shrugged his shoulders. It didn't happen—why think of it?

Daniel raised his eyebrows. "Thank you. . . . May I just say that—if I'd been right—you would now, if you were alive, be an embittered exile, a man without a country, without a future, one of history's bad jokes, a farce. Not even that. History would ignore you. The defeated have no history."

Jean smiled at him. "Perhaps. But I should have been free."

"Free!" The shrunken face became an image of contempt. "Free from everything except poverty, solitude, impotence. And I'll tell you something else, my boy. When there actually was a degree of freedom, people didn't theorise about it. They lived it. They don't live it now, they talk of—it's an idea, a thesis, dead, a ghost. . . . You don't really imagine that a poor clerk, a poor greengrocer, cares a loaf of good bread about freedom? If it were only yourselves you conceited patriots got killed! But you kill! All the simple men and women you delude into getting themselves arrested and hanged or maimed. And for what?"

His breath came thinly and brokenly, a thread of air blowing through a crack.

"You're tiring yourself," Jean said unemotionally. "And it's a waste of time. We don't understand each other. We never shall."

But, he thought, after all, for what? For almost nothing. For that weak flicker of—call it what you like—conscience, freedom, love, which a whole world of calvinistic dictators, big and little, wants to put out. For that helpless innocence which is so dangerous to them that they have to prove it guilty. . . . Bored now by listening to a sick man, his mind darted aside. One day, at one of these wonderful political trials, there'll be a miracle. The crushed broken trembling human rag in the dock will lift his head, spit in his accuser's face, and shout: I'm not guilty. . . . Even without a miracle, who knows what goes on in their hearts at the last minute? . . .

"No," his uncle said, in a gentle voice, "we never shall. I'm unlucky. . . . Tell me—what happened to the priest?"

Jean frowned. "The priest? You mean Father Baussan? Do you want to see him?"

"He came back, then, from—where was it?"

"Dachau," said Jean curtly. "In bad shape, but he came back." He thought unkindly: Why not tell him? "When he heard that you'd been tried and sentenced, he said he was very sorry he hadn't got home in time to speak for you."

"Kind," Daniel said, without expression.

Jean walked across the room, rapidly, so that he need not limp as he passed the couch. Turning in the doorway, he said,

"You must try to be as comfortable here as possible."

"My dear boy, why not? It won't go on forever."

CHAPTER 8

Alone, DANIEL MONNERIE LET HIMSELF SLIP
down a little against his pillows. His weakness and exhaustion
had become part of him, as much part as his dry smooth skin.
He no longer felt them as distinct from himself. He was
no longer, as he had been, conscious of the labouring of
his heart when he made an effort. But he felt the relief,
the pleasure, of linen pillowcases. He felt, too—and this
he had not expected—disappointment, bitter and aching.
He had imagined every sort of homecoming except just
this—to be given, as a leper might be given, every attention,
a place to live, food, linen sheets, and, like a leper, be cut
out of the body of the family. As Jean—for once neither
mocking nor ironical—had said.

He felt no pity for himself. Self-pity was not one of his
habits. Even when he heard his sentence he had only felt
like a man surprised by a catastrophe of nature. A catastrophe of human nature. He had no desire, not the smallest,
to be offered sympathy. That he would have considered
impudent. But he longed—my God, how he longed—for
someone he could talk to.

With smiling regret he thought: Ah, if only Otto were
here. . . . He had been sitting in this room—no, no, in the
library—when the door opened and a speechless Amélie
showed in the German officer. She must have expected every

63

sort of horror, anything—except his cry of welcome and
delight, his outstretched hands . . . "Otto! My dear Otto!" . . .
A moment later he had collected himself. "Dear me, what am
I thinking about? You're an enemy, you've invaded and over-
run us again—it's a really shocking habit you've fallen into.
What's wrong with your country that you can't stay in it
peacefully?"

Otto crossed his long legs, and folded brown slender
hands on his knee. His smile ran from his eyes—blue, clear,
candid—to his fine mouth. "If you knew the trouble I've
taken to get myself sent to Tours to be near you, you
wouldn't scold me." He sent a smiling glance over the book-
cases. "I've come, of course, to pillage. This room."

They were old friends, used to each other rather than
intimate. All their memories were of pleasures they had
shared—boar hunting, music, pretty women—yes, they
had shared women. In the whole lot there was not one
painful or disturbing memory. No doubt that was why
more than anything their friendship was an extremely
pleasant habit; and one which Daniel Monnerie, the man
of taste, lover of any music except modern music, man of
the world, his world, saw no reason to break. What harm
did it do?

What harm could it possibly do for two old friends to
sit drinking, gossiping, talking quietly about everything
except the war and politics? Not that Otto had avoided
these. At the very beginning he said bluntly that he detested
and despised the men now in control of Germany—ugly
brutes, some of them; the others at best ambitious rankers,
or fanatics. "Then why," asked Daniel, "do you serve them,
you and your friends?" Otto shrugged his shoulders in his
admirably cut tunic—at the moment unbuttoned. "Why
not? One serves—that's all." He went on to remark with
energy that—although nominally in charge—he was, God
be thanked, completely absolved from having to take an
interest in the activities of the police. The chap in control

ran his own job. . . . "A frightful fellow, my dear Daniel, with one of those Prussian necks, and an East Berlin accent. I'm told that in civilian life he's a pastry-cook—what do you think of that? It means, I hope, that he has a light hand with the sinners he arrests."

The vision of a pastry-cook in colonel's uniform struck both of them in the same instant as irresistibly comic. They shook with laughter. If anyone—if Marie—had happened to be walking through the hall and heard this schoolboyish outburst. . . .

Would she, would anyone, believe it was only now, years after, that the echo of their laughter in this room rang in his ears strangely, dubiously? That only now it struck him how adroitly they had both evaded knowing just what the pastry-cook was up to? Once, and only once, a crack opened in the evasive silence. It had to do with Father Baussan, the parish priest, a stunted, scurrying little man, vaguely sympathetic, with no graces, to whom Daniel Monnerie was always extremely polite. An atheist, he approved of the Church. One Sunday evening, crossing the priest in the village, he had stopped to talk. He must have lamented the fanaticism and violence that were ruining the world, because the little shabby fellow fixed a pair of blazing eyes on him and said, "Indifference is a sin, too." The next day he heard that the priest had been arrested. He spoke about it to Otto, who reflected a moment and suggested that they might invite the pastry-cook to dinner, "and try to talk him into opening his jaws and letting the hare drop." So they invited him. He came, and he opened his jaws, but not, alas, to the benefit of the poor hare. Instead, he had treated them both, his French host and his commanding officer, to a lecture—earnest, as fluent and dull as if he had been neither colonel nor pastry-cook but a pedantic professor—on the pure Nazi doctrine. It lasted through the meal, and through coffee and liqueurs afterwards, until rising stiffly and saluting, he excused himself for leaving at once. He had,

he said, "to be present at an interrogation. A duty, *my* duty—
I might say, my virtue. You allow me to go, sir?" . . . Otto
came out of a stupefied inattention to say, "Yes, yes,
allowed. . . ."

Alone, they had stared at each other in silence for a
minute, until Otto breathed, "But the man's mad, stark staring
mad! They must all be mad." Even the room, the familiar
room, its windows open to let in the autumn sound and
scents of the Loire, seemed to have swollen beyond measure;
chairs which had been at ease here for a couple of hundred
years now stood awkwardly as if they had been fitted with
high boots and breeches too stiff to move about in. The
door opened again and Amélie came in to take away the
coffee cups. At once, when the old Frenchwoman's hand
or glance touched them, each chair, each object, returned
to its proper size and remembered what it had been made
for. A few seconds after she had gone, Otto said meditatively,
"The old hag never looks at me, I should really like to
have her thrashed." It was a joke, of course it was a joke. . . .

Suddenly restless, Daniel pushed the blanket away and sat
up. The effort made itself felt in every vein. He waited another minute, then, with immense care, got off the couch.
He was possessed by the need to touch things in the room,
the waxed arm of a chair, a glass, the stone moulding round
the fireplace. The grain of polished boards under his bare
foot gave him a voluptuous joy, sharpened and deepened
when he was able at last to run his finger along the grooves,
fine, curving, worn down to the smoothness of marble,
in the grey stone. The shock in him of this joy was too
severe. He saw the fireplace. He saw nothing, a blackness.
He would have fallen if François, coming in that instant,
had not raced across the room to catch him in his arms.
The Englishman was with him. Leaning on them, he waited
until the room steadied round him, then walked back to his
sofa, slowly, dragged at by the leaden weakness of his body.

"You mustn't do that sort of thing," François reproached him, "you'll kill yourself."

He smiled into the young man's face. "That would be absurdly unnecessary."

"You're awfully brave," said François ingenuously. "I do so admire you. I'm glad you've come home." He glanced at Hartley. "You know Captain Hartley, don't you?"

Adam felt in his own shoulders the effort it cost the old man to turn his head very slightly, with a look of pleasure. "How nice to see an English face. But I don't know you, I'm afraid, do I?"

"I was here once during the war."

"Ah—we didn't meet then."

"I rather forced myself on you," Adam said smiling, "and left without thanking you for your hospitality."

Though weak, Daniel's voice came out as clear and flexible as a child's. "Surely Madame Regnier told you at the time that if I knew you were in the house I should hand you over to my German friends?"

Looking at him, Adam marvelled that he was able to summon the whole of what clearly was an extremely shallow reserve of strength, and direct it where he chose. At this moment it was all in his eyes, lively, gleaming with spiteful amusement, the eyes of a younger man. He said quietly,

"I never felt safer in France anywhere than in this house."

Daniel laughed, a thread of sound. "And there are people who doubt whether English diplomacy is the finest in the world! I should like to assure you, Captain Hartley, that I had only one German friend. He was as tactful as you are—very tactful, very correct. He used to dine here with me most evenings, but we never discussed the war—we talked about fishing, music, books. Invariably. . . . I was sorry when he left France. He was an attractive fellow. I daresay you won't believe that?"

"But of course I do," said Adam. Not without malice, he added, "We all know at least one attractive German. Mine is, was, a German colonel we hammered at in Normandy for eight days, trying to crack open his strongpoint. It must have been merry hell for him. I took his surrender, I'd meant to make some civil remark or other—but I didn't. We were both too tired."

What he had begun in malice ended in a simple regret. He had moved his chair back a little, so that he could watch Daniel without seeming rude or inquisitive. He was fascinated by the way in which a thought, an emotion, moved across the bloodless old face like a shadow behind glass: there seemed to be no barrier of flesh to trap them.

"General Kettler had courage," said Daniel coldly. "He volunteered to go to Russia, and was killed. Rather a pity. . . . You'd agree he was charming?" he said to François.

Adam glanced discreetly, amused and curious, at the young man. Which way will he somersault now? . . . A look of embarrassment, not very profound, crossed François's face.

"I? Oh, I hardly remember him." He hesitated, and with a gesture of his graceful hands said, "After all, I never spoke to him."

Adam's curiosity sharpened quickly. . . . Why the devil is he lying? Since the old boy knows it's a lie. . . . Without moving his head he looked at Daniel's face: a shadow of irony crossed it, followed instantly by sadness. Speaking very slowly, Daniel said,

"My dear child—yes, of course—I won't forget that."

"How good you are," François cried. "I do love you, you know."

Between these affectionate phrases, a sentence had been dropped out. They understand each other very well, these two, thought Adam. . . . The truth was much too obvious to miss. Except old Daniel, no one in the family knew that François had met and liked the German—and the old man needed no clearer appeal to be discreet, or warning, than François had just given him. Obvious—and rather lamentably sordid. Why on earth need the young idiot have given himself away to me, wondered Adam? Because he wanted to put himself in a good light with me? Probably.

Daniel's hand, the skeleton of his hand, rested for a moment on François's arm. "I hope, my dear, you're going to stay at home now. I should like to have a friend in this house. It's not necessary, but I should like it." He glanced politely at Hartley. "Are you going to be here long?"

"For a few days," Adam said.

Daniel's glance moved to the unshuttered windows. "With the lights on I can't see out. It must be a lovely night."

"It's not bad," said François gaily. "And do you know, they're floodlighting the chateau—an absurd idea and it looks quite wonderful. The ghost of the fourteenth century, without its squalor and cruelty."

"Ah," Daniel said. He smiled. "In my young days it wasn't a ghost, it was alive and lived in. . . . There were dances, then we changed and had breakfast, and rode out— the women, too, as fresh as if they had slept all night. That wasn't the Middle Ages; it was only yesterday; it was the world as it used to be before fanatics ruined it."

CHAPTER 9

NONE OF THEM HEARD ELIZABETH COME IN. Turning his head, Adam saw her in the doorway. To catch sight of her without warning gave him the same shock of excitement, painful and absurd—with the difference that now he knew it was absurd and tried to defend himself against it. As she moved towards the couch, her dress brushed his knees: he had the sensation that the warmth of her body was passing into his through the thin folds, and felt for a moment suffocated by the blood beating in his temples.

This was the first time since his return that she had seen Daniel: she gave no sign of being startled by his frightful gauntness. At this moment, as though he had used up too much energy, he was lying perfectly still, fleshless head sunk in the pillow, eyes vacant. Lifting one of his hands, she spoke to him as if he had never been away.

"We're going to walk down the road to look at the chateau. What a pity you can't come with us. There's a wind and it's quite cool."

She has no great liking for him, Adam thought, and no sympathy; she is being polite to an old gentleman, so old, so infinitely old and decrepit, that she can hardly see him as real. Neither is she pretending: she's polite, friendly, modest, because anything else would be an effort and unnatural. Yes, yes, he thought, with grief, this is where she

belongs, in the politeness and warmth of this countryside—
la grâce et la douceur tourangelle....

Daniel kept hold of her fingers. "I shall be quite happy
here. It will be dark and cool, I shall be alone—and outside—outside . . ."

Elizabeth freed her fingers gently. Turning to Adam, she
said,

"You'll come, won't you?"

"Certainly. If I may."

She looked at him gravely. "Do come. Unless it bores
you."

It gave him ridiculous trouble to speak in an ordinarily
calm voice. "There's nothing in the world I should like
better."

With surprising distinctness Daniel said, "Of course he
wants to see it. It's dead history, and the English adore
that, it flatters them to think how easily they survive. Besides,
he wants you to take him."

Adam looked at him. His glance crossed one so full of a
sardonic malice that he was slightly disconcerted. "It's true
we have fewer monuments than you French," he said civilly.
"Now and then I find myself thinking that you've kept
too many, you might move easier and farther if you weren't
struggling to prop up all that weight of the past—the often
brutal past."

"Is it any different in your country?" Elizabeth asked.
She was smiling.

My love, he thought with anguish, my only love. "Quite
different."

"And to think I shall never see it!" she said in a light
voice.

"Why not go there with Captain Hartley when he goes
back?" Daniel said. His profile at this moment had the
ferocity and slyness of a bird of prey. "He'll be delighted to
take you."

Adam looked closer at his face, this mask stretched over

a malice springing from the devil knew what depth in the broken body. He realised with a slight shock that Daniel had assumed, with the cynicism and edged clairvoyance of the very old, that he was in love with the young woman, and did not forgive him for it. Was not likely to forgive him for still being able to suffer, in spirit and body, from a mere emotion.

"That's quite true," he said smoothly, "I shall be delighted —when Jean brings his wife to England, as I trust he'll have the wits to do—to show her as much or as little of our past, our modest past, as I can."

The fall of Daniel's eyelids gave back to his face its bloodless severity. When he lifted them again it was to turn towards Elizabeth a gaze infantile in its unfocused serenity.

"Give me your hand again," he murmured.

She gave it to him without hesitation or marked kindness. A feeling of repugnance seized Adam at the sight of her hand lying in the feeble clasp of Daniel's dead fingers—they had all the appearance of death. He looked away. Jean came into the room at this moment, and Daniel said,

"As you see, my dear boy, I'm doing what I can to corrupt the young."

Elizabeth drew her hand away gently and turned her back on him. "You're coming with us to look at the chateau, Jean, aren't you?"

He shook his head. "I'm afraid not."

"Ah, do come," she said.

"I'll come some other night," he answered, smiling down at her.

"Do you promise?"

"Yes, yes, I promise."

As if his indulgent voice angered her, she turned away from him, quickly, slipped her arm into François's and, smiling into Adam's face, said gaily,

"Come along then, we'll go."

As he closed the door Adam caught the first words only

of a phrase drawn out of Daniel's inexhaustible, almost impersonal malice.

"You would have done better to go with them——" the
door shut—"your Englishman is not without charm, for all
his intolerable air of being equal to any situation. How I
dislike that! But it has its attraction, especially for an ignorant
young woman. Elizabeth has seen too few men, It's unwise
of you to throw them together."

A barely noticeable smile crossed Jean's face. Standing
beside the couch, he said,

"I came to put you to bed. Would you like anything
before you sleep?"

"Sleep? My dear boy, I gave up sleeping a long time
ago."

"Really?" No one ever, he thought sceptically, gives up
sleeping.

"I mean, without help. The prison doctor—a boor—
finally gave way and allowed me to send to Martinon in
Paris for some proper pills. I put them—where did I put
them?—there's too much room here. Living in a cell or a
prison hospital saves a lot of trouble. . . . They're in the
big pocket of my coat. On the back of the chair." He
watched Jean put his hand vainly into all the pockets. "Aren't
they there? Well—ah, I know—look in the flap of my letter-
case."

Handling the fine soft leather—across one corner, Daniel's
four initials in gold—Jean wondered where he had kept
it in this famous cell. He found a flat round box.

"Is this it?" He slipped the lid. "They're very small."

"Yes. Small, but extremely efficient." He sighed. "I only
take one. Do you think I could have something to send it
down? My throat isn't very obliging nowadays."

"Yes, of course. What do you want? Water? A glass of
wine?"

A plaintive, almost childlike expression came over
Daniel's face; his lips trembled slightly together, like dry

leaves. "D'you know what I'd like? A cup of lime tea. Cousin Marie used to make it for me, do you remember?"

"I think I could make it," Jean said.

He strode towards the door, and reached it as it opened. Cousin Marie came in.

She took no notice of him. He was too surprised to do anything but stare at her as she passed him. She walked as though a single impulsive movement had carried her from her room to Daniel Monnerie's couch. Her black dress, the one she had worn at dinner, covered her from neck to ankle: it was an old dress, one Jean had seen a score of times, but, astonishment sharpening his eyes, he noticed for the first time that it had been made on the lines of a Greek dress. In the same instant he saw that she had added to it, since dinner, an elaborate old bracelet. This unlikely touch of coquetry astonished him more than everything else. For less than a moment he felt alarmed. She might, he thought, do anything. With a vague idea of protecting Daniel, he came back into the room.

Daniel remained placid. He had perhaps reached a place where nothing disturbed him. Looking at her with an air of amusement he said,

"So after all you're too polite just to bolt."

"I had to see you," Cousin Marie said quietly.

His look of amusement and irony vanished. He said simply, "That was kind of you. I feel—happier."

"Kind?" She stared at him with as much surprise as contempt. "I only wanted to look at you."

After a moment,

"I see," he said with an effect of indifference. "Well, my dear, it's quite plain what being in prison did to me. And now are you satisfied?"

She moved a little nearer his couch. She was tense, her arms rigid at her sides; she held her head up, looking at him from lowered eyelids. Again Jean felt a prick of fear, but this time obscure and confused, premonition rather than

fear. Or a savage fear, lying dormant in his nerves, of the
danger created by a hatred as bitter as hers; mightn't it
spread farther, destroy more than one fragile old man? He
had an impulse to interfere, to stop her before it was too
late. And a vexed sense that they would both of them
consider anything he said as completely irrelevant. Hate,
like love, creates its own strictly closed world.

"No," Cousin Marie said in an even tone, "no—you should
have suffered. They should have made sure you suffered."

Daniel Monnerie smiled. "And you think I didn't?
Well——"

"I know you," she interrupted him. "Cold, sceptical,
selfish. You have always guarded yourself from any feeling,
any thought, that might hurt. But I wonder . . . did you
never, never once—in all these four years—see yourself as
you are? Ah, but you wouldn't admit it."

"This passion of yours for improving me," murmured
Daniel. "You and Jean! And when I think that I shall have
to spend my few remaining weeks with you. . . . I might
as well be back at school, kept in on a fine evening as a
punishment." He ended on a nearly inaudible laughter, a
whisper of pure merriment.

"Invite any friends you have here," she mocked him.

He was unmoved, except to a more biting gaiety. "Ah,
yes. I discovered when I was being tried how many friends
I had among our neighbors. They all turned out to be
patriots—even—no, especially the ones who had an innocent, excusable, oh, so excusable and easily explained little
moment of collaboration on their sour consciences. Praying
God that no one would hear about it and ask them to explain.
And comforting themselves by pointing at me. . . ."

He closed his eyes. Against his will he saw rising behind
them the faces that had obsessed him during his first weeks
in prison until his contempt managed to drive them from
his sight. He resented their return, bitterly. The disturbance
they started in him wrenched the nerves round his heart.

And he had so little strength. . . . One of his judges was not only a neighbor but an old friend, a man who, he knew, had been at best very lukewarm about rejecting the occupiers. This man raged against him like a devil—a very vulgar devil. Then there was the village chemist, known, everyone knew it, for treating his wife and children with sadistic unkindness; throughout the Occupation he had prudently ignored any chance of annoying the Germans, and so had four years bottled-up venom to get rid of. There were others. The thin clever schoolmaster with political ambitions. And a woman whose plump cheeks quivered suddenly in a gust of compassion—"Ah, let him off, what's he done, after all?" Did she have to pay afterwards for her moral collapse? he wondered: I hope not. . . . And then the face, the one face he was never able to evade for very long. . . . Opening his eyes, he saw it within a few feet of his bed.

"I don't remember what you did, my poor Marie."

"I didn't speak," she said drily.

"I'd forgotten. . . . But I haven't forgotten your face. That was—shall I tell you what you were like? You looked exactly as I always imagine Dante's face in hell when he was watching one of his old enemies being disgustingly tormented—pale, noble, perfectly serene. Nothing, I suppose, gives a hanging judge such a delicious feeling of serenity as the thought that his victim is being purged morally as well as in his shivering flesh!"

To be ignored, as if he were a chair or an infant, irritated Jean. He tried to break through the tension isolating these two enemies. If in fact they were enemies.

"Why must you go on tormenting each other like this? It's useless and rather horrible. Cousin Marie . . ."

The movement of Cousin Marie's hand brushed him negligently aside. "Simple people don't judge like lawyers," she told Daniel, fiercely. "They are like children, they see through lies, they know whom to hate, and who deserves to be killed." She drew herself up, shaking. "They hate—and their hatred rushes into filthy rooms and cleanses them. That's all."

"Wonderful," Daniel murmured, "wonderful, wonderful. A great actress was lost when you married Guy Regnier. And you mean every word of it! Yet you can't—I swear you can't tell me what I did to deserve to have a bathful of cleansing hatred emptied over me. Can you? Four years of—I don't want to exaggerate, you do it so much better—of a mitigated hell. And what had I done? Conducted myself like a civilised human being——"

"Like a traitor. Ah, if there were only a simpler word for what you are. . . ."

She stopped. And did a thing Jean thought very strange. Coming to the side of the couch, she laid one hand lightly on Daniel's chest. In a low voice, almost a whisper, she said,

"If you were sorry—and said so—you needn't any longer be an outcast in your own family."

Daniel looked up at her with his ironical smile. "How you would like to see me on my knees at your little feet!"

She jerked her hand back as sharply as if he had bitten it. "No."

"Yes," he said mockingly, "yes, my dear Marie. You came into this room tonight in the hope that it would happen. You had no other reason."

She did not answer at once. Watching her, Jean saw with horror that she had been seized by a craving to strike the helpless old man. Her arms lifted slightly, hands outspread and rigid. They fell again to her sides. She said softly,

"If you weren't dying—nearly dead—I wouldn't have tried to make things a little better. You're quite worthless. Your heart must be small and rotten—like a maggot. No wonder it is giving you up."

There was a long silence. It was a curiously sudden silence, and in Daniel's eyes the walls of the lighted room

wavered and thinned out like the smoke from burning
leaves; through it moved elongated shadows—as though
the immense silence and solitude of the darkness outside
had entered the house. He tried to lose himself in this
darkness, but the walls contracted again and hardened. He
felt a cold worm of anger moving in his body. Anger was
one of the pleasures he had forbidden himself; he could no
longer afford to borrow from it a brief energy, and he
thought he had left it behind in prison, with other ruinous
and futile emotions.

He glanced from Cousin Marie's face to Jean's, heavy
with a disapproving pity. "That's your judgement on me,
is it? Both of you. And yet—I didn't betray anyone, I
didn't give anyone away."

"You weren't given any chance," Cousin Marie said
calmly. "Until this evening you didn't know we'd had the
Englishman hidden upstairs for five nights. If you had
known . . ."

"I should have handed him over—is that what you think?"

"Of course."

Jean touched her arm. "You're hurting yourself more
cruelly than you can hurt him," he said gently.

Daniel's glance moved past him to fasten a weak claw of
energy on Cousin Marie's face. He could only just focus it.
"Are you going to say next that if I had had Robert in my
hands I should have betrayed him?"

"Why not? You were capable of it." She stopped. Her
own words had released in her an extraordinary feeling of
giddiness, as if she were looking into an abyss; she stiffened
slowly from feet to head; her eyes dilated, she began to lose
control at the same moment of her thoughts and her tongue.
Her voice rose.

"Yes, you knew he was here that night! Perhaps you
knew he was going to Orléans next day. Perhaps you spied
on us, listened. I ought to have questioned you at the trial. . . .
My God, oh my God. . . ."

There was nothing in Daniel now except his will to use the thin residue of life in his veins to punish. Punish her. The pleasure of letting himself go in a jet of hatred was almost too great, too sharp. He breathed carefully, as carefully as a woman draws a thread of silk through the too small eye of a needle.

"If you had done that, my dear, I might, perhaps, have told you to ask your beloved Babba about it."

"Babba? she echoed, stupefied. "You—what do you mean?"

Jean made an abrupt movement. He had been listening for the last minute to something he could hear approaching; he did not know what it was, it was still obscure and faceless, but it moved; pushed its way upward; and he felt it about to press on his body with a frightful, a quite insupportable weight. As well as fear, he felt an intense shameful curiosity. He shook both off. With the same coolness, he shook off his almost superstitious sense that what was going on here was beyond his control. What nonsense! His strongest habit of mind—that of the professional soldier he had wanted to be—took charge. If there were anything—anything at all except malice and the desire to hurt—in Daniel's retort, it must be forced out. Now. At once. He glanced quickly at Cousin Marie and realised that she was in her most uncompromising mood, will and spine both rigid. As for the fragile old creature in the bed, he was paying his energy out in tiny sums, like a prudent gambler. And probably too angry to care what he told.

"What do you mean?" he asked quietly.

"Ask your brother yourself what he knew," Daniel said under his breath.

"What could he know? He was in Paris then."

Daniel's tongue flicked across his upper lip. "Ah, yes—the famous printing press. Such a pity the Germans smoked it out so easily! And how lucky that François's part in it

was really so subordinate and casual—for all his boasts—
that his name wasn't even mentioned. . . ."

"You have a filthy tongue," Cousin Marie said.

"Please leave it to me now," Jean said. He looked at
Daniel Monnerie's eyes, the only part of him which seemed
alive: tiny shadows followed each other across this narrow
ford. "You're lying, aren't you?" he said coolly. "Just to
amuse yourself."

There was a silence, then Daniel muttered,

"Yes, I was lying."

"If you weren't . . ."

Daniel was exhausted. The effort of the last few minutes
had been too costly: no longer to be described as bloodless,
or emaciated, his face had become only planes, sharply
tilted, sunken, of light and shadow: all the life in it, and
the life of his body itself, was concentrated in throat and
lips. He managed his voice cleverly, at the expense of every
other effort. His eyes, although he turned them towards
the sound of Jean's voice, were dead.

"But I was," he said.

Jean watched him. "I would never have expected——"
he hesitated, and did not find the word he needed—"such
baseness," he finished.

Incredibly, Daniel smiled. "Really? But why not? You
know what I am! Nothing I do or say ought to surprise
you."

Cousin Marie spoke suddenly, with horror. "No, no, Jean—
there's something he hasn't told us. He does know something about Robert. About François." She turned on Daniel.
"Tell me what it is," she demanded. "What's in your mind?"

He closed his eyes. "Nothing. I should like to sleep now."

Losing control of herself completely, she stretched her
arms out, hands clenched, and shouted,

"Tell me—you've got to tell . . . to tell. . . ."

"Take her away," he said in a low voice to Jean. "She
wearies me to death."

Jean pushed aside any pity for him. "You've only to tell her the truth."

For another moment Daniel lay still, his eyes shut. The shadows laid across his face by the lamp were more living, warmer, than the thin layer of flesh below them. When he opened his eyes it seemed he had found somewhere a reserve of strength. He spoke clearly, with a peculiar fluttering lightness.

"The truth? Don't be absurd. You can expect nothing from me except lies, baseness, frivolity, cynicism—and so on and so forth—the whole noble patriotic scale."

Jean felt baffled. There was a note in this deliberate sarcasm which was not, to use Daniel's own words, frivolous or cynical. He thought briefly: The old devil really is hiding something. What?

"Uncle Daniel, for God's sake——" he stared directly, heartlessly, at the done-for old eyes—"you've accused François of knowing something about Robert's arrest. You can't leave it at that."

The glance his uncle returned him was quite placid and indifferent. "She made me angry. I was trying to punish her."

"So it was a gratuitous lie."

Daniel smiled. "Yes."

Jean considered this, steadying his mind. "You never told lies," he said slowly, "you have too little kindness for people to lie to them. And you never had that sort of inferiority—you never wanted to impress anyone, or be approved. You didn't even take the trouble to defend yourself before the tribunal."

"I'm sorry, dear boy," his uncle said distinctly. "You must forgive me. This time I was telling lies."

Still staring, talking to himself, Jean muttered,

"I wonder if I can believe you."

The hand Cousin Marie laid on his for a second was

stone cold; it made him jump. "Jean, go away," she said unemotionally, "leave me to talk to him."

"My dear Jean, I hope you'll do nothing of the kind," Daniel said mockingly. "It's quite a respectable death, being torn to pieces by women. Or so they say, our romantics. But I'm an ordinary reasonable man and I should prefer an ordinary death."

"Unfortunately, I can't tear out your brain and read it," she said drily.

"Dear Marie. I'm sure you would if you could. . . ."

A sound—the criss-crossing of voices outside, in the garden—broke into the room. . . . Jean was thrown back six years, to the night when he was walking along a road he did not know, north of La Flèche; he had become certain he was lost and might at any moment stumble into one of the patrols he knew to be out. And suddenly, where he had thought were only hedges, a thin stem of yellow light flowered; it widened to a prudent two inches, and a voice, the rough dragging voice of a countryman, spoke to him from the door of a cottage, a hovel. "Is that you, guv'nor?" At once, what had been inimical, bewildering, evil, became familiar and safe. . . .

The voices outside became indistinct, died out. Inside the room there was silence. Then, quick footsteps crossed the hall; the door opened; Elizabeth, her face unguardedly radiant, came in quickly. François came in on her heels.

Behind them, Adam Hartley hesitated in the doorway.

Looking into the room from the wide ill-lit hall, he saw it with painful sharpness. He still had behind his eyes the cool night, the spectres of trees, and the sounds born in the darkness—noise of tearing silk when a family of partridges rushed across the road in front of his face, soft bound of a hare less than a yard from his ear.

He watched Elizabeth walk directly to Jean and touch his arm, smiling into his face. "We came back for you, it's so lovely. Come and look."

"Sorry—I can't now," he answered. He leaned slightly back, hands on his waist in the attitude of an old washerwoman resting her body. He looked down at the girl with franker sensuality, thought Adam coldly, than he knew.

With an unshaken gaiety, she persisted. "Oh, please change your mind."

"Do. Do change it," Daniel echoed. He laughed, a shocking sound, startling even Jean. "You see," he went on in the silence, "she came back for you! She's afraid to be out there without you."

Jean lifted his head brusquely, and gave Adam a cool glance. Adam shrugged his shoulders.

"You really are missing something," he said quietly.

"Yes, my word you are," exclaimed François. "Do come, Jean. Both of you. . . . Mamma. . . ." He turned a brilliant smile on Mme. Regnier.

Although she had had her eyes, wide open and gleaming, fixed on him since he came into the room, it was a moment before she seemed to grasp that he was speaking to her. All she did then was to make a little gesture with her hand, the gesture of warding off a troublesome child.

"We're all too tired," Jean said rapidly and tonelessly. "Too tired, too old. Run away—all of you."

"Oh well," said François. He yawned, with a shameless abandon. "I'm very sleepy."

"Then go away to bed," his brother said again.

During this last minute Adam had become aware that only the tension in his own mind had prevented him from noticing the even sharper tension outside him, in the room. Not sure where it came from, he looked at Cousin Marie: she had moved and was leaning against a window, her black dress lost in the dark folds of the curtain—like a bat, he thought. He looked swiftly away from her.

"No, Jean," Elizabeth said, with her widest, most radiant smile, "you can't send us off to bed as if we were still in the nursery. It's the most splendid night you ever saw. The

scent is extraordinary—pines, clover, wood smoke, the freshness from the river. Ah, do come."

She was using, deliberately, Adam thought, every charm
she had, the seductively light movement of her hands, the
changing tones of her voice: lifting her head she looked at
Jean through her thick eyelashes. This was not like her.
It was not like her to act; the comedy, charming as it was,
struck him as intolerable. A silly and vulgar lie.

"I'm very sorry," Jean said. At its deepest and most
brusque his voice had a disquieting resonance. "Some other
night."

He rested his hand on her shoulder. Before he could
draw it back, she had bent her head swiftly and brushed it
with her lips.

"You disappoint me," she said.

Without glancing at anyone else she turned and went
quickly out of the room.

Jean's face as he looked after her gave away only an
impassive tenderness. The tenderness disappeared, wiped out,
when he turned to listen to François. Stretching himself,
yawning again widely, the young man was saying,

"Oh, very well then, good night." A little hesitantly he
added, "Good night, Uncle Daniel."

In a kind weak voice Daniel answered, "Good night, dear
boy."

Adam forced himself to shake off his feeling of uneasiness:
it sprang from his confused irritated sense that he was
stumbling about blindfold among ambiguities to which he
had no clue. His natural scepticism, as well as his good
sense, were outraged. I'm beginning to make mysteries out
of nothing, he told himself. The fact is I'm too tired to
think. . . .

François moved towards Cousin Marie, meaning to kiss
her. As if by accident Jean stepped between them: he gave
his brother a gentle push towards the door.

"Run along, my son," he said.

The young man raised his eyebrows and went through a delicate pantomime to show his amused understanding that Mamma was in one of her states, then slipped quickly away, blowing her a kiss from the doorway as he went.

With a brief good night, Adam followed him. He had the clearest possible impression as he passed her that he had only forestalled by a second a request—an order— from Cousin Marie to take himself off.

For a moment after he had gone, no one said anything. Jean decided brusquely to get rid of Cousin Marie. "I think——" he began.

She turned her head like a woman coming slowly awake, but ignored him, and said quietly and coldly to Daniel,

"Now—the truth."

Daniel made an attempt to answer her with decision. But now he could not bring even his voice under the control of the will fluttering visibly behind the skin of his temples. He managed a broken murmur.

"Every night for four years—how many nights—count them, Marie—I've imagined this night. Let me have it."

"You must let him rest," Jean said curtly. There was no need to add: He is, after all, a sick dying man.

"Why should I be sorry for him?" she said. "He's not worth being pitied."

"Perhaps not. But that has nothing to do with it."

She hesitated, then without a word moved to go away.

Jean held the door open for her, and followed her out. In silence he let her go upstairs. As he walked along the passage to the kitchen, he had the sense that his own footsteps were following him over the stone floor. Filling a glass with water, he hurried back with it.

"I'm sorry," he said formally. "I thought you'd rather have this than wait any longer while I tried to make lime tea."

"Thank you," Daniel said. "Would you—do you think I

might have that window open now? You could draw the shutter across it."

"Yes, of course."

He set the glass of water on the table at the head of the sofa, and placed the box of sleeping pills next it, then turned out every light but the one small closely shaded lamp on the table within reach of Daniel's hand. The breath of air that came in when he opened the window was noticeably salty, as always when the wind blew from the west. This faintly maritime air, flowing with the dark Loire below the scent of pines and cut grass, was soft and voluptuous.

He turned round. "Is that all right?"

Daniel did not answer. He had closed his eyes; his face showed no sign that he had heard, or would ever hear anything: it had the stillness and inhumanity of time-eaten stone heads above the doorway of an old building, an outline of coldness, contempt, delicacy, ruthlessness. Jean hesitated. There should be some word to carry as far as the thin stream still runing under this stone. In the end, tired, deriding himself as an imbecile, he went away without finding it.

Daniel Monnerie lay still for several minutes. Then with a deep sigh he opened his eyes, and slowly, fraction by fraction of an inch, pulled himself up until he was leaning against the back of the couch. Looking at the window, he tried, frowning, to recall the phrase hanging about timidly on the very edge of his mind. . . . "What is it, what is it?" he whispered. "What—ah! . . . *La Loire est une reine et les rois l'ont aimée*. . . ."

Satisfied, he stretched his hand out and closed it over the box of tablets. Before he could open it Cousin Marie came into the room; he put it down again on the table.

CHAPTER 10

Since she did not at once speak he thought: Poor Marie, she can't accept the irreparable, she goes on tearing her hands on it, as if it would be disloyal to turn away. . . . He wondered whether he had enough strength left to protect her as well as himself.

"Marie, haven't you any pity?" he asked gently.

As he had expected, she said, "No, not for you."

"For yourself, then, my poor girl."

"Do you mean anything by this nonsense?" she asked drily.

"You hurt yourself," he said. "And you torture me."

"Robert was tortured."

He knew he ought to keep silent. His feebleness spoke for him. "Poor boy."

"Don't pity him—you have no right," she said in the same dry cold voice, "you were a friend of the men who did it."

She was, he knew, past being reached by irony, but he said,

"Yes, I know, I know. But even if it were true, what good are you doing—to Robert's memory, to our family—by looking for new victims?"

Her eyes gleamed. "You can easily make me ridiculous. I *am* ridiculous—a woman of my age who nurses all her worst memories—and talks about justice. Anger makes me ugly, doesn't it? I ought to be like other people, sensible rational people, ready with a little dust to throw over the past—then brush it off my fingers and be happy. I could be happy—why not? I could shut my ears to Robert, close my eyes against his last minutes—and against all the other cruelties. I should keep my looks. And you—you would smile and say: Dear Marie, how much gentler and more charming she has become . . . I hope I shall never be gentle. Never."

Her vehemence revolted him a little. It was so female and ill bred.

"After all, you are like everyone else. You want to be paid for all you've lost. But why call that justice? You used to be more honest."

"You're very clever," she said contemptuously, "very, very clever. And an accomplished hypocrite. I'm too simple to be amused by your cleverness. Keep it for your equals."

Daniel did not speak. In prison he had become used to this sense of not belonging to himself, so much so that he was very often two men, the one who submitted and the one who watched him, with more amusement than contempt, submitting, preparing to submit. This evening the split had deepened abruptly, and he did not know whether he were thinking his own or the other's thoughts. He—or was it the other?—was willing, no, aching to tell her the truth. And not merely so that she would go away and leave him alone. There is a terrible temptation about the truth, when telling it will bring on a catastrophe: the taste for catastrophes is as old as sin. But could he trust her with the truth? Would she use it decently, or only murderously? . . . He had lost all confidence in his power to make a decision; his thoughts rushed away like smoke. He said wearily,

"Marie—isn't peace worth having? Let's anyhow have peace here. In this house."

"I would rather," she answered, shaking, "set fire to the

house and destroy every stick in it than have peace when peace means that Robert's murderers can creep back into the daylight, take good warm bread into their mouths, have children, smile at them, do with their apes' hearts and hands all the things that human beings do. . . . No, no, no. . . ."

Daniel smiled at her. "You were always all passion."

What she took to be contempt in his sunken eyes vexed her. "And you always detached, selfish, without warmth or honesty."

In a meditative voice he said, "You were very beautiful— but you frightened me. You're still beautiful, you know, although you're burned out. Burned down."

Anger struggled in her with some other feeling she refused to look at.

"Don't. I won't have you speak to me as if we were friends."

"We used to be," he said gently. "If you had said a word, one word, for me at my trial they would have treated me less severely."

"Did you expect it?"

"Yes. I did rather," he murmured.

For a moment her small colourless face was purely cruel. "I should like that to be true—because then you were disappointed."

The little strength Daniel had drawn from allowing his mind to drift was slipping away from him, with each breath. He remembered, very vaguely he remembered—and what the devil was this trivial memory doing here now?—a November evening when the Loire was in flood, and he had leaned far over it, trying to look into the dark vortex of a whirlpool: he had turned giddy and drawn himself back just in time. . . . With immense labour he said,

"You know—the instinct to punish often has very disreputable roots. At the trial you thought you were punishing me for Robert. But are you sure? Are you sure you weren't punishing me because a long time ago—years since—when you first came here—you loved me more than I cared to love you?"

She kept her eyes fixed on him with a look in them he failed to understand—he was too tired.

"I never loved you," she said calmly.

This made him smile. "Ah, Marie, Marie," he said, with the utmost gentleness, "and you called me a liar."

Nothing moved in her face; you would have said she was not listening: even her voice became dull.

"You are lying now."

How well did I ever know her? Daniel wondered. Perhaps she was always simpler, more vulnerable, than I imagined. A very beautiful woman—or a woman whose beauty is of the challenging, gleaming, almost malicious kind—rouses something like cruelty in a man too lazy and egotistical to surrender to it. Cruelty? But who could have helped it? It is true I was frightened. She would have been a devil of a handful, she was far too wilful and striking. What sensible man wants a wife who looks for all the world like a young St. George on the day of his victory? . . . There had been one evening when, from the window of his room, he saw her cross the lawn to the bank of the river, and stand there, her arm on the low wall. Then, too, she was in black. It must, he thought, have been soon after she came here, she was still wearing mourning for her husband—but her arms were bare from the shoulder, and on one wrist she wore the same antique bracelet made of seed-pearls she was wearing now. After a time, since she seemed fixed there, he joined her. It was a very warm night, the Loire as still as glass, but soft, soft, more a dark shadow than water. Standing beside her, he became aware that she was waiting, her body tense with its waiting, for him to say: I love you. Or for some word. Or some touch. Even apart from her certainty—she was certain—of her triumphant beauty, she had some reason to expect it. He had been showing her all the attentions of, well, perhaps not of a lover, but at least of a man who is deeply impressed. And now, abruptly, at the very moment when everything—the soft night, her nearness, her bare arms—should have turned him into the lover, he felt detached and cold, unwilling, very definitely unwilling, to commit himself. He began some argument—of no interest—he had forgotten it completely. After a few minutes of it she left him and walked back to the house alone. . . . Did she, he wondered, lie awake a long time? Humiliated? Arguing with her humiliation? She had—she has—an intellect as well as passions.

Almost without intending it, he said,

"Can you remember an evening—oh, years since, many years—when we were out there—" he moved his head very slightly—"you and I, and you wanted, you were hoping, that we should fall into each other's arms—a great passion? . . . It's so long since, you can let me say it, and I can say it —look what I am now—without being insufferable."

"Yes, it is true," she said under her breath. "But it's another life. It happened to another woman."

"But she went on living in you."

"No." She shivered a little, and crossed her arms over her chest. "No, she died at the same time as Robert."

"Look again, Marie. More carefully."

There was a silence. Letting her arms drop, she said,

"Perhaps she is alive."

Daniel sighed.

Her face changed suddenly, becoming dull and shrunken. "But she wouldn't fetch you as much as a glass of water."

"Then why did you come?"

"Why? You know quite well. I came to get the truth out of you. Jean would let you off, but—" an extraordinary smile of mockery and triumph crossed her face—"I shan't let you off."

The weariness he felt was more than a weakness of his body; it was outside him too, a river washing round him.

He had only to throw up his arms to drown in it—and what relief!

"Listen, Marie," he murmured, "suppose the boy—suppose that François made a mistake, would he be to blame? Entirely to blame?" He smiled with a little irony. "He had me as an example, you know. . . . And even Jean—you haven't forgotten that Jean used to call himself a pacifist, and talk to the child about war as murder and lunacy—which it is. . . ."

She cut him roughly short. "Jean was a soldier and a resister. What do you mean?"

"He was older than François—twelve years—old enough to become what he chose." Shadows crossed each other behind his eyes; a heavy weight dragged at him, at the back of his head; he resisted it with difficulty. "I heard stories when I was in prison about very young men—boys—being sentenced to death as traitors, who were obviously not traitors. Not even scoundrels. But dupes—" he lost the thread of his sentence— "children—terrified, begging at the last second not to be killed. In tears. Dupes."

He must have fallen away for a moment. He could not see the room clearly, and he was not sure of the woman near him. Who was she? Her voice stung him into attention.

"Are you telling me that François was duped into some treachery or other? What? And who duped him?"

"Perhaps I did. Or his nature——" he frowned—"he was very young then—when the war started. Sixteen. You expect too much of the people you're kind enough to love." He paused, and gave a clear weak brusque laugh. "When they disappoint you in some way, you're angry. It's shocking egoism, my dear—and really rather vulgar. There's a good deal of the peasant in you—you want your love to show a profit."

An astonishing smile forced open Cousin Marie's sallow lips—like a crack opened in a finger by the cold. She said quietly,

"Tell me the truth and let me judge for myself."

Daniel listened for a moment to himself breathing, a thin irregular rustle which had an independent existence somewhere near him.

"You love Jean," he muttered, "you respect him."

"Yes—you know I do."

"Then have a little pity on him, Marie, don't stir up what's done with—to break his heart."

She asked sharply, "Is that why you kept quiet?"

Have I been keeping quiet? he wondered. He felt confused. "You made me angry, you know, this evening. I'm so tired. I lost control of myself. I'm ashamed of it. . . ." He let his eyes close. "Be sorry for François. We can't all be heroes."

He had no idea how long the silence had lasted between them before he heard her saying,

"No one had any pity on my son. . . . Tell me the truth."

Now he had the idea that he was using a terrible force to push up a stone covering him; his other, his watching self, nudged his elbow; he saw first the edge of the sheet, then the woman's black-robed body—but only for a second.

"No, Marie," he said, faintly querulous—but with a sly smile. "Whatever François tells you will be the truth. Ask him." And let that be enough, he thought.

She bent over him. "Open your eyes. Look at me." He opened them and she saw that they were without colour, as if seared in his face. "Tell me," she repeated. She had to stoop lower to hear his answer.

"Let me sleep, Marie, I'm terribly tired."

She felt that she was biting into an acid fruit; it puckered the skin of her lips. He has always evaded everything, she thought. And tomorrow morning I'm going away. An angry despair seized her: she drew a chair up to the couch and sat down facing him.

"You shall sleep when you've told me." She spoke as if she were driving the words into a stubborn child. "Not until then."

His face, in its withdrawn stillness, became ironic. "Why, Marie, you take to torturing like a duck to water."

"How unfair," she cried, "and how like you!"

He made a gesture which surprised her. Stretching his hand out he touched her wrist. His fingers, for less than an instant, took hold of it, a light dry cold pressure, little heavier than a leaf. "Please, my dear Marie, please. Just this one night—you can't imagine how tired I am."

She struggled not to feel sorry for him. During a minute or two she sat swallowing tears. The silence of the house—a silence made up of a multitude of tiny sounds in the panelled walls and in the joints of old heavy cupboards, and filled by the thoughts of dead and living Monneries, the dead more insistent than the living, since their questions remained unanswered, unanswerable—narrowed to a few feet of space, to the womb of light enclosing the two of them. She said gently,

"But it's your own fault—you're so obstinate."

"No, no," he whispered, "I only want to sleep."

She gave way to a simple tenderness. "Sleep then."

"Ah——"

This sigh of relief so vexed her that she not only mistrusted him again, but lost suddenly every last rag of self-control. She sprang to her feet and bent over him, gripping his arm.

"No, no, you are a devil, a devil. Answer—answer me."

He did not answer. She shook him, and went on shaking him for a few seconds, then, coming to herself, stopped, looked at him; raised her hand to her mouth.

After a moment she hurried across the room and opened a shutter. A cindery light, weak, yet stronger than the light of the lamp, spread everywhere: in it, the room, like the man lying on the sofa, became quite different.

CHAPTER 11

COMING DOWN IN THE MORNING, ADAM
Hartley crossed a young servant, old Amélie's grand-
daughter, at her daily task of rubbing the stairs with a woollen
cloth: centuries of wax had produced a surface like blackened
amber, and only a little less dangerous. The door into the
courtyard was open: he went out, sauntered through the
kitchen gardens to the front of the house, and across the lawn
to the river. In this early sun the water was a greenish gold,
darkening to bronze in the shallows where pebbles and sand
seized and held the rays of light. The wind had dropped,
there was only the fine smiling light which stretched the
horizon to infinity on all sides; in its summer laziness the
Loire was as calm and cloudless as the sky; its curving banks
held it firmly—nothing soft about them, nor about the islands
lying warm and quiet between their sandy shores. Everything,
every stone, every leaf and idling water-bird, had been etched
with strong sweeping strokes. Without knowing it Adam
smiled. A morning in France like this one had on him the
effect of listening to Mozart; it made him believe he could do
anything.

He turned to look at the house. All the windows of the drawingroom stood open on to the garden. They've taken him
away, he thought. He walked slowly across the grass, and as
he approached the room saw someone in it—François—wear-

ing a sleeveless shirt and light trousers. When Adam stepped inside he hurried forward, smiling.

"You've heard the news? Has someone told you?"

"That Monsieur Monnerie is dead—yes, the servant told me when she brought my coffee. I'm sorry."

"Oh, there's no need to be sorry," François said pleasantly. "I'm not, I can't be—it's so much the kindest thing that could have happened to him."

"Did he die in his sleep?"

"Yes. Well, I suppose he did. The doctor says so. No one was there. He was dead when Mamma came in very early this morning. She called Jean, and Jean carried him upstairs—to his old bedroom." He glanced at the ceiling. In a lively voice he went on, "Just imagine—he used to be a heavy man —graceful, but very heavy. Now he's so light that Jean carried him alone easily. And that's what prison did to him. Awful! Poor old boy, poor Daniel!"

"How old was he?"

"Sixty-nine. He looked much older, didn't he? Well— I'm glad it's over." He looked at Adam with his charming smile and went on quickly, "Do you know, I lay awake for hours last night, worrying over the things I said yesterday. You must have thought I was mad—or neurotically silly."

Adam felt disinclined to help him. "Why, what did you say?"

"Oh, but surely you remember? I told Mamma you'd mistaken me—all the things I said to you about Uncle Daniel and his German general. You hadn't, of course, you were quite right. What can you possibly have thought of me? It wasn't until I was in bed that I had time to think about it, and then I worried myself to such a pitch I could hardly wait for morning to see you and explain. I felt simply terrible."

Although he was speaking easily, and smiling, he was plainly very anxious. Yet it was too small an incident to rouse this excessive anxiety. It's part of something else in

his mind, thought Adam. What? . . . A grotesque image—
the tip of a cat's tongue coming round the door—jumped
into his mind. He suppressed an indiscreet smile.

"There's nothing to explain," he said calmly. "I was tactless. That's all. It was stupid of me."

"No, no," exclaimed François, "it was my fault. I spoke
to you very carelessly and, you know, I hate to upset
Mamma—so then I was driven to get out of it as best I could.
But you must have been surprised and shocked by the awful
way I behaved."

"Good heavens, no," Adam said. "How absurd."

"Really? Do you mean that? Oh well, I'm very relieved."
With a swift return of his vivacity, he waved a hand at the
window. "What a magnificent morning! Isn't it? Not a
morning to be dead."

Adam stared and smiled. "I hadn't thought of it like that."

Jean Monnerie came into the room. Beyond nodding at him
he took no notice of Adam. Speaking with a sharp authority
to his brother he said,

"Will you catch the bus into Tours and get several things
we must have—oh, and leave this letter at the Vezins for
me."

"Yes, of course I will. What d'you want?"

"Good," Jean said curtly, turning away. "You'll find the
list lying on a chest in the hall." He began speaking, in a
warmer voice, to Adam. "I can't tell you how sorry I am
this has happened now——"

"I suppose I'd better change my clothes?" François interrupted in an easy voice.

"Yes."

As the young man went out, Adam said hurriedly, "I'm
damned sorry to be here in your way. I'll push off. Shall I try
to see Madame Regnier, or will you give her my thanks
and say goodbye to her for me? And—" he hesitated briefly
—"Elizabeth. Is she up?"

His instant feeling when the servant told him that old

Monnerie was dead had been one of overwhelming relief.
. . . Thanks be, I have my excuse to go. . . . To get away—
to turn his back on an experience not less bitter and humiliating because no one except himself knew about it—was all
he wanted now. He felt a crazy impatience.

"I hardly like to ask you not to go——" Jean began.

"But of course I'm going," he interrupted. "At once."
Realising that he had let his dismay show much too plainly,
even arrogantly, he added, "Perhaps you'd let me look in on
my way back. I'm driving south. I have business in Marseilles
—a customer."

He had no intention whatever of coming to the house
again.

Without moving a muscle of his face Jean said, "I want
you to stay now—if you will."

"But surely . . ."

"No, no," Jean said with a cold smile, "I'm not being polite.
I want you here." He stared in his least reassuring way. "In
fact, you must stay, I need you. . . . I'll talk to you about
it later—this evening—tomorrow. . . . There's too much to
think of now."

As he spoke, his hand had been moving absently among
the things scattered over the table. Now it closed on one
of them. He held it out on his palm.

"These shouldn't be left lying about," he murmured.
"The poor old boy's sleeping pills—unpleasant things, I
never need them myself."

He dropped the box into a pocket of his coat.

Feeling trapped, Adam said, "It's kind of you, but I'd
better go."

"Nothing to do with kindness. . . ." Elizabeth came in;
he turned to her. "Ah—you can deal with him," he said.

She looked at him with an air of surprise, very charming.
"What am I to do?"

He was already moving towards the door. "Persuade him
not to run away," he said over his shoulder.

He went out.

The girl turned to Adam with a polite smile. "Were you going?"

"Of course I was going. You can't want me underfoot now."

He watched her cross the room to a window. Without knowing it he was trying to see her as if for the first and last time—the young energy breaking awkwardly through the lightness, the soft youthfully unfinished line of cheek and jaw.

"Is it such a trouble?" she was saying. "He had his one perfectly happy night, and went quietly to sleep. Can you think of anything better?"

Adam started. "No. Yes. A great deal. Being alive this morning, for one." He had lost control of his thoughts and was talking at random. "Doesn't a day like this make you want to live forever?"

She shook her head. "No, what a dreadful idea!" She laughed, a clear laugh without malice. "Think of it. Either your friends will be immortal, too, and how unbearably bored you would get with them. Or every fifty years or so you'd find yourself with a fresh lot. And can you imagine anything worse than waiting for them to reach the point where the others left off! Thank you—no."

Is it only her foreignness that makes her enchanting? he wondered. Am I—it's more than likely—one of your English monomaniacs who give their hearts to a France which doesn't exist except for them? . . . He did not believe this. For all he cared she could be a Kalmuck—if Kalmucks have thin strong legs, and flecks of green light in magnificently dark eyes. . . . She was leaning against the frame of the open window. Outside, the heat must be intense. A ray of sun struck through a rent in one of the blinds stretched above all four windows, and a dust of tiny flies moved up and down, up and down, in this thin torrent; every now and then the leaves of a tree, an acacia, shivered in a light breath from the river.

If I don't go at once I never shall go, he thought. His indecision exasperated him with himself.

"I must go," he said. "What were you saying?"

Turning from the window she came to stand in front of him, smiling, with lifted eyebrows, each a smooth black feather. He forced himself to listen to her. Her nearness had the effect of making him feel heavy, as if the blood had thickened in his veins. As if he had had a slight sunstroke. No, I'm sunk, he thought drily.

"I was talking nonsense," she said, "But don't go. . . . It's strange that I find it so easy to talk to you—no, not strange at all."

Too much of his attention was going into memorising the movement of her thin wrists, the turn of her head on its long neck, and her voice, light, almost always a little mocking, but without a hint of malice. No one, he reminded himself, is ever able to recall as if hearing them the actual tones of a voice. Not even when dreaming. A pity. But after today it would be enough for him to catch sight of marguerites blazing in thick grass and hear the warmth of bees moving in and out of lime-trees, to see in the same instant, with hallucinating clearness, the movement of a wrist, a hand pushing off the forehead a fold of hair, a smile too young and candid to be, as it half seemed, equivocal. . . . Suddenly it struck him that she was not in reality so calm as he had thought. The part of his mind used to listening to the other person's desires and fears came to life sharply: for the moment it pushed back his sensual trouble.

"Yes?"

She looked away. "During the war, you know, when we had to do so many unlikely things—and lead an abnormal life—I didn't mind in the least, because, then, to be living a normal life would have been the wrong, the unnatural thing. But now—now I should like everything to be simple, even dull."

"And isn't it?"

"You know it isn't! You've seen Cousin Marie. Any house, any family with Cousin Marie in it, would always be—what do I mean?—restless, uneasy. I love her—oh, very much—I admire her more than anyone in the world. Except Jean. But I don't want to live in that uncompromising way always. Do you know?"

"Yes, I think I do."

He had an impulse to shake her gently, as you would a child who is having a nightmare.

A look of fear and exasperation clouded her face, giving her the air of a mutinous schoolboy. "And there's another thing. I have a hateful feeling of suspense—as if a spring which has been tightly wound is beginning to unwind. And it isn't only because a tired old gentleman who wasn't wanted, even in his own family, is lying upstairs dead."

"Nonsense," he said, smiling.

She laid her hand on his arm. "Did Jean mean that you want to go away altogether? Don't go."

He set his teeth to endure her touch. "I'm afraid I must."

"Oh, but why? You mustn't go." She moved away from him again, restlessly, and walked about touching things, the carved back of a chair, one of the horrible crochet mats on a table, as if trying to reassure herself by their commonplace existence. "There was something I wanted to ask you—a question—about Robert."

"What is it?"

"Nothing very much . . . Would he, do you think—if he had been alive would he have been as angry with Uncle Daniel as Cousin Marie is? Would he have wanted him punished?"

"How do I know?" said Adam. "But I think not."

She nodded soberly. "I'm sure you're right. And that makes me feel sure, too, that he wouldn't blame me at all for"—

she paused, lifting her hands lightly, half smiling—"oh, for being alive, and for . . . no, never mind. . . ." She bit her lip. "You know, when he died—and when we knew how he had died—that pain . . . and I thought if I had loved him better it might have protected him. . . . I felt such grief I didn't believe it would ever stop. It went everywhere with me, every day, every night. And then—and now . . . Oh, even if it's cruel, I must live, I must touch something living, I must feel the sun on my arms——" she held them out, thin brown. "And I enjoy riding and swimming and eating, and I've forgotten far too many things no one ought to forget."

"Are you always happy?" he asked ridiculously.

"Of course not! That would be absurd." She laughed. "The truth is, we should be much happier if Cousin Marie were less wonderful."

He had himself under control now; his violent sensations of a minute ago struck him as faintly idiotic. Only a complete fool lets himself suffer beyond the point where he can halt the process.

"We?" he repeated. "You and Jean? . . . When are you going to be married?"

She did not at once answer him. He wondered if he had offended her, and didn't deeply care. What could it matter? After a moment she said briefly,

"September . . ." She had gone back to the window. Lounging against the window, in an attitude that was graceful only because of her youth and thinness, she began rapidly, gaily, "Imagine it—we had you hidden away here for five days, if you had been found we should all have been punished, perhaps shot—they shot one of the Duvosquel girls because she was wearing an English parachute cord she had picked up—yet I know very little about you. It's all wrong. Tell me something. Anything."

"What can I tell you?"

She was, he realised it acutely now, on edge. Why?

"Your parents—tell me about them. Your father."

"I don't know much about him, he left my mother soon after I was born."

"He never wanted to see you?"

"I really don't know. I saw him once. When he died he left me the family business—but whether out of kindness, or duty—or simply inertia—I don't know; I have no idea."

"If he were like you—it was kindness." She came to stand in front of him again, abruptly. Her eyes, widely open, had filled with tears. "Yes, you're kind," she said in her lightest voice, "and obstinate and self-centered. And you always know what you want, and what you can do. But you're not"— she hesitated—"not in the least self-satisfied."

"Why are you crying?" Hartley asked. He spoke coolly, but it was an effort: the air between them seemed to have been drawn tight, so tight that any careless movement would snap it across like a fiddlestring.

"I'm not." She shook her head vigorously.

"Why?" he repeated.

Carefully, knowing what he was doing, he put his arms round her. He held her gently. I mustn't frighten her, he thought. After a moment she drew herself quickly back, but she still held his arms with both hands.

"No, no," she murmured, smiling and trembling. "Don't touch me again."

He knew that she was trembling only through the hard pressure of her fingers. Without a second thought he gave himself up to the inconceivable relief and pleasure of taking her frankly into his arms: he felt the warmth of her body, then nothing, only the relief, the discovery with all his senses of another human being, shoulders, small slight breasts, rounded knees. At first she only submitted, but in a moment she turned her mouth to his and held him with all the strength, astonishing, of her thin arms. She said something he did not catch.

"What?" he asked, with difficulty. "What did you say?"

She forced her head back. "How long is it?"

"How long . . . ?"

"When did you begin to love me?"

The foolishness of the question made him smile. "Yesterday."

"Oh," she murmured. "But I loved you when you were here—all those years ago—and ever since."

"Does it matter?"

"Yes, of course it does. Think how wicked it was . . . poor Robert. . . ."

She threw herself into his arms again, but he had reached the point of not being able to stand it. He held her gently away from him. "My love, my little love, nothing in the world matters—except ourselves. Except this."

Startling him, she broke away. "How can you say that? Everything matters—Jean—everything—Cousin Marie . . ."

Instinctively he picked up the least dangerous line. "Cousin Marie has nothing to say in this."

She interrupted him. "Someone is coming across the hall——"

As lightly and easily as you please she walked across the room to a window and turned to face the door. It opened briskly: Mme. Regnier came in.

She gave Adam a look at once unfriendly and self-possessed. "Are you staying with us, Captain Hartley?"

Before he could answer Elizabeth said, "Yes, he'll stay."

"I'm delighted," Mme. Regnier said. Never was a word less apt.

The ease—or did it only look like ease?—with which the girl had taken hold of herself and of the situation, astonished Adam. They are all born comedians, he thought with a faint touch of contempt. He turned to Mme. Regnier and said stiffly,

"If you're sure I'm not too much in your way?"

"You are in the way," she answered calmly, "but not too much." She glanced at Elizabeth. "You must do your best to amuse him. Perhaps he would like to see the vines, or the cellars, it's the sort of thing, I believe, Englishmen do like. But not now, please. We owe some respect to Monsieur Monnerie, after all. Be careful, won't you, that no one sees you out today, don't go into the village. There'll be plenty of time to fish later, if Captain Hartley would like to try."

From the corners of her eyes Elizabeth sent him a look of young complicity. "Would you like that?"

"Of course."

"And now, Elizabeth, please," Mme. Regnier said peremptorily, "I need some herbs. Will you get them for me and bring them to the kitchen?" As the girl moved to go out through a window, she raised her voice. "Your hat, Elizabeth, get your hat."

With a smile, Elizabeth stepped back into the room. "Is it more respectful to Uncle Daniel?"

"I was thinking quite as much of your complexion," Mme. Regnier said coldly.

"I hardly think that matters," the girl answered, still smiling. "But I'll get it."

She ran across the room, opening and shutting the door into the hall carelessly. Mme. Regnier watched her with a half-indulgent displeasure, then glanced sharply at Adam.

"Girls nowadays are either doubtfully moral or tomboys. Elizabeth will be steadier and more sensible when she's a little older."

"I hope not," he answered, polite and absent.

"Or when she marries," Cousin Marie went on inflexibly. "It's high time she was married. She and Jean, as I daresay you know, are going to be married—in September."

Was she warning him? Probably. He said slowly, "Shouldn't she—she hasn't after all, had very much freedom——"

As soon as he began to speak he knew he was being unwise. Mme. Regnier's eyes gleamed with contempt. She interrupted him in a harsh voice, so vehemently harsh that he felt certain she was not thinking only about Elizabeth.

"Freedom? What rubbish! You talk like—like an Englishman. A young woman is free to wait, quivering like a fish, day-dreaming, harming herself with her idiotic dreams, for some man to come along and make love to her. But d'you think that makes her happy? Rubbish! A house to look after, children, something she has to serve and go on serving—nothing else will give her life the only sense it can have."

Her almost brutal manner with him—he was becoming used to it—scarcely brushed Adam. At the moment he was too sunk in himself to pay very much attention to her. The thought that he was going to have to talk to Jean obsessed him. He felt a mixture of pity and disgust—above all, disgust. However well or badly he takes it, he thought harshly, it will be abominable. The taste of treachery in his mouth sickened him.

His mind was so demoralised that he had been staring through a fog of dissatisfaction and anger at the lawn and François Monnerie crossing it, for some moments before he saw them. He saw them suddenly. A flash of lightning behind his eyes jerked a whole buried landscape into vivid relief. The young man, still in his open-necked shirt and flannel trousers, was sauntering past the windows, an instant in full sunlight, the next instant standing in the light shade of the acacia, his head lifted, so that sun and shadow played across it and across his white shirt in a rippling shifting disjointed pattern.

Adam drew a sharp breath. . . . Now I remember him. . . .

The significance of what he remembered swept over him with such overwhelming surprise that he exclaimed,

"Good God, do you see him?"

Mme. Regnier stared at him, and lifted her eyebrows. She turned to glance through the window.

"See. . . ? See what, Captain Hartley? Are you talking about François?"

Vexed by his idiocy, he could have bitten his tongue out. In a mild voice he said,

"Did I startle you? Do forgive me, I thought for one

second that François was a man I knew during the war and haven't seen for—oh—it must be six years." He laughed. "I was very surprised."

The mocking look Mme. Regnier turned on him reassured him. So long as she takes me for an ill-mannered fool, he said to himself.

"You're in rather a nervous state, aren't you?" she said smoothly.

Glancing briefly at François, he asked,

"Was he in Paris the whole time during the war? No, of course not. He was too young."

"He was still at school in Tours when the war started. He didn't go to Paris, to the Sorbonne, until '42. . . ." With a movement of her hand, she dismissed François. "I must speak to you frankly for a moment, Captain Hartley. At any other time I should have been happy to try to keep you here—though no doubt you find us very dull—for as long as you cared to stay. But——"

She broke off as the door opened. The old servant stood there, staring at her, without a word.

"What is it, Amélie?" she asked with impatience. "What do you want?"

Amélie's voice was exactly the same whether she were announcing the end of the world or a fine day: it never varied its low dragging tone, except for the trace of satisfaction that crept into it when the news she brought was bad.

"There is no butter."

"What do you mean?"

"It's what I've told you—there is no butter—that old Grasset refuses to sell any, the sinner." She chuckled under her breath, delighted—for all her devotion and loyalty to what she always spoke of as "my" family—that one of her own sort, an old nothing of a farmer, was holding out on it.

"I'll see about it," Mme. Regnier said in a voice of menace.

She hurried out. As soon as she had gone Adam leaned out of the window, and called,

"Aren't you too hot out there?"

François Monnerie turned, laughing, and strolled towards the house. Adam stood aside to let him step into the room.

"No, it's marvellous," he cried. "I adore heat."

"Really? You remind me of Robert. He could stand as much heat as a lizard."

"Poor Robert," François said lightly. "Such a shame he had to die, he enjoyed everything so much." He stretched his hand in the ray of sun, moving his fingers. "Did you know he was a champion skier, among other things?"

"He didn't have to die," Adam said coolly, "he was murdered. And before that he was betrayed. Someone denounced him, you know. Probably—no, certainly—one of his own countrymen."

François pulled a disgusted face. "Don't talk about that," he said with energy, "it's too awful."

Adam watched him. "Did you see much of him during the war?"

"I? No. After I went to Paris I didn't see him at all. Yes, once"—a frown drew the thick eyebrows together over his sparkling eyes—"I saw him once."

"Where was that?"

"In Paris. We had dinner together at an amusing little restaurant I knew on one of the quays. The most delicious people—girls in pullovers with not a stitch under, and fellows who might have been anything, acrobats, writers, I don't know."

"You only saw him once?"

"Oh, well"—he pouted his lips—"it might have been twice —or even oftener. I forget. . . ." He threw his head up with the liveliness of a colt on a fine day. "What a morning! I must fly, though—if I'm going to swim before I do my errands." He laughed. "If Jean catches me still here—no swim for me this morning!"

He was out of the window in a flash, and across the lawn.

CHAPTER 12

Adam watched him until he disappeared behind a bank of willows. "No, no, I'm certain of it," he muttered. His hands were shaking, and he thrust them in his pockets. Think. I must think. . . . For a second, he saw Elizabeth's face; her clear eyelids were lowered, calm, abandoned to him. With an effort, he pushed her to one side, as if he had shut a door, and brought his whole mind to bear down on the problem he had to answer—and answer quickly.

Why, in the instant of recognising François, had he felt so certain that he was in Orléans that evening only because of something to do with Robert? It could, he warned himself, have been chance. . . . His instantaneous conviction was still there, unshaken. That young man knows something, he thought, probably not much, but something. . . . Wasn't it possible that, at the same time as he was running a clandestine press, he was involved with a group of resisters which at some point or other touched Robert's? It was perfectly possible. But why had he never said so? Perhaps because something went wrong. Not all resisters had been brave, devoted, or even decent men: there was a resistance underworld where private or political accounts were settled brutally, and common neurotics and criminals amused themselves. It was possible that, in his innocence, or only out of carelessness—he was surprised to discover what a low opinion he had of François Monnerie's good sense—the young man had stumbled into and out of one of these *cloaques*. Nothing about the resistance was too tortuous or too fantastic to be true. . . .

He thought coldly: The only thing is to ask him: Why were you in Orléans?

The door opened behind him. Jean came in—moving, as always when he was preoccupied, his head sunk between his shoulders, like an animal too massive to need to look where it is going. For a moment Adam saw him again for the first time. Before he became a face or a voice he had been this dark purpose moving quickly and steadily across the field in the lighter darkness of the summer night.

"You're going to stay, aren't you?" he asked.

"Yes."

"Good. Thanks."

You have nothing to thank me for, thought Adam drily. "I want to talk to you," he said. He stopped short. What ought I to talk to him about first? he asked himself. Again he felt a sour taste on his tongue.

"What about?"

Before he opened his mouth, Adam felt, for the first time, the whole weight of his responsibility. For less than a moment he considered holding his tongue. For less than a moment. It might be wiser, kinder, but he could not do it. With a painful clearness he saw Robert Regnier walking away from him in the early sun of a Paris street, turning for one instant to smile and lift his hand. No, no, he thought, I must find out what I can.

Almost roughly, he said,

"I told you I'd seen your brother somewhere before. I've remembered where it was."

Jean stared. "Where did you see him?"

"In Orléans. The evening I waited there for Robert."

"Impossible."

Adam faced his coldly intimidating stare for a moment,

then averted his eyes. His consciousness of this stare resting on him sharpened his voice.

"Forgive me, I haven't had time yet to get it straight in my own mind. . . . I can tell you the facts. . . . It was when I was walking to the station. I crossed one side of a very small square with trees, and I noticed the young man who was standing under one of them. . . . I noticed his face. . . . Extraordinary tricks one's mind plays. I suppose—the anxiety I was in at the time drove it into my mind—and then blacked it out. Just now—two or three minutes ago—I saw him out there in the garden—" he jerked his head—"in exactly the same attitude—and the light coming through the trees. Exactly the same."

Jean had not made a movement. "You must be mistaken."

"No." He looked at Jean again. Except that its lines had deepened, as though withdrawn into the dark flesh, his face kept its air of impassivity and absence. "My dear Jean, you know me better than to believe I make mistakes of this sort."

"You're sure it was François? After all, it's some years ——" he stopped, and moved his hand sharply. "Yes, yes, of course you're sure. . . . Did he see you?"

"No. Just as I passed him a child racing a hoop ran head first into him and fell on the gravel—he picked her up and dusted her knees, and smiled at her. She was crying." He added, "You all smile alike in your family. Even Monsieur Monnerie."

Jean asked coldly, "What do you propose I should do?"

With something like irritation, Adam frowned and said, "Why d'you ask me that? . . . Surely there's only one thing to do? Send for François and question him about it."

Jean lifted his head: his eyes were hard, calm, attentive.

"Are you suggesting that he denounced Robert?"

Adam looked at him, stupefied. "Good God, no. Of course not."

"Then why question him?"

"Why? But—simply to find out what he was doing in Orléans that evening—of all evenings." He added slowly, "And what he knows."

"Why should he know anything?"

Adam did not answer at once. How could I, he asked himself, have been so abominably obtuse and naïve as not to expect this? There is something missing in me, he thought, with remorse. Why didn't I remember immediately that François isn't only his brother, he's more like his child, an only child. . . . He was appalled by his egoism. In the same moment he had to suppress a feeling of impatience. There was now no drawing back. The thing must be got clear—and the sooner the better.

"Listen, Jean," he said with energy, "there's no question of François being guilty. Or"—he caught himself back, not able to be less than exact—"if it's anything at all, only guilty of knowing something he hasn't told us. . . . If he knows nothing, why did he never tell you he was in Orléans that day?"

He waited. Silence.

"He knows something—it may be only the least, the most insignificant detail—but even that—in such complete bewildering darkness. . . . It might be the first real clue to fall into our hands in the whole of this vile business."

"Vile?" Jean repeated. "Vile?" His voice had sunk to such a depth, was so devoid of any change of tone, that it could be keeping the same time as the throbbing of the blood in his arteries. "Would it be any viler than the way you persist in tearing the bandages off a wound—poisoned—suppurating? . . . And what's the use? What good is it? All that happened in another life—over and done with. It might never have existed. We're living in another world, the world of simple respectable people who made profits out of the war —our farmers, old Grasset who sold the Germans all his butter at ten times what he would have got for it from women who couldn't buy it for their children, Georges Fargue who cheated them year after year and put the money under his mattress—there were plenty of others who found the Germans a wonderful gold mine. . . . Or my dear second cousins in Tours, the Vezin family, lawyers, who jumped from side to side of the fence with the agility of fleas, according to the news they picked up on the B.B.C. . . . They make a magnificent story of it now, believe me, the risks they ran listening in at night in a cellar so well buried that not a rat could have found it, let alone a German. . . ." He pulled a mocking face. "Robert got himself tortured to save men like these, pantaloons like Daladier and Reynaud. When I think of it now, I laugh."

He was not laughing.

"All perfectly true, no doubt," Adam said quietly, "but——"

"Yes, yes, I know what you're going to say—the courage, the sacrifices, the miracles of goodness and heroism and simplicity, are just as true, just as much the naked human being. I know, I know. But I'm through, I've stopped playing. I'm through." He took a step forward, with an unconscious air of menace. "Forget it, forget Robert. Let it alone."

"My God, I don't understand you," Adam exclaimed.

A gleam of life broke through Jean's fixed gaze, the explosion, silent, of a malicious laugh.

"You don't? Rubbish! You're not a fool, not naïve, you understand perfectly well that the one hope of a tolerable life in this house is to let us forget what happened six years ago." He paused, and went on rapidly, with the same repressed passion. "I asked you to stay here—instead of letting you go away, as obviously you wanted—because I hoped that, with you in the house, Cousin Marie would be forced to keep quiet about a thing that happened last night. Something Uncle Daniel said to her about François. Whether he meant it or not, God knows, I don't. The truth is she maddened him until either he didn't know what he was saying or didn't care. My belief is he didn't care. What I hoped"

—he smiled briefly and without kindness—"was to use you as a brake, a sedative, something that allowed Cousin Marie time to calm down."

Adam scowled. He was going to have to give way. It would be impossible to question François unless his brother agreed. Impossible, too, to go on insisting. It was unkind— and in bad taste. I'm a guest, he thought, irritated. Very well, drop it. . . . He prepared to drop it—but with the worst possible grace.

"If you think I'm making a mistake——"

Monnerie cut him very short. "Understand me, I don't disbelieve you. François was in Orléans that day. Very well, he was in Orléans. But since not even you believe he had anything to do with Robert's arrest, what is the good of starting trouble? Tell me that."

"Why should a few questions——"

"Because Cousin Marie is like that, because if you give her a shadow of an excuse, a shadow of a reason to believe that someone—François—anyone on earth or in hell—had any part—at fifth, sixth, fiftieth hand—in betraying her son, she won't rest until she has torn out of François whatever secret"—his voice sank—"whatever worthless little secret he has been keeping from us. . . . Let me tell you something you don't know. She was with Daniel when he died —questioning him. . . . That's what she is. Unmanageable. Impossible. Impossible."

Just because he was defeated, Adam shut his ears to the undertone of humiliation and grief in his friend's voice. He said stubbornly,

"Madame Regnier? I don't see why she need be brought into it. . . . And I don't see any good reason for not asking François, quite simply, what he was doing in Orléans. It may turn out to be nothing at all. Take us nowhere. But it's the obvious and sensible thing to do."

Jean's stare gave away his contempt with so much mocking indifference that it was an insult.

"You always know what is the sensible thing to do, don't you? Other people make mistakes because they're ignorant or stupid, you make them only from the purest motives. You talk, you're always talking, about the need to be tolerant and you have as much tolerance as a stone. Like all Englishmen. . . ." Leaning over the table, both hands pressed on it to support his weight, he smiled. "And at the bottom of it, all you want is to be morally comfortable. To be certain it wasn't you who made some fatal, some idiotic mistake. You're like the rest of us, a hypocrite, but a polite hypocrite——"

After all, he is going to agree with me, Adam thought. His victory—which he had ceased to expect—filled him with something between remorse and tenderness.

"You're quite wrong," he said gently. "The one thing I can't stand is knowing that at this very moment a man is living somewhere who can move his hands, feel the sun on them, take up a piece of bread in them, lay them on a woman . . . and Robert's hands . . ." Instinctively, he moved his own.

"Very touching. I never knew you were a poet."

Adam laughed. "Call me any dog's names you like——" The thought of Elizabeth sprang into his mind. He felt a confused shame. Not now, I can't my God talk about that now. He was unwilling even to think about it, or about Elizabeth. One war at a time, he thought briefly. As briefly, it brushed his mind that he would have done better, in effect done less damage, if, as a younger and less disciplined man would have done he had dropped everything else and gone straight for—for what?—for his happiness. He let the thought sink without trace.

"If I ask you—as a kindness to me—to me, not to Cousin Marie—" Monnerie was speaking between his teeth, closed in on himself like a man who has been wounded in the stomach and has to avoid any but the most cautious movements—"to hold your tongue? . . . I realise what I'm asking. It's not possible for you to forget you saw François in

Orléans that day. The very day, the very evening Robert was arrested there. But I——"

He stopped, turned his head slightly, and stared over Adam's shoulder at the window open on the lawn. Adam swung round.

How long had Cousin Marie been standing there?

CHAPTER 13

I N A DRAGGING, CURIOUSLY REMOTE VOICE
she said, "What are you talking about? François was in Paris
then, not in Orléans."

She came in, slowly.

"He was in Orléans," Jean said.

"What? What nonsense. How do you know?"

Jean looked maliciously at Adam. "He was seen there. Our
friend Hartley saw him."

The turn on its slender neck of Mme. Regnier's head, and
her eyes, fixed on him as a hawk fixes a young bird, effec-
tively steadied Adam. He looked at her, waiting for her to
question him.

"Captain Hartley, is it true?"

"I'm afraid so," he said.

Her lifted eyebrows gave her a fine air of amusement.
"May I ask why, why you've only just decided to tell us
this—this astonishing story?"

Before he could answer, Jean said,

"Don't take the trouble to go into all that, my dear. I've
had the story, from beginning to end." He went on in an
even voice, "I have no doubt, no doubt of any sort, that
François was in Orléans that evening. About that there's no
question. The question is what we ought to do." He turned
his head to stare coldly at Adam. "If we ask Captain Hartley

to hold his tongue, not to speak of it again, he'll probably agree. He's very conscious of the debt he owes our family——"

Adam could not stop himself saying,

"You could have begun there. Why didn't you?"

"It was hardly necessary, was it?" said Jean smoothly.

"No." Adam smiled with a sarcasm directed strictly at himself. "It shouldn't have been necessary."

With a light cutting impatience Cousin Marie said,

"What Captain Hartley owes us—or chooses to think he owes us—is completely irrelevant. . . . Where is François?"

"Cousin Marie, the simplest thing we can do is to do nothing," Jean said brusquely. "Make no enquiries. Ask François no questions. Bury it when we bury Uncle Daniel. . . . I beg you."

There was a short silence. Without looking at him, Cousin Marie said,

"Have you really the—" she spread her hands out—"call it strength of mind—it could be cowardice—to do nothing? . . . You believe you could rub out the picture of François strolling about Orléans the very day Robert fell into their hands? Not even ask him what he was doing there? Not ask anything?"

"It would be the best thing," he said, with difficulty.

Now she looked at him. "No. I can't."

"I beg you," he said again, softly. "What will be the use?"

She moved slowly to a chair, and sat down in it, her back as straight as always, hands resting on the arms.

"You agree with me, not with Jean," she said to Adam coldly. It was not a question.

He hesitated and said, "Yes, I agree with you. . . . But I'm perfectly willing to drop it. . . ." He looked directly at Jean. "Only—if you drop it, if you don't question your brother, you won't forget it, you know. There'll always be a doubt in your mind—poisoning you. . . . Do you suppose you can stand that?"

Jean smiled. "I should have known I could count on you to be sensible—as always."

Adam made no reply. With a feeling of dissatisfaction—indefinite, attached to nothing—he thought: I've said all I can. . . . In the end, the decision was not his. It lay between the other two. As unobtrusively as he could he retreated to the back of the room, and stood there against a window —watching. He was not simply a spectator, not even only a witness; he was involved, deeply. But with me, he thought suddenly and bitterly, it is almost a question of nerves: the nerve of pity for Robert, of—call it love for him; for what he was. With them, it is a matter of the heart and the blood it sends through their veins, of their bodies, minds, the past, the present, the same hatreds, the same silences. . . . He watched Cousin Marie get up from her chair and stand in front of Jean, arms hanging and rigid.

"You're asking too much of me, Jean. In any case—tell me, why should I spare François?"

"He's very young."

"He is one year older now than Robert was, when they were . . . hurting him."

Strange that the anguish she must be feeling, Jean thought —surely she felt it?—gave her this false air of youth; her face was smoother and less haggard, her mouth full and soft. What was it Daniel said about the terrible serenity of a hanging judge? Unjust: and yet true. She was as single-minded, as innocent, as Electra sentencing her mother to be butchered. . . . When we were children, he thought abruptly, she never made any difference between us. . . . *My three children.* . . . No one who saw her carrying François, with Robert holding her by the skirts, would have guessed that one was her son and one not; she loved both, she punished both, with the same justice. As now. . . . A profound pity for her seized him. Against it, he felt utterly powerless.

She had brought her hands together, gripping them. He took them in one of his, noticing half absently that they were cold, the skin covered with fine lines—an old woman's hands.

"At least leave it for a few days," he murmured. "Leave it until after the funeral."

Freeing her hands, she walked about the room for a minute. He watched her, trying to guess the thoughts behind her white face—trying and failing. She turned suddenly and looked at him without kindness.

"No." In a gentler voice she added, "And what's more, Jean, you agree with me."

Do I? he asked himself. Involuntarily he shuddered—goose walking over his grave. He felt certain—in spite of her woman's obstinacy and incorruptible anger, he felt certain that if he chose to use his authority as head of the family he could shout her down. . . . Am I going to try that? . . .

A frightful weight seemed to have fastened on his will, dragging it back. I spoiled him, he thought. . . . All through his brother's childhood, and when François began to grow up, the boy had only to ask eagerly for something, or beg to be let off a dull duty, and Jean gave way. He could close his eyes and see himself in the clumsy uniform of his military service year being hurried along a side street in Tours, François pulling at his hand, to look at the very expensive bicycle the child wanted—and against all his elder brother's saner instincts, got. It was always the same. Who could be harsh with a child so affectionate, so charmingly eager to please? No mother had ever indulged a son more crazily than he had indulged François, protected him from the anger of tutors and schoolmasters, forgiven him when, with floods of tears, he confessed to taking a hundred francs from the drawer where old Amélie kept a little money. He knew he ought to dock it off the boy's pocket-money. Instead, he replaced it himself. . . . And when the lively loving little boy became an adolescent, with an adolescent's slyness and reserve, he turned his eyes away from every sign that François was capable of being selfish and irresponsible far beyond the natural egoism of a

young man. Even the affair of the clandestine press. . . .
What Daniel had let drop was no news to Jean. Ever since the
end of the war he had known that his brother had been boast-
ing when he told them about "my press"; he had had very
little to do with it, almost nothing. Even this Jean had refused
to look at squarely—very much as a woman will refuse to take
any notice of a pain nagging her body.

Why? Out of weakness? Out of love? . . . Who knows
how deeply a man or woman is to blame for being soft with
a child? Any more than you can be sure, sure, that a wise
thoughtful sternness is what it thinks it is—and not simply
cruelty in disguise.

They are waiting for me to decide, he thought. Both of
them. But he knew already what he had decided. This sick-
ness at his heart—François had become just that—must at last
be looked at. Even if . . .

He did not finish his thought.

"Very well," he said in a low voice, looking at Cousin
Marie. "You have the right to be merciless."

He has given in, Adam thought. . . . He had no feeling
of pleasure. A feeling almost of disaster. He was struck by
the movement of Cousin Marie's arms, sudden and violent,
like a cry of joy breaking from her silence and rigidity. . . .
She would certainly hold her tongue under torture, she has as
much courage in her little finger as most of us in our whole
body, but what have I let loose, my God, in this house? . . .
He pressed his lips together over an unsought and uncomfortable doubt. No, no, he answered himself, let's get at
the truth. . . .

"You're satisfied now, I hope," Jean said to him. He was
smiling, a derisive but not an unfriendly smile.

"I don't see what else you could have done," Adam said
quietly.

Jean shrugged his shoulders. "When are you going to
talk to the boy?" he asked Mme. Regnier, harshly.

"This evening. You must give me your word to say nothing to him before then. Do you promise?"

He stared. "Yes."

She insisted. "You promise really?"

"What promises are not real?" he asked, smiling.

"Those one makes to oneself," she said swiftly, "to be loyal, generous, tolerant, happy."

"I know nobody so loyal as you," he said.

She walked quickly towards the door. Reluctant to call attention to himself, Adam let her pass him and did not move: she had reached the door before Jean was able to shake off a feeling of indifference, deathly indifference, as paralysing as extreme bodily weakness. She looked back at him as she was going out.

"The worst disloyalties go on inside. No one sees them."

She went out.

After a moment Adam said,

"Why can't you and I talk to François alone? Why make a family affair of it?"

Jean looked at him. "It is a family affair."

"I don't see it."

"There are a great many things you take care not to see."

The best I can do now is to take myself out of his sight, Adam though drily. He moved to go.

"There's one thing I must say—again. I don't imagine— I don't believe for one moment that François behaved treacherously. What I do believe is that he knows more than he has ever told anyone. He had—" he hesitated—"he may, during the war, have had untrustworthy friends. All your people were not models of loyalty and courage. Any more than ours would have been in the same circumstances."

"Than yours?" Jean mocked. "Good of you."

"At the very worst," Adam went on calmly, "he may have been careless. . . . Or—he may have gone to Orléans to see a girl. Why not?"

"Perhaps. But he didn't tell any of us he had been in Orléans that evening."

"It isn't possible to tell the truth always—or at a given moment," Adam said bitterly—a bitterness his friend felt was unnecessary and out of place. "It's not even always decent."

He turned and went out of the room.

Alone, Jean sat down heavily at the table and rested his head on his hands. He was not able to think. He let himself drift into an oppressive no-man's-land of consciousness, darkened by a vague feeling of insecurity and doubt: his house, his whole life, had become dubious, without meaning or shape.

He was roused from his absurd state by François, who put his head into the room, said "Oh, there you are," and came in. He had changed into a thin dark suit, one he might have worn in Paris when he needed to be elegant. Lifting his head, Jean forced a smile, less for François's benefit than his own, to hide from himself the momentary anguish he felt. He had a crazy impulse to say: Get away—anywhere. Only go, take your thin graceful energetic body and lively face into safety. None of it is your fault, so why should you be punished? . . . Instead he asked calmly,

"Have you been to town?"

"Not yet," François said gaily, "I'm just going. I went down and had a swim."

"You've been swimming—this morning?"

"Oh, why not? It's a perfect day for it."

Yes, after all, why not? Jean shrugged his shoulders without answering. François gave him a confiding smile and said,

"There's something I wanted to ask you. I was going to talk about it yesterday, but with Uncle Daniel coming and then dying and all that——"

"Yes?"

Except that he was not a child, François's smile, coaxing

manner, the look of merriment in his dark eyes, were those of the attractive little boy. In his eagerness he stammered slightly.

"Is there any point in my living here? I hate farming really. And even the vines. . . . I enjoy the river, and fishing, and going out after hares, and the rest of it. But I'm frightfully bored otherwise. And you don't need me, do you? After all, it's you the place belongs to really, you've lived here longer than I have, you like it—and when you marry——"

Jean interrupted him quietly. This was so unexpected a turn that he had a sharp feeling of relief, as though the pressure on him had lifted.

"What could you do?"

A flame of gaiety and enthusiasm sprang in François's eyes. "What I'd like to do is to go to New York—no, it's not as mad as it sounds, in fact it's extremely sensible. Jacques Bonfant is going—you know his father's firm has an agency there, Jacques has to learn the business, and if I went with him I could have a job, too. Nothing very grand, but a beginning, and then——"

Frowning, Jean interrupted again. "Bonfant? Wasn't there some story?"

The half-sulky, half-pleading look that came into the young man's face was familiar. "You mean about his being a collaborator? It isn't true. In fact it's a damned lie—he was never tried, or anything."

"He may have been lucky," Jean said in an ironical voice.

"Well, I like him," exclaimed François, "he's a good sort, amusing. And I should like to go to New York—get away from here, a new life, a country where people really live. I'd have a chance to do something there, be someone." Smiling, he put his head on one side, with a charming diffidence. "I know Mamma will scream—but talk to her about it, Jeannot, won't you? It's what I really want—more than anything in the world."

Like the bicycle, thought Jean. Like the expensive camera he never had the patience to learn to use properly. The fencing he lost interest in when he discovered that to be good at it involved long arduous practice. . . . All bitterly true. And in the same breath he found himself responding, warmly, helplessly, to his young brother's eagerness and energy, and wanting to give him what he craved. As so often before he felt convinced, almost, that this time it was decisive, this time it was the thing, the one thing which would harness François's restless intelligence. Half automatically he said,

"We'll see. We'll talk about it later."

"But soon," insisted François. "I can't wait long. Bonfant wants to know."

They must have been planning it for some time, thought Jean. The thought hardened him.

"And I want my letter to Vezin delivered," he said coolly. "D'you think you could now?"

"Yes, yes, I'll go."

He made a waltzing turn on the polished floor, chanting in what he imagined to be American the first line of a song he had picked up on the radio.

"François," his brother said gently, "don't sing as you go upstairs."

"Oh, my God, I forgot," he cried. "I'm sorry."

But the door slipped out of his grasp and slammed, and he had to reopen it to say again that he was sorry. . . . Jean watched him with affectionate derision. No, it's not so bad, he thought brusquely: Hartley's right, there's some explanation, disreputable perhaps, or silly—a girl—he wouldn't want it to be known he was in Orléans on that particular day amusing himself. . . . The worst is never true. . . . His war-time creed. And like all such, believed without regard for the facts. Not that he ever denied facts their seriousness: he was not a fool; and he never needed to make

light of danger by cocking snooks at it. But, below everything else in him, below his seriousness, his terrible lucidity,
below even his habit of mockery, there persisted a smiling half-
puzzled simplicity, the simplicity of a man who would rather
work well than be liked.

CHAPTER 14

THE PRIEST HAD WALKED FROM THE VILLAGE
in the late afternoon heat—not a great distance, but for a
man so crippled, far enough—and spent an hour on his knees
beside Daniel Monnerie's bed. Now, on his way out of the
house, he allowed Jean to persuade him to sit for a few
minutes in the drawingroom and drink a glass of wine, one
glass. He might have refused it if Mme. Regnier had not
brought it in herself: not out of complaisance—she did not like
him—but because, parish priest as he was, she did not
like him. And because he had suffered in Dachau attentions
which turned a robust broad-limbed peasant into this
shuffling wreck. Not that Father Baussan had ever been a
beauty; he was short, with blazing prominent eyes, a wide
mouth, a nose so broad and flat that the nostrils spread across
his cheeks, and an adam's apple the size of a walnut moving
under the skin of his throat. But he had been sturdy and his
body well knit: it was now frail and lop-sided, dog's-eared
at the corners, shrivelled like an old man, and it jerked as
if held together by wires.

He sat sipping his wine, the lump in his throat rising
and falling like a ball caught in a jet of water. His skinny
twisted legs ended below his cassock in boots covered with
chalky dust. From barely opened lips Cousin Marie dropped

a few civilities of which he took no notice. He was certainly the most tactless priest in France. At last, fixing on her the glow of his large eyes, he said,

"I hope, Madame Regnier, you were given the chance to forgive Monsieur Monnerie—and be forgiven by him."

Cousin Marie met his glance with an unflinching brightness. "I haven't the faintest idea what you mean," she said coldly.

Before he answered, Father Baussan took another sip. "I needn't ask you what *you* mean," he said. "You didn't forgive him."

"Certainly I didn't. And I don't. Why should I?"

"For the simplest of reasons. That neither you, Madame Regnier, nor I nor anyone, has the right to refuse to forgive any other human being. To a person of your sensibility it ought to go without saying."

Amused, as it would have amused him to watch two skilled fencers at each other, Jean said,

"Are you including your guards at Dachau?"

He knew what the answer would be, but he wanted to hear it, and Cousin Marie's reply.

"Certainly," retorted the priest. He waved one of his twisted hands. "I'd like to know what else you could do with them except forgive them?"

"I myself," Cousin Marie said calmly, "if I had liberated Dachau and the others, would have shot them all. At once. Before any imbecile of a lawyer could get there to save them."

A sharp smile crossed Father Baussan's broad lips. "I daresay. And you would have been wrong. Why? Because in each of them Christ is waiting, and what right have you to ruin His chances?"

Something—a belief, was it?—or a bitterness he could not for the moment turn into irony—moved obscurely in Jean Monnerie. "Is that what you would tell a French soldier, called up for the second time to throw out the same, always the same docile inspired brutal invader? Aren't you—forgive me—a little too exacting?"

The priest turned on him a newly sorrowful look.

"Alas, no," he said softly. "I know that sometimes one must kill. But it was something else we were talking about. About forgiveness and punishment. And I was saying, to Madame Regnier, that no one is allowed to kill *as a punishment*. Who knows what the rest of the cruel fellow's life might have been saving up for him?"

"More cruelties, perhaps," said Jean drily.

"This is delicious wine," the priest murmured.

"Let me give you another glass."

"No. Thank you." In the same voice, low and more than a little harsh, with the dragging inflections of his birthplace in a lost village of the Morvan, he went on, "It might be something utterly different. We all—even the stupidest of us, like me—know that there is always a chance of the coward turning brave or the broken man becoming whole. So why shouldn't the wicked man live his last half-hour as a saint? It's not impossible. Nothing is impossible. Let me tell you something . . ." He hesitated. Did it just brush his mind that once again, and this time really monstrously, he was about to prove his want of tact? If it did, he paid no attention. . . . "You are, let us say, being tortured, you have become nothing but your body, which is in pain. That is what your sadistic guard wanted, he wanted you to understand that you are only this black swollen face, this miserable body—which belongs to him. And at this moment, which seems the last—and ought to be the last, if you were not an animal of my sort, unable to die—suddenly you escape, you look at your man and you see that he is defeated, there is positively nothing more he can do. And he knows it. At the last minute, ugly brute that you are, up you jump." He coughed before allowing himself his sharp smile. "I speak figuratively."

He's only telling me what I knew, thought Jean, but why

talk about it in front of Robert's mother? Without moving
his head, he watched her, confident that she did not see
him. She had listened with seeming calm to what might
have been her son's story, gleaming eyes half closed, exactly
as she would fastidiously have endured a bore. Abruptly—
by some secret compassion—he realised that whether she
spoke or held her tongue the dispute was strictly between
her and this priest she didn't like. And that she wanted it
to go on.

"I believe you," he said coolly. "There is something—
some energy—in reserve at the lowest level. But what is
it?"

Just as coldly, Father Baussan said, "God."

"It's possible." Jean smiled. "But do you need your highest
card? Couldn't it be the one single proof, the only one we
have, that there is something we call our freedom . . .?"

"Put there by God," retorted the priest. "What you call
an instant of freedom is Christ. The instant when—for less
than an instant—He lives in you."

The slight gesture Cousin Marie made startled both
men. She had called up a look of tired amused pity. "So
you forgive your guards! How—if I may say so—how
exalted and unreasonable of you."

"Oh, but I have splendid reasons," he answered eagerly,
almost merrily. "Let me give you one—my best. My Nazis,
poor fellows—and you could say the same thing about
Monsieur Monnerie and our other so-called traitors and
collaborators—see, everywhere they turn, a brute force at
work. They obey it instinctively, as a blade of grass does, or
a dog. And like grass and dogs they are part of this world—
and so one loves them. The world is there to be loved. One
pities them, too, of course—they're so ridiculously mistaken
about what moves the world. . . . As for you, my daughter,
and your little quarrel with God—a quarrel inside the family—
I know, I know—you expected an answer to your prayers
for Robert. . . . I will love You if You save my son; if not I

shall dislike You. . . . But exactly, exactly—" his eyes blazed
with eagerness and triumph—"like a man with something
to sell! . . . I have named my price. . . . Or a child bargaining
with his parent. That's not how to persuade God to wipe
away all tears—no, no, no."

In a pitying condescending voice, such a voice as she used
sometimes with old Amélie, Cousin Marie said,

"My poor Father, I don't suppose He wiped your tears in
Dachau, did He?"

She goes too far, thought Jean. The priest obviously did
not mind.

"No, of course not," he said simply. "Why should He have
interfered between me and His other children who were
tormenting me? He made the world and left it to us, you
know." He glanced reflectively at his legs, dangling like
two dead branches. "I don't mind telling you," he said in a
brisker voice, "that at the time I had a fearful job remembering
it. . . . I don't blame you. I'm only giving you from my
experience—from Robert's, too, poor child—believe me—
the answer to those questions you lie awake at night asking.
Prayer is only prayer when there is no answer, the love
that hopes for a return isn't love. . . ."

He began to get up from his chair, an involved process,
since he had to place each foot exactly where it would take
the distorted balance of his body. It needed most of his
attention, but he went on talking.

"You'll see. One day you'll send for me to tell me that
you've decided, since there's no reason why you should, to
believe that God is good, and to love Him—in your miserable
human way. Since there's no reason. . . . Ah-h-h," he ended.

It was a sigh of contentment; he had achieved his balance.
He moved at once to go away, making a clumsy gesture
towards Mme. Regnier. She stood up, and bent her head
stiffly, without a trace of friendliness.

Jean walked with him as far as the courtyard. "If you'll
wait a minute I have an English friend here with a car. I'll

fetch him, and he'll run you home. Mine cracked up again last week."

"Oh, thank you, but I'd rather walk," said the priest, smiling. "Now that I've got back the use of my legs I should be a scoundrel if I didn't use them. Besides, it keeps me fit."

And off he went, moving in jerks, like the toys children wind up. Jean did not stay to watch him, but went round to the front of the house. On any other day he would have walked part of his way with Father Baussan. Or at least would have turned over in his mind what the priest had said—not so much as priest but as man, a man intelligent enough, and who had been to the very end of human courage and cruelty. And who, without any false modesty, had something to say about both. But today he had no patience, even for this priest he respected. The thought of what lay in front of him this evening was too much: he could hold it at a distance, he could call up reserves of hardness and irony; but that was the most he could do.

It was close on seven o'clock, the air so clear that leaves, grass, the slates of the roof, were traced in it like veins: the Loire disappeared into the distance, an immense distance, with no loss of clarity; as far as the eye followed it it was as sharp as glass. The trees at the side of the house, transparent and luminous, formed a cliff of tawny light, the very colour of evening. Jean had a sense of astonishment. A prisoner suddenly set free and taken to the edge of the sea would feel as astonished, as overwhelmed by its vast calm. And with this feeling of release his confidence began to come back, even his gaiety. He found that he was smiling.

CHAPTER 15

WHEN ADAM PASSED IT ON HIS WAY
downstairs the door of Daniel Monnerie's room was partly
open. He could see that the nun was back in her place by
the bed; she was reading her prayer-book—or is it what
they call a breviary? he wondered. He knew nothing about
Catholics. For less than a moment he saw his dead mother
lying on the bed in her room. Three days, he thought, she
was alone there for three days. Now and then, when he
could manage it without being seen by anyone, he went
in and spoke to her, whispering in her ear—so that she should
not feel herself absolutely deserted. Her icy cold, her unnatural unmeaning smile, the coldness of the room, created a
sense of loneliness, neglect, abandonment, he had found harder
to bear than anything else. This other way was surely kinder?

The drawingroom when he came into it was empty. The
sunblinds had been raised and all the shutters folded back
to let into the room a light tinged with saffron, beneficent,
pouring down from the half-hoop of clear sky and reflected
from the river and its unmoving poplars and willows.
Adam stood staring through a window. No ghost, however
restless and demanding pity, could survive in this light, he
said to himself, not even in this house. . . . He shook off the
unwanted memory. The vague feeling of guilt it had started

in him persisted. Coolly, he turned his back on that, too:
he refused, his common sense refused to think that
possibly he had made an error this morning. If I had been
less than absolutely certain, he thought, it would have been
unforgivable to say anything to Jean. But I am certain.
And so—what else could I have done? . . .

He caught his breath as Elizabeth appeared, running
towards him from the direction of the arch leading to the
inner courtyard and the barns: she kept close to the house,
as if trying not to be seen from the upper windows.

"Ah, you're here," she said, out of breath, "we have only
five minutes—and everything still to say."

"Everything has been said." He meant it seriously.
Impossible, with her cheek on his, her warm fingers gripping
his wrists, to think that he had ever been separate from
her or could be again. "I know everything about you—" he
freed his hands—"from here, from your eyes—inwards to
what you are thinking." He passed his fingers over her
eyelids, moving his hands gently down to close them round
her chin; its fine bones rested in his palms like the hard line
of a sculpture.

"If it were only true," she said, smiling, a desperate young
smile. "If we only had more time."

"We have all the time we need," Adam said with energy,
"time to live together for fifty years at least, time to plant
trees, work, travel, time to grow old and sit in front of a
fire in the evening, reading, and warming our old feet."

"No." She shook her head.

"Yes, my darling, yes, yes, yes. Don't be absurd."

He took her in his arms. She completed him—as if all
these years he had been a man without a centre, without a
heart. He felt calm and lucid, sure of her and himself.
Never to be without her again, he thought, with a light
shock: to be happy with her, amused, surprised, bored,
enchanted, content, angry—a happy life is full of quarrels,
even bitter quarrels, and of anguish, disappointments,

boredom, and there are always, until the last of them has come and gone, reconciliations and another morning and night. To have children, to have no time and no place in his life for other women. . . . He realised abruptly that she was trying to free herself from him.

"What is the matter?" he asked. "Don't move."

She drew back. "I came to tell you—we can't possibly love each other——"

"But we do," he interrupted, unable not to smile, "you're talking terrible nonsense."

"Yes, we do! I love you with all my heart and soul, but no one must know, we mustn't tell anyone. And you must go away."

"Why?"

"You know why. Because of Jean—because of Cousin Marie—because they took me in here and were kind to me, kinder than they had any need to be."

"Who wouldn't be kind to you?"

"A young woman without parents and without a penny?" she cried vehemently. "You don't know what you're talking about, Adam. . . . Cousin Marie treated me from the day I came here as if I were her daughter. And Jean——"

She broke off, with a light helpless gesture of her hands. Adam said gently,

"I know. I'm not a fool, I know what it will cost you to hurt them. . . . You don't imagine I like it any better, do you? But you're not going to give me up to marry Jean. That sort of thing—sacrifice and all that—is senseless and shocking. And completely futile."

She looked at him with amused reproach. "But you were ready to sacrifice yourself in the war! You even came here when you could have stayed safely at home for another two years."

"That's altogether different," he said, with calm sincerity. "What you do in war time—or for an idea—that's not sacrifice, it's a matter of course. Nothing to do with any

sentiment about sacrificing your happiness to make someone else happy—it's pretty certain you'll make them pay for
it!"

"How arrogant you are!" Elizabeth cried.

"Arrogant?" he said, astonished. "I? If you knew how
humble I feel when I look at you. . . ."

"And if I had been married to Jean by the time you got
here?"

"That would have been another matter," he said curtly.
"I should have run for my life."

She threw her hands up. "No, you are impossible," she
murmured. She laid her palm on his cheek, forgiving him.
"I love you and you are impossible."

"Listen to me," he said, "we have no time now to argue
about anything, anything inessential. I'll tell you what I
propose to do. You can't stay here afterwards—after I've
spoken to Jean. I have a friend in our Embassy in Paris,
quite a good friend; he's married, his wife is a sensible woman,
intelligent, kind-hearted. I'll take you to her; she'll be
delighted to look after you until we can be married—I don't
know how long it takes to get married in France. But everything's quite easy, quite simple."

Her lips trembled as if she had been crying. She smiled.
"How do you manage, the times when you're not able to
pretend that things which are horribly difficult are simple
and easy? You frighten me, Adam. You're too sure of
yourself."

After all, he thought, chilled, I'm talking to a stranger.

"That's not true," he muttered. "I'm very uncertain. I'm
selfish and self-centred as well, as you already noticed. I
shall probably hurt and disappoint you—again and again.
If you're afraid of me . . . I can't do anything. . . ."

Elizabeth threw her arms around him. "But you love me,"
she said fiercely, "you love me. You're sure you love me?
Yesterday you were sure. Hold me, please—no, no, closer
than you have ever held me. Hurt me. Quickly!"

The moment of agony when his confidence had failed him vanished in an access of pity. After a minute he said,

"I thought I'd lost you."

Something, her eyelashes, moved against his cheek. "No, Adam."

"I understand how much you care for Jean," he said. "And how hard this is for you. But it's impossible for us not to seize each other. Quite impossible. You see that, don't you?"

"Yes. Yes."

She thought for a moment of Jean, seeing him in the icy light he himself turned on things and people. Any woman he loves, she told herself, will always, for all his love, come under his judgement, his *appraising* judgement. He can't help it. . . . Adam, far less reasonable, in one way less intelligent, was less disconcerting, his illogical certainties easier to live with and, in the end, less dangerous to their possessor. Not, she thought quickly, that he was simpler than Jean; he had his own subtleties—with which he didn't make any play: he ignored them, but they were there, the profound source of his strength. He took care not to know himself too well . . . Jean handled himself with the skill, control, and coldness of a good actor. It failed to strike her that if he did not appraise himself as coldly, as brutally, as he appraised everyone else, she would hardly have been able to see him with so little pity or sensual trouble. . . . Never to be dupe, even of himself—what a weight to carry about for life! . . .

She drew back to be able to look at Adam clearly. "I don't believe you know why I love you—selfish, self-centred as you say you are," she said, smiling. "In the end, at the very end, you're peaceful and solid. I like that."

"Don't count on me to be either with you. Besides, we're not at the end."

"You won't speak to Jean yet, will you?" she said swiftly.

He frowned. "I can't. Not before tomorrow—we've got

to get through this evening first. I suppose you know about that?"

"Oh, yes, I know all about it," she said, with a flash of impatience and exasperation. "Cousin Marie told me this afternoon when we were taking the cream off the milk. Poor François! I hate these family inquisitions. And I feel very unhappy about this one. It's going to turn out badly, I know it." She added quickly, "And for us, too."

"Why for us?"

"I don't know. But I feel it will."

"Nonsense, my darling . . . I detest, I must say, this idea of putting the young fool through the hoops in front of us all. It's not what I expected—or wanted. And I can't believe it was necessary. But it will turn out all right. I promise you."

"Do you think so?" she murmured.

"I'm sure."

He turned her face to his to kiss it, and abruptly released her. Someone, outside in the hall—it must be François—had begun to sing. His voice, unusually clear and pure, lent the tune of what was only a foolish new song a strange poignancy. He stopped as he opened the door. Poking his head into the room he said gaily, "Dinner's just going in—come, my chickens, come at once." He laughed and added, "That's what Mamma said when we were children, you know."

CHAPTER 16

"Bᴜᴛ ᴡʜᴀᴛ's ɪᴛ ᴀʟʟ ᴀʙᴏᴜᴛ? ᴡʜʏ ᴀʀᴇ ʏᴏᴜ asking me these absurd questions?"

The young man's voice was alert, vigorous, frank. Watching him, Adam was struck, as at first sight, by the extraordinary brilliance of his eyes; they might have been made from something hotter and less ephemeral than flesh— from black bubbling pitch. His slender body was tense with energy.

A feeling familiar to him all his life seized Adam, a needle-point of expectation, the certainty that something decisive was on its way and a sense that he himself had become coldly perceptive and adroit. He was still convinced that François had been hiding an essential piece of information, not important in itself, but revealing and significant when dropped into place. . . . A sudden memory—the man, a Belgian, suspected of being a spy, whom he had helped to interrogate one hot evening in July, 1944. He saw the man with great distinctness, dark face, small sunken black eyes and thin mouth, against a vague background, the white-washed walls of a country schoolroom, a petrol lamp, a moth, its wings singed, turning madly round and round on a sheet of squared paper. The man defended himself very cleverly, his face insolently calm, but his hands, Adam

noticed suddenly, were contracted like a pair of claws. . . .
Involuntarily he glanced at François's hands, and in the
same instant remembered his revulsion, the jet of shame,
almost grief, when the Belgian broke down, confessed, and
was taken out. Not that he cared about the fate of the
wretched man: it was the thought of the pleasure—it was
that—he had taken in trapping him. For others to finish off
in the school playground. . . .

These family councils, he thought drily, are the devil.
They are part of the rites and sacrifices the French devote to a
demi-god which has taken the form of the family. It is perhaps
on the point of falling on its face, like Dagon, but will that
be entirely a good thing? And what will they set up to serve
in its place?

Outside, the night was not dark enough yet to reflect the
lights in the room, but small and large moths came to beat
themselves against the windows; they knocked, flew off in a
circle, came back. Adam watched them for a minute with a
slight feeling of distaste, then looked away, round the room.
Empty coffee cups stood about on a table, with a decanter
and glasses, but no one was drinking. Cousin Marie had
seated herself directly opposite François, on the sofa: she
had an air of complete serenity. You couldn't have said
that Jean Monnerie looked serene, although his face
expressed little more than a heavy frowning attentiveness.
With a sharp pang, Adam recalled his voice speaking about
his young brother one night when they shared the bedroom
of a village schoolmaster—you would have said a father
talking. . . . He could see Elizabeth only if he turned his
head: he had taken care to sit next and a little in front of
her, with the ridiculous idea that his body afforded her
the shelter she needed—a young bird hidden trembling
under a rock from the hawk overhead. That she was not
trembling, and had claws of her own, failed to spoil his
absurd satisfaction.

"For your sake," answered Jean quietly, "to clear up"—

he paused and went on without any change in his full, deep, monotonous voice—"certain doubts."

"But where," cried François, "did you get them from—these doubts, as you call them?" Frowning, he looked from one to the other, then slapped his hand on the table. "I've got it! Someone has been telling you that the printing press in Paris was bogus, because it never distributed anything. . . . What rot!"

With even more gentleness his brother said,

"But, my dear child, no one said anything of the sort."

Very little taken aback, the young man retorted, "You implied it."

Jean moved his head slowly. "I asked you to tell us more about it. That's all."

"But it wasn't my fault if the brutes got their hands on it before we'd properly started. No more than it's my fault I was lucky enough not to be there that night!" He went on talking quickly and easily, waving his hands. "I really was lucky. I'd tossed up whether to take a cab or the metro, and it came down for the metro, so I went in at the Etoile—and walked straight into a round-up. I stood for three mortal hours against the wall while they looked at papers and arrested two people—and in the end it was so late I decided I'd go home to bed. But for that. . . ."

He is being too adroit, Adam thought. He looked covertly at Jean and Mme. Regnier, trying to detect, in their eyes fixed on the young man, what they thought of his fluency. He learned nothing. Jean was eyeing his brother with a heavy, almost sorrowful stare; Mme. Regnier's gaze was quite dispassionate, as if she were barely interested. But it was she who spoke as soon as François's rapid voice stopped.

"You never tried again," she said calmly. "And in fact, no one ever saw anything you had printed."

"That's not true! I still have a set of proofs of the pamphlet we were getting out at the time—the set I had in my room. Why, I showed them to you." He jumped up. "I'll get them, they're in my bedroom——"

"No," ordered Cousin Marie. "Sit still."

François turned on her in a quivering fury. "I won't be treated like this. It's abominable." He controlled himself. Sitting down again, he said quietly, "I beg your pardon, Mamma. But you really have no right to criticise me— either of you. I did what I could. I suppose, if I'd given all my time to it, I could have done more. But you were always—both you and Jean—writing to me: Get on with your work, don't neglect your classes. . . . You're being extremely unfair."

Jean watched him with the same sorrowful attention. "You're not to blame for anything to do with the press— except for pretending you were running it, that it was yours. You did that to make yourself look important." In a lower voice he went on, "And that was my fault—for expecting more of you than you had it in you to do or be."

"Dear me, you're very sententious this evening," the young man said in a tone of easy sarcasm.

Jean smiled briefly. "Perhaps. I'm sorry. But——"

François cut him short. Pointing at Adam he said,

"And why is *he* sitting here staring? If he hasn't the decency to take himself out of a family squabble, you ought to tell him. It's not his business."

Adam had expected this. Listening, as closely as he was, to the high-pitched young voice he had caught a note that was not anger: it might be desperation. He felt momentarily sorry for the young man, and irritated by the cruelty of this inquisition. He said quietly,

"You're forgetting, aren't you, that Robert was working with me."

"I don't see the connection," François said in a puzzled voice.

Leaning forward slightly, her back an unbending line, Cousin Marie said,

"Never mind about the press. It's not important."

He looked at her with the same air of bewilderment. "Then what is?"

There was a short silence while she stared into his face, her own grave, without malice. "The only important thing is to know why you were in Orléans the evening Robert was arrested there."

"What are you talking about?" He spoke quickly—no trace of hesitation.

She repeated her words.

François flung his hands up. "But this is mad! I wasn't in Orléans during the whole of the war. Not once."

Almost imploring him, Jean said, "Think very carefully."

If ever I saw candour in a face . . . Adam thought. This very candour roused him, it was too clear, too free of any of the trouble of innocence defending itself. My child, you're overdoing it, he thought without kindness.

François repeated his denial, word for word, in a firm voice.

If I had been allowed to talk to him alone, thought Adam, this is where we should have started. He leaned forward.

"Forgive me," he said, "I saw you there."

François turned on him a smiling insolence. "You have me at a great disadvantage. The sillier the lie the less possible it is to deny it."

"You do, don't you, deny it," said Jean Monnerie, slowly, heavily.

"Of course I do!"

Jean turned to his friend. "Are you sure? Quite sure?"

He half closed his eyes—afraid, perhaps, that he was giving himself away.

Adam did not answer at once. He had a horrible moment of indecision and stupor. Can one be sure of anything? The wildest improbabilities are no more improbable than an absolute certainty. . . . At this moment he caught sight of the young man's left hand: no one else could see it, he had turned in his chair and flung that arm over the back, but the fingers, instead of hanging slackly, were stretched like claws, and jerked in time to a violent irregular pulse. The temptation seized Adam to lie. He could quite easily do it, he had only to hesitate, stammer something about his own state of mind in Orléans, beg their pardon for making a fool of himself—and get up and go out of the room, leaving François to make the most of his triumph; the young ape would do it very well, a fine performance.

He forced himself to think calmly. What should I have achieved? . . . Jean's peace of mind. His happiness—since I should be handing Elizabeth back to him when I went away, as I should have to go. At once. I should go away leaving everything exactly as it was before I came into the house. . . . And without knowing—never, I should never know—how Robert was trapped. Who trapped him. But, after all, is the knowledge worth this—this execution? . . .

Looking up, he caught Jean's eyes fixed on him in a hard penetrating ironically accusing stare, and knew that he had been seen through. Knew, too, that he could not do his friend the kindness of lying to him. It meant repudiating too much that had been created between them. A loyalty and trust created not without pain. To deface it would be too indecent. He said,

"Yes, I'm sure."

Standing up for a moment, François twisted his face and body into a caricature, offensive and mocking, of his graceful deference to an older man.

"Thanks! This is twice you've tried to make trouble for me. What's the point? You're either mad or a peculiar sort of liar and mischief-maker—which is it?"

"That's enough," his brother said sharply.

Adam pressed his lips together over the direct question he wanted to thrust at François. This, now, he thought with energy, is the moment for it. . . . But it was Jean, not he, who had the right to ask it. Or Mme. Regnier.

From her face, its delicacy hardened into an absence of any expression, feeling of any sort, he could guess nothing.

"Forgive me," he said coldly, "but can't you tell the boy what he's accused of, and finish?"

François laughed bitterly and wildly. "Dear me, don't you have family gatherings in England? Do you mean to say you don't make a habit of prying, digging over graves, opening private letters, bullying? Wonderful!"

"That's enough," Jean said again—this time with so much kindness that a flame of hope, or anger, sprang in the young man's white face. He struck a clenched hand on the table and shouted,

"Very well. Unless you tell me what you're getting at I won't listen any longer. It's monstrous—all of you sitting round me like judges. . . ."

"One of your judges is not here," Cousin Marie said.

She had spoken calmly, so calmly that it disconcerted the young man. He looked at her as though he were not sure whether he had been hurt. "What—what do you mean?"

She stretched her head forward.

"I mean that before he died yesterday your Uncle Daniel told me all he knew about you."

Did he? wondered Adam. It struck him as highly unlikely. Jean, at whom he looked interrogatively, returned him an inexpressive stare. His own impatience and exasperation were reaching a point where he would not be able to control them.

François's efforts to steady himself gave him a sulky and defiant air. "But what? What could he tell you? There was nothing. Nothing to tell."

Elizabeth spoke, abruptly and coldly.

"If you'll excuse me, Cousin Marie, I'll go. I don't like this, and I don't see that there's any need for me to be here."

Cousin Marie looked at her for a moment with surprise.

In a light voice, its smoothness touched with contempt, she said,

"Of course you must be here. You were going to marry my son—or have you forgotten that now?"

Elizabeth did not answer; and stayed where she was. You old devil, thought Adam sourly. He moved his chair back a cautious few inches, bringing himself close enough to Elizabeth to lay his hand on her arm for a second. She gave him a quick glance. In the same moment when he felt a spurt of anger that he had no right to protect her, he saw that she did not need protection, his or anyone's.

Cousin Marie wanted more light on the table which stood between her and François. She ordered Jean to move two of the lamps. They were heavy old-fashioned brass monsters and threw down swathes of yellow light in the centre of the table. In the darkness outside there were now two broken flames; it seemed that the moths circled between them, clinging desperately with beating wings, then falling helplessly back into the distorted reflection.

When he had placed the lamps so that they satisfied her, Jean did not sit down again at once. He leaned against the table. The light from the nearest lamp threw into shadow his eyes under their heavy lids: his long mouth, the ends drawn down, enclosed between deep lines, expressed at the same time tenderness and a hard reserve. He said in a low voice,

"For the last time, François, I ask you to tell us anything you can. All you can. I promise you it's the best thing."

There was a long pause. The young man seemed to be going through a struggle with himself. . . . *Is* he? Adam wondered. Or is he only acting out all the emotions of a man going through a struggle? . . . Surprised, he found himself believing this.

For the first time, he faced the suspicion that François might be more than carelessly guilty.

He glanced at Jean Monnerie. . . . Does he think the same

thing? . . . He was standing as Adam had seen him stand scores of times when he had a difficult problem to settle, hands on his waist, big head lowered slightly, frowning, all his intelligence and anxiety concentrated in the fixed stare of his eyes under their heavy lids.

Adam waited. Abruptly, since Jean remained silent, he decided to strike.

"May I remind you of something? You told me, the first evening I was here, that you had known General Kettler well, and liked him. Later, when you were talking to Monsieur Monnerie, you made it very plain to him that you were counting on him not to give you away—to keep it a secret. But now that Monsieur Monnerie has let you down . . ." He paused.

The blood rushed into François's white face. The effect of this was in some way more shocking because of his natural pallor. It receded again at once. A grimace which became a smile twisted his mouth. He began to speak in his normally quick charming voice. He turned pointedly away from Adam to speak to the other two, his glance darting between Cousin Marie's face and his brother's with a confident appeal.

"Oh, I've been a fool, an absolute idiot. You'll never forgive me. I know you won't. I ought to have told you about it, but I daren't, I simply daren't." He moved his hands in a fluttering gesture. "I didn't dare tell you I'd got to know some Germans in Paris—they were friends of the Bonfants, I met them at their house. And they were really such decent friendly intelligent types. You won't believe it, I know, but they *were*. One of them was in the Intelligence, he turned out to be the son of Uncle Daniel's friend. His name was Helmuth—Helmuth Kettler. He was the one I got really friendly with. . . . Oh, I know you don't approve—you couldn't—but Uncle Daniel did, you know! I told him, and he quoted Stendhal to me, the very thing *you* used to quote, Jean—don't you remember? . . .

Des deux côtés, la même duperie. . . . And there was something else, something about not being able to turn into a blockhead between one day and the next." His eyes sparkled. "There *was* a time, Jean, when you would have approved of my having German friends—when you used to tell me that there would be no peace in Europe until we were reconciled with the Germans——"

Jean interrupted him.

"There's a difference between neighbors, friendly or unfriendly, attractive or unattractive, and the same neighbours when they break your door in and begin murdering."

"I know, I know," his brother retorted. He stretched his hands out, small beautiful hands, finer than Elizabeth's. "Please forgive me. . . . No, no, don't forgive me, scold me as much as you like. I deserve it for being so happy when you were all unhappy . . . I was careful. I really was careful —surely you believe that? And Kettler—I mean *my* Kettler—Helmuth—never asked me any questions." He smiled, a diffident little smile, and added, "And, you know, it was quite a good cover—having a few German friends."

Adam thought: He has begun to give himself up. He felt an ignoble satisfaction. And in the same breath an unwilling movement of admiration for the young man's adroitness and rat courage. Pulling himself up, he thought soberly: Where do you draw the line? There is a level of human relations on which invader and invaded can meet and touch hands. But François, smilingly shaking hands with an officer in the uniform of the Security Police, was as far from that tragic simplicity as from any—he was almost certain—any deliberately schemed treachery. It would have been the same, he thought ironically, in London or New York—the two or three fashionable drawingrooms discreetly opened to well-mannered well-connected "occupiers," the ambitious disappointed writer seizing his chance to make appreciative friends, the one highly placed ecclesiastic, the mob of greedy male milliners with something to sell. . . . But

François? . . . How guilty is he? Guilty of anything worse
than frivolity? . . . He glanced again at the young man's
hands. Now that he had ceased to gesticulate with them
the fingers were once more turned inwards, closed con-
vulsively—over what?

"A good cover?" he repeated. "That depends. What did
you keep under it?"

With a sudden swooping movement, Cousin Marie snatched
up one of the lamps and brought it close to François's
face. . . . Outside, in the darkness of the garden, a flame
circled up, then down, like the rushing flight of a gull.

"Why go on lying?" she said.

The young man stared at her, his lips parted. After a
moment he moved them as if he were speaking, but no
sound came.

"You have a second judge who isn't here," she said.

"Robert?" he stammered. "You mean Robert? He wouldn't
blame me. He wasn't like that."

"No," she went on quietly, "he doesn't trouble to blame
you. He only looks at you—surprised. He looks, he . . ."

For the first time she seemed to find it hard to be calm.
Recovering herself, she set the lamp down on the table.

"Whatever Uncle Daniel told you, it wasn't true," François
said inaudibly.

Adam saw that Jean Monnerie was going to speak. An
impulse too powerful and insistent to be disregarded drove
him to speak first.

"Listen to me, François. You may only have been hiding
—from your family, from your brother—the discreditable
fact that you had German friends during the Occupation.
Discreditable to you. One lie told about it would force you
to tell a second and a third—I've known just such small
cowardices or vanities ruin better men." He paused and
went on with a cold gentleness. "But—you were in Orléans
that day. Why?"

The young man's breath escaped in a ludicrous squeak. "I wasn't. I wasn't."

"It would be much better to tell us yourself."

François let his arms fall on the table: he rested his head on them, lifting it again with an effort, to look pitifully, not at Adam—at his brother. His face twitched. He drew his hands down it as if that would wipe off marks of fear or exhaustion.

"I didn't mean to do any harm, Jean. You know I didn't. It was an accident . . . Something I said without thinking——"

A low sound, half groan, half cry of triumph, came from Cousin Marie. "Ah-h."

Jean said nothing, but his silence was like a beast entering the room.

"Go on," Adam said evenly. "Don't be afraid. Tell us the rest of it."

"I didn't do it on purpose. I didn't do anything on purpose. They knew all the time—Helmuth Kettler knew Robert was working against them."

Now, Adam thought. "How do you know that?"

"They—they were pretty sure he was. But they thought it wasn't very serious. Not like—not like——" he swallowed a constriction in his throat. "They knew that someone called Bastide was important. . . ." He stopped.

"How—when," Adam asked, "did they decide that it really was serious, the work Robert was doing?"

A sudden shock of certainty, the jerk of a nerve inside his head. He went on,

"They didn't know, *until you told them,* that Robert and Bastide were the same man. You told them."

François's voice rose. "I let it out by accident. . . . It wasn't deliberate, it was an accident, I wasn't trying to help them. You can't think that!"

A spasm of anger released Adam from his paralysing hatred of the young man in front of him. He bent over

him, gripping his shoulder, shaking him. "You half gave
Robert away, only half. Not bad as a beginning—promis-
ing. . . ." He controlled himself as Jean moved, and stepped
back. "I'm sorry. I'm very sorry—he's yours, not mine."

He was vexed with himself. Elizabeth had pressed her
hand across her eyes: dropping it, she looked at him with
something like grief, but it was a grief without fear or
blame. He glanced at Mme. Regnier—and was startled by a
change in her face. It was taking place inwardly, below the
surface: something, some energy at work there, without darkening the serenity and delicacy of her face was taking possession of it. She looked older—no, archaic. The thought struck
him that later he might regard her with horror for her
cruelty; at this moment he could see in her only an amazing
simplicity—as if a force of nature had invaded her. He
thought strangely: But a pre-Christian nature. . . .

The effort it cost Jean Monnerie to speak was given away
by his voice, by the immobility of his eyes below the wrinkled
forehead with its film of sweat.

"How did you know," he asked, "that Robert was Bastide?"

His brother's face became strangely simple and furtive,
the mask of a hunted little beast. "I found out. I forget
now how I found out . . . Something Robert said to me—
and I put two and two together with something Helmuth
told me. I wasn't even sure. It was just something I thought
—a theory."

In the same unemotional voice, dragging the syllables,
Jean said,

"And you had to share your theory with your German
friend."

"It—it was an accident."

"Did Uncle Daniel know all this?"

François nodded. "Yes. I told him." He rushed on with
an astonishing vivacity. "When Robert died I was so unhappy
—you don't know how unhappy I was. I had to tell someone. He was awfully kind and understanding, he said it

wasn't my fault at all, it was one of those things—a fatality, he said—and it would be silly to go on thinking about it. . . . I can't tell you how kind he was." He closed small white teeth over his lower lip. "Not like you."

Jean shook his head. "It wasn't kindness. It was indifference."

So, he thought, all the time when we were condemning him, he had this in his hands: he could have struck back at us with it. And didn't. His moment of grace. . . .

"I don't care what you call it," cried his brother, "he was kind. Kinder than people like you and Mamma—who never made a mistake, and don't understand."

There was silence, brief, lasting long enough for Adam to hear two sounds, both very faint. Some tiny crack opening in the old wood of a cupboard behind him. The frantic tapping of the moths. Looking at Jean, he realised that, at least for the moment, he was sunk.

Very calmly, Cousin Marie said, "Why were you in Orléans?"

"They—they asked me to go."

"Why?"

François stared at her for a moment, then burst into tears. He did not try to stop them; he sat still and let them pour down, his mouth working.

"You went there," Cousin Marie said, "to give him away."

Still crying blindly, he stuttered, "No, no, I knew . . . before . . . before I went. I knew they were going to arrest him."

"You knew, and you didn't warn him," Adam exclaimed. He was stupefied.

"But by the time I knew, it was too late! You don't understand! He was in the train. They said—Helmuth said the police in Orléans didn't know him by sight, they wanted me to go there and just point him out. If we went by car, we could beat the train. He said he would like to take me. . . ."

It had not been in the least necessary. Drily, Adam said,

"Were they so anxious that you shouldn't miss any of the fun?"

He was not proud of his jibe: it came from the emptiness of his mind now that its excitement, a little shameful, a little ugly, had dropped. The chase had run to earth a little beast almost as pitiful as he was detestable.

Nearly inaudibly Jean said, "As you know, they always tried to involve an informer, a traitor, as deeply as possible. I think it must have amused them."

"But why do you call me that?" his brother cried. He was mopping at his face now with a large soft white handkerchief. "I was a fool. A fool to take you and Uncle Daniel seriously, a fool to get myself mixed up with *them*. But I wasn't a traitor. You can't say I was!"

For what was probably the first time in his life Jean spoke to him without any trace of kindness.

"What did you think you were doing to Robert?"

François was only too eager to explain. "Helmuth said they would arrest him for his own sake. A little lesson— to keep him out of trouble in the future. They'd treat him well, he said, since he was my—my friend, my cousin. He *promised* me no harm would come to him." He looked at Cousin Marie. "I didn't betray him. You know I didn't."

Without moving, she said,

"The court will decide that."

Adam remembered the *drôlesse*. He felt a violent movement of repugnance, and thought: Is that where we are?

A look of horror and incredulity came over François's face. "But—you're not going to give me away?"

"Ah." She smiled, without irony. "You don't like being given away? You think such things shouldn't happen to you —you?"

"Don't, don't smile," he stammered. "Let me go away. I'll go right away—you need never see me again. . . . Jean, say something . . . Elizabeth. . . ."

Adam suppressed his impulse to interfere. The girl was very pale, but she spoke calmly and steadily.

"I think you should let him off."

Cousin Marie looked at her as if she were a mischievously rude child. "Why?"

"I'm not sorry for him," Elizabeth said. "He's detestable." She hesitated and said in a lower voice, "He's detestable in a way you don't understand—you're too old."

The air of mockery which crossed Cousin Marie's face made it younger and less formidable. "Yes, I'm an old woman. I'm fifty-seven. There's no hope now of my being able to follow your subtleties. I must do the best I can with the ridiculously narrow ideas of right and wrong I was brought up with."

François said, choking, "You're going to destroy my whole life for a single mistake."

Adam's discomfort—it was scarcely more than that, the intimation of an illness hatching obscurely in the body—sharpened. So they're going to turn him over to the lawyers? Well—after all, why not? It's what he deserves. . . . He admitted to himself that he had not expected it. . . . Then what did I expect? . . .

"But is it really necessary to hand him over to a court of law?" he asked, looking at Cousin Marie.

"May I ask you to keep out of this?" she answered. "It doesn't involve you."

He controlled the anger her voice roused in him. "Forgive me, but I am involved. I involved myself. . . ." In a gentler voice he said, "You don't, you know, need to remind me that anything I feel is a shadow of your—grief. . . . But you must let me say this: we've been treating the boy—" he looked at François, flattened like a beaten little dog in his chair—"as if he were a murderer. To be fair, we could remember that he didn't mean to kill, he didn't know he was killing."

Mme. Regnier examined him coolly; her eyes were so widely

open that their whites gleamed. "What is a murderer? . . .
My son was a soldier—I believe you were one yourself—he
was fighting the invaders of our country. This—" she pointed
at François—"betrayed him to them. What does your senti-
mentality call it?"

Adam was silent. I wanted to get at the truth, he thought.
. . . His heart was like a stone in him. What he had got was
the truth, certainly, but it was something else as well, something peculiarly distasteful. Without allowing himself time
to reflect he said,

"We know the truth now. Why not leave it at that?"
Mme. Regnier's smile shocked him. He went on, "You can't
do any good, can you, by punishing him too severely?
Why not give him a chance to—" he hesitated, seeking the
phrase least likely to rouse her derision—"a chance to redeem
himself?"

Cousin Marie fixed him in a smiling contempt and indifference. "How charming you English are. Your first idea,
after a war in which the Germans were just not able to
finish us off, in 1918, was to comfort them for being defeated.
And again now. . . . But this—this is for François's family
to decide."

Without troubling to glance round Adam knew that Jean
Monnerie had lifted his head to be able to watch him:
he knew, too, that there would be nothing but curiosity
in his hard stare, not a shadow of an appeal. At the same
time he knew, knew without doubt, that he was saying for
his friend the one thing Jean would not say himself.

"Call it what you like," he said curtly, "charity—
mercy——"

"Nowadays there are plenty of charming names for
treachery and cowardice," Mme. Regnier said tranquilly.
Her eyelids flickered. "Charity is only one of them. I'm
surprised you don't quote the Bible—especially since the
English, I'm told, believe they wrote it." Her face changed,
losing its wilfully smiling derision but not its atrocious

serenity. "I don't pretend to know anything about divine justice. How could I? But I can see to it that human justice is done."

François made an inarticulate sound, less human than animal. It was overlaid by the noise of Elizabeth's chair when she got up, pushing it carelessly back. She was trembling, but she spoke with a light defiance.

"I told you I don't like this. I don't—and I'm going." She turned her shoulder on Cousin Marie. "My poor Jean, you can despise him as much as you like—who cares? Why can't you be satisfied with that?"

Jean did not answer. Almost imperceptibly, he shook his head. There was a look of incredulity on his dark face, like a man refusing to believe that the friend he was joking with an hour ago is dead. Still watching him, Elizabeth stretched her arm out, groping with it towards Adam. He moved, and she gripped his hand.

"Can't you do anything, Adam? I knew it would turn out badly. I told you."

"I've done all I can," he answered inaudibly.

He looked down at her without the least effort to hide what he felt. Short of taking her in his arms in front of them all, it was a confession, as explicit as if he had made it in words.

Jean was watching them. He said calmly,

"You'd better leave this to me, Elizabeth."

She looked at him as if he had startled her, seemed to hesitate, then walked quickly across the room. As she passed him François caught at her skirt: without a glance at him she pulled it out of his grasp, and went out.

Adam wrenched his mind from her. He tried to believe that anything he said would be understood. He did not believe it. The last minute or two before Elizabeth's intervention had reminded him, sharply, disquietingly, that he was not in his own house.

"Need we drag in the law? After all, the boy is being

punished—the worst conceivable punishment—by knowing
that you all know what he did. He'll carry that with him
all his life. The humiliation—frightful . . . Isn't that enough?"

A very strange expression crossed Jean's face—affection,
irony, amusement, an almost gentle smile. "You believe,
do you," he drawled, "that people go on suffering for a long
time from what's only moral humiliation? After all, you're
very innocent."

"Captain Hartley," Mme. Regnier said, "oblige me by
going away now."

He looked at her again, at the colourless face, at the implacable brightness of her eyes, even of her lips. Anything
he could say to her was futile. Turning to Jean he said,

"Possibly you were right."

The slight movement of Jean's eyelids conveyed his ac-
knowledgement and his inextinguishable irony.

"Possibly."

From the door Adam glanced over his shoulder. It seemed
to him that the three he was leaving in the room were
fastened together inside a circle which excluded not only
the stranger but every other person, and time and place as
well. And yet it was rooted in *this* minute and *this* house in
the wide dark valley through which the Loire ran in a silence
broken only by the barking in the courtyard of a dog and
the echo of it sent back from the other side of the river.

CHAPTER 17

As THE DOOR SHUT, FRANÇOIS SPOKE TO Cousin Marie in an imploring whisper.

"Please let me go away. You don't know what you're doing to me."

"Nothing, no sentence you will get now," she said very quietly, "will be severe enough. If you had been judged four years ago—when *he* was—you would have been sentenced to death. And that would only have been just."

With a little more confidence, he tried Jean. "You don't think that—do you?"

"You can consider yourself lucky," his brother told him in a forbiddingly controlled voice.

"But it will be a horrible disgrace," he said, his lip quivering again. "To you as well as to me. You can't want that to happen!"

"That's in Cousin Marie's hands. It's she you did worst to."

Impulsively, like a child, clasping his hands in front of him like one, François ran to her.

"Please, please, oh, please forgive me . . . I'm your Babba —have you forgotten? You can't mean it, Mamma. Mamma. . . ."

Cousin Marie moved away from him. "Don't call me that

again," she said drily, "I only had one son." In the doorway
she looked back at Jean. She was smiling, a smile of extraordinary brilliance. "Try," she said in the same voice, "to convince him that crying in public won't do him any good. It
will only make him a laughingstock."

She had forgotten to say what every spring, summer, and
early autumn night since she first came to the house she had
said before going to bed. "Don't forget to close the shutters.
. . ." In the provincial town she came from, windows staring
nakedly through the short summer nights would have been
considered imprudent, even disreputable. With the half-
formed idea of bringing things back into order, Jean went
round the room unfolding and closing the inner shutters. At
the single west window he stood for a few minutes, flattering
the grain of the wood with his fingers, and staring into a
darkness less dark than that in the lighted room. He was
letting himself look in it for what he knew was not to be
found there—peace and an answer to his questions. There was
peace of a kind. Whatever anxiety might be tormenting and
keeping awake some few in the sleeping countryside it was
not the fear of being taken from bed by an alien police: the
single light he saw moving far off along the bank of the
Loire could be nothing more menacing than a poacher. Happy
the Loire, Cher, Indre, Vienne and the others, when the
only unlawful shadow moving among their reeds is that of
an innocent French poacher. . . . There had been many
days during the resistance when he could feel it as a clear
simple quarrel between him and the invader. But more than
once, even then, he had not been able to help stumbling
over a root creeping obscenely just under the soil. Of treachery
or a mean caution. In this house itself, he thought bitterly,
in my own family. But how? Why? . . . Daniel Monnerie
he understood easily—an elderly man who had enjoyed everything that Europe has, had, to offer money and a cultivated

taste and felt no patience with another boring interruption. But François?

He turned round. His brother lay, as if thrown down there, in an armchair, a high-backed round chair covered in shabby leather, his favourite when he was a little boy. He seemed creased and small, his narrow shoulders drawn up, his head turned sideways, cheek pressing the leather. Jean's heart contracted with remorse, pity, love.

"How much of this is my fault?"

François said nothing and did not look at him.

Frowning, he went on, "It's true—when you were a child, I tried to make a pacifist of you. I was one myself."

He saw very clearly the fine-drawn attractive face of the form-master in his school, a young man badly crippled in the 1914 war, who with wit and passion had taught his pupils that war is the worst of evils—and a crashing bore. We swallowed it whole, he thought. And afterwards, I passed it on to an impressionable little boy.

"But François," he said gently, "did you never think for yourself?"

"You always told me what to think," François said sullenly. "I believed you."

Even as he felt, with surprise and pain, that his brother meant more to him than any human being in the world, more than Elizabeth, his mind noted coldly that François would take any advantage possible of his weakness.

"I blame myself—severely—for the way I talked to you and brought you up. But I can't take all the blame. I have too much respect for your—your intellect." As he said it he thought: But without a well-brought-up heart what use is intellect, except to mislead?

"Respect?" said François, with a childishly exaggerated sarcasm. "What nonsense. You despise me."

"I'm horrified by what you did."

"Oh, dear, why don't you listen? I didn't mean to do

anything very dreadful. It was pure carelessness—I wasn't
thinking."

Jean felt despair. He controlled himself to say,

"Don't dodge away from it, my dear. Carelessness? You
told Helmuth Kettler that Robert was a man they wanted
badly, not just an unimportant little resister they might have
arrested—but wouldn't have tortured in the hope of getting
his secrets."

"But why need he have driven them to that?" François
cried, almost screamed. "Surely he could have told them *something?*"

The shock, pure grief, caught Jean in the pit of his
stomach, twisting the nerves. He thought: He's rotten to
the bone. After a time he muttered,

"No, I can't talk to you."

"You see," his brother said peevishly, "it's what I said—
you despise me, you hate me."

"Don't you understand at all?" Jean asked him in a low
voice.

"I know I made a dreadful mistake. I was a fool," François said quickly. "But, you know, Jean, I didn't approve of
the resistance. Not really, not in my heart. And you see I was
right! Why, people are already saying that we must make
friends with the Germans."

People? thought Jean. Yes, of course—the Bonfants.

"There was a certain lack of elegance in making friends
with them just when you did. Or don't you think so?"

"Oh, you can be ironical with me," cried his brother.
"But if it's sensible now it was sensible then. . . . And if
what you mean is that I'm a coward, say so."

Jean moved his hands helplessly. "Do you imagine that
Robert, and I, too, weren't afraid? The truth is, Robert was
afraid the whole time. He was imaginative, he knew what
they were capable of doing. Well—they did it—and he didn't
speak."

François said in a fretful voice,

"I can't help it, Jeannot, I'm not like that."

How is it possible to pity, no, to yearn over someone, as they say, and in the same moment to see in a dry light every mark of disgrace on him?

"No, you're not like that," he said gently.

"I'm simpler. All I want is to live a peaceful life."

Not a big traitor, thought Jean wearily, only a little animal wanting to keep warm and unmolested. And nothing—I had given him nothing, no idea, no faith, that could have pulled against his fears and lusts. Not even enough love for the future of this one house, for these few yards of the Loire. But perhaps between big and little traitors is only a question of degree? All of them rootless, greedy, and conceited men? As for ideas—the cleverer they are the more readily their minds provide them with reasons which make their treachery look respectable. "Poor little devil," he murmured.

François sat up quickly. He smiled at his brother with a warm trustful eagerness, and in his softest voice said,

"I didn't, oh, I didn't mean to do wrong. Why can't we forget about it?"

Not able any longer to keep his contempt out of his voice, Jean asked,

"Can you?"

"I do nearly all the time. And if I get away—to America, you know, I'll do everything I can to make up to you for the trouble I've caused you and Mamma. I'll be different. I promise."

"I wonder. . . ." He had to turn his head away: the confident excitement in the young man's face was unbearable.

"I know I should. I *know*. Oh, Jeannot, help me. . . . Mamma will do what you tell her, she always does in the end, you have only to bully her a little."

"And you think you'd get on there?"

"Yes, of course, of course I should," said François with energy. "I told you—Jacques Bonfant and I can both have a job in their agency. I'll work hard. And people do like me, you know," he said smiling.

"Yes." He felt something like horror that his brother's smile had not changed. Who in their family had given them this smile—self-satisfied, ironical, joyous? How many scores of years back? "You always liked to be liked."

"Now you're sneering at me again," exclaimed François.

He shook his head. "No. I was only remembering. . . . Even as a little boy you had a sort of insincerity, you told each of us what he wanted to hear. You won't remember it —you were about eight—the two little girls you played with had quarrelled, and you went between them, inciting them both, telling each what the other had said to you. . . . At the time it seemed amusing—rather touching."

A pettish look came over his brother's face. "I don't see any point——"

Jean was not conscious of cruelty. He felt only that at last—at last—he was telling himself the truth about the charming little boy he had brought up so badly.

"Even then," he said slowly, "you knew how to run with the hare while you hunted with the dogs. And now—no, you weren't even a dupe, you admired the Bonfants and Uncle Daniel's worldly wisdom, but you weren't misled. You were unlucky. Your sort of mildly venal insincerity and self-seeking usually isn't punished. In easier times you would have got away with it. You would never have been pushed on and on, to—to the moment when you pointed Robert out to your German friends. . . . Before that you were trying to please me by involving yourself a little—very gingerly—in the resistance." He watched François with an inhuman coldness of penetration, seeing him as a construction in bones and flesh in which, somewhere, was buried the spring of an inconceivable meanness. "Did that affair really break down? Or did you give them away, too?"

Trying to get as far as possible from his brother's menacing body, the young man cowered back in his chair.

"The press?" he stammered. "It was found out. I swear it was."

"All right," said Jean, "I believe you. Because I want to, and because I'm fairly sure you wanted to please me. Just as you wanted to please Helmuth Kettler and impress him with your cleverness and all you knew." He closed his eyes for a moment. "Such a little traitor," he said. "You betrayed out of—my God, out of what?—frivolity—vanity. And a little out of fear—once you'd got yourself involved with Kettler."

"I'll do better in America," whispered François. "I promise."

"Why not here?"

"No, no! I want to get away." A pitifully eager look of cunning came into his white face. "You ought to understand that. How would you like to stay in a country where everything reminds you that you behaved like a fool?"

"You didn't do the country any harm," Jean said softly. "You couldn't."

"Well, then——"

"What you sinned against was—" he hesitated—"men themselves. Humanity. Brotherly respect."

François pulled a pleading, ruefully ingenuous grimace. "You do use such grand words," he sighed.

Against his will, the elder brother was touched by this childishness. "Oh, my God, François," he exclaimed, "do you think I don't know that I might have behaved just as badly? I don't know what I might have done under torture."

All the young man's lively charm sparkled again in his dark eyes. "Then you don't hate me?" he said in a coaxing voice. "And you'll help me to get away?"

It was nothing worse than he had already said. . . . Nothing worse, nothing worse, Jean repeated—then why, suddenly, this explosion inside his head, blinding him for an instant, of rage and contempt? He bent over François, hands clenched in his pockets, his face darkened by the blood rising in it. The young man gazed at him in dismay.

"Can't you," he said very quietly, "see that you must be punished? If some wretched boy in my group had given Robert away, to save his own skin, the others would have been forced to kill him before he could betray anyone else. . . . You weren't even saving your skin. . . . You'll go on living. You'll be part of the future. If you'd been tried in '45 you'd have been torn out of it."

"It would have been horribly unfair," François stammered. With something like stupefaction, Jean said,

"No. No, you don't realise at all what you did."

"I didn't do anything on purpose," François said sullenly. "It happened. That's all."

"François———" he began. He stopped. The most frightful bewilderment and despair had seized him. "For once—for one minute—look at what you did. Robert was as much your brother as I am, and you sent him to be killed, horribly. *You pointed him out.*"

The young man looked at him with the obstinate refusal of a schoolboy determined not to understand a word of the lesson. "You pretend to love me, yet you want to ruin my only chance of—of retrieving myself!"

Jean thought flatly: He's beyond me, I might be talking to a deaf mute. At this moment he felt that nothing was left, nothing was of any importance. And there was nothing to be said. Even his anger had vanished without trace. . . . Yes, there was still something.

"My poor boy," he said in a barely audible voice, "I do love you."

François smiled. "Then you *will* tell Mamma not to spoil my whole life?"

"It wouldn't be any use."

"But, Jeannot———"

"Listen, my dear," he interrupted gently, "I can do a great deal with Cousin Marie, but this is one thing I can't do. Robert was her son. She owes it to him to punish you. And against that I can do nothing, nothing at all."

François's eyes dilated. "They might decide to shoot me!"

"No, no, they won't do that. You can be sure of that now. They'll give you a prison sentence—perhaps not a long one. And afterwards you'll be able to begin again."

"But you don't know, you can't possibly be sure," François cried. "Oh, it's frightful—and the disgrace. . . . And I might get years! Think of it—years taken out of my life. Oh, no, no!"

All my life, thought Jean, I've loved the idea I had of you. I expected things of you, achievements, success. And it's only now, when I see how little there is in you to be respected or admired, or liked, when I can't love what you are, when I *know* what you are, that I love you.

He went down on one knee beside the chair, to bring himself on the same level as his brother, and looked closely at the jet-black eyes and delicate colourless face, so much younger than his twenty-six years.

"It won't be too bad," he said gently. "I promise you that."

François groaned. "But it could be for years and years."

Jean put an arm round him. "I don't think so. But you'll be brave and quiet." He touched the young man's cheek with a finger. "I said something about your vanity. *You* were mine, you know. We're both involved in this."

After a moment François said, almost calmly,

"We were always happy when you came home for the holidays. D'you remember?"

"Of course. We'll be happy again."

His brother gave him a long bright look. "Yes. . . . Yes, why not? I'll try, Jeannot. I want to do something for you. You look so sad."

The exultance Jean felt swelled in his throat, it was as much pain as joy, but it was joy. This moment paid him for everything, for all his disappointment in François, and for the agony of finding him out. Indeed, he was overpaid. . . .

He tried to think of something, some phrase, that would restore to François a saving measure of self-respect.

"You mustn't be ashamed. Remind yourself all the time that what's waiting for you is trust and gaiety—exactly as it used to be."

François's face changed with a shocking abruptness. It seemed to break up, his mouth went slack, tears poured from his eyes. He threw himself down in the chair, crying and whimpering.

"No, I can't," he said in a choked voice, "I can't bear it. I shall die in prison, I know I shall. Jeannot, let me go away. Please, Jeannot. You were always kind to me, you used to beg me off being punished—don't you remember? Help me now. I could hide for a few weeks and then get away, if you help me. Oh, you will—you will!"

Jean stood up swiftly. For a moment he was not able to think. "Hush," he said automatically, "hush, François. Wait, wait a minute."

But François was past all. "Why did I have to be born now?" he cried hysterically. "I'm not a hero, I never wanted to be heroic. Why couldn't I have been born in some country where you can live a decent life without being heroic? It simply isn't fair!"

Jean's own voice startled him, coming as it did from the darkness at the back of his skull. "You'd do the same things again tomorrow—in the same circumstances—wouldn't you?"

He walked across the room. Running after him, François went down on his knees and caught his brother round the legs.

"Help me," he sobbed, "help me."

Jean freed himself. The young man crawled after him, imploring incoherently. He seemed to be going mad with fear.

"Get up," Jean said.

He watched François stumble to his feet and sink down at once into a chair, where he lay crying loudly and pitifully. There's only one thing I can do, he thought. He felt calm. He felt calm and without hope. He said gently,

"Very well."

François's tears stopped. Turning his head he said in a weak voice, "You'll help me?"

"Yes." After a moment he added, "It will be better for you to go away—out of danger." Danger to come, danger of behaving badly again.

Relief and joy together sent a flame into the young man's eyes. Repeating himself like a child, he said,

"Thank you, thank you. Thank you, Jeannot. Good kind Jeannot. . . . When can I go?"

"Tomorrow."

"Are you sure? And Mamma—what if Mamma won't agree?"

"I'll see to that," Jean said briefly.

"But you said—just now you said you wouldn't be able to do anything with her!"

"Don't worry. I'll manage."

"There you are, you see," François said. He laughed. "I knew, I knew you could if you wanted to." His excitement made him reckless. "I knew you didn't mean it. Oh, when I get to New York I shall have a wonderful life, everything will be all right, you'll see it will."

He had thrown off everything, his fears, his guilt, Robert, the whole of the past. It was a frivolity so deeply in him that it was incurable.

To refuse to have any memory, to tear it up, to tear up and mock the past—that's what is wrong with us all now, Jean thought bitterly.

"We need a drink," he said. He limped to the table.

"Yes, yes," cried his brother, "we'll drink to the future, shall we?"

Jean put his hand on the decanter; drew it back. "No," he murmured, "that's not what we want. I'll get a bottle. Wait."

He went out. Alone, François stretched himself in the chair, with little twitches of his meagre shoulders, like a thin young animal waking up; points of light danced in his eyes. Without any malice he thought: I can always get round old Jean—and anyone else. . . . His glance moved from one heavy sombre piece of furniture to the next, and across the shuttered windows. He blew them a kiss, triumphant, spiteful. Never again, he thought, praise be, I shan't see you again. . . . A fountain of light, which was New York, sprang up behind his eyes. He almost laughed aloud.

Dear old Jeannot, he thought with complacence, watching his brother come across the room balancing a kitchen tray holding a bottle and two glasses already filled. They had been filled to the brim, so that he walked slowly. His heavy face, its lines deepened by fatigue, had the look François knew best, a grave concentration and kindness.

"When you've drunk this," he said gently, "you must go straight to bed and go to sleep."

"Oh, I shall sleep," François said. He smiled into his brother's face. "I say, will you tuck me up and stay with me until I'm asleep—as you did when I was little?" That will please him, he thought affectionately. He really wanted to give his brother pleasure.

Jean lifted his glass. "Yes. I will."

CHAPTER 18

J EAN CLOSED THE DOOR OF THE LIBRARY
behind himself and Georges Lardeau, the policeman from
the village.

Oppressed by his errand, and by the sense that there were
things he ought to have said—afraid, too, that his foot, as
it did when he came in, would slip on the pitilessly waxed
floor—the man stood still in the middle of the drawingroom.
All the windows were open: he could see the Loire, slow,
tranquil, its surface the colour of the sky, and beyond it,
beyond the level meadow, the clump of trees marking one
of its distant curves. Early in the day as it was, not yet ten,
the heat was too great, a desert of heat stretched between
the earth and a white-hot sky.

"It's been far too long without rain," he said.

Jean Monnerie nodded. "Very hard on the vines."

"Sunday they prayed for rain," the man drawled. "I don't
know that anyone up there has noticed."

Monnerie smiled briefly. "It takes time."

Lardeau glanced at him from eyes as patient and bleached
as the sky. What an animal, he thought, with shrewd respect.
A regular bull. . . . Clearing his throat, he said,

"Well, you may perhaps come on a reason why this un-
fortunate young man should, h'm, take his life."

"It's possible."

"As at present, you can't think of any." It was a statement.

"None," Monnerie said, "none at all."

"He hadn't seemed unhappy?"

"No . . . that is—" Monnerie lifted his head to look with a friendly complicity at the other's sun-blackened face—"you know what young men are nowadays, they go in for ideas as you and I used to fish for shad down there."

A sly smile narrowed the man's eyes. "Oh, you haven't forgotten! I can still see you, your head shaved like a cannon-ball, your knees torn, your feet and legs full as dirty as mine. We must have been about ten, eh?" He reflected that these memories were not entirely in order, and passed a hand over his face to bring it back to a proper lugubrious gravity. "Yes, yes, Mr. Jean. The fact is we had a similar case a few months ago—at La Charité. A young fellow, not badly off, no love affair, no vices, nothing, shot himself through the mouth. When his brother was giving evidence he said one of the silliest things I ever heard, and in my job I hear plenty. He said: Our José, you know, was an existentialist. . . ." He ran a calloused finger along the line of his jaw. "You might explain that to me, Mr. Jean."

"Another time."

"Of course, of course. You've enough on hand. But—" he could not bring himself to let it go: he would blame himself later for his misplaced garrulity, but it was so seldom he had the chance to talk to an intelligent man—"to jabber all the time about existence and then blow your brains out —it's not logical!"

"I agree," said Monnerie gently.

"It always strikes me that what they need is a trade. Eh? There's an old fellow—in fact, a cousin of my grandpa— he's spent his life, eighty years, he's eighty-nine, working the vines. That's what he says, you know—*I must go and work the vines.* He's bent like a hoop, absolutely like a hoop, from stooping so long pruning, hoeing, dressing, weeding.

Worse than any woman with her first in its cradle. He hardly takes his eyes off them, for fear. Yes, and nobody ever taught him anything. He has, you might say, the knack . . ." He hesitated, he had lost the thread of his thought. With a sigh, he prepared to move, to plunge from this almost cool room into the dry furnace outside. "I'll give you as little trouble as possible, Mr. Jean. You know that."

"Thanks." Monnerie rested his hand for a moment on the man's shoulder, with the same shrewd friendly air.

"Your uncle's funeral is for this afternoon, isn't it?"

"Yes."

Lardeau nodded. "You have too many worries."

"At least," Monnerie said, "I'm not likely to die of boredom."

A little, but only a little, taken aback, Lardeau muttered, "I can tell you that Inspector Labbé certainly won't ask to see you before this evening."

"Good."

"And it's possible, of course, that it wasn't suicide."

Monnerie gave him an absent look. "Eh?"

"He might have swallowed them out of, as you might say, devilry—or thoughtlessness. Scatterbrained as they are at that age—always making trouble for themselves."

"Yes, that's possible, too."

"If you'd just ask the doctor to let me have his report as soon as he's finished it, I'll give it to the inspector when he comes out, or I'll take it to him. . . . Goodbye, Mr. Jean. I should say Mr. Mayor."

"I'll see you out," Monnerie said warmly.

He walked with the man across the hall, ready if Lardeau slipped to grasp his arm, but, sweating a little, the policeman put his feet down like a bear. "Goodbye, Mr. Jean," he said again, in the doorway, "my sympathy."

Smiling, Monnerie patted his shoulder. "Goodbye, Georges. Off you go."

Turning, he saw Cousin Marie on the stairs. She came

swiftly down and went into the drawingroom. He followed her. "You should be resting," he said.

She looked up at him with—no, not a smile, with a strange, glittering half-triumphant light in her widely open eyes and in the upward curve of lips so colourless as to be striking.

"I don't need to rest. Why should I? A burden has been lifted from me, Jean."

Without irony, he answered, "I'm glad."

She would never compromise, he thought: she belongs to the race, small enough—or where should we be!—of the faithful-unto-death. Beyond death, if that's allowed. . . . He had a brief almost amused vision of his Cousin Marie arriving in the fields of the dead. The instant they heard her soundless step, all the old enemies who had been lying comfortably side by side, Germans by French, the murderer beside his victim, would draw hurriedly and guiltily apart. She would never rest nor let others rest in so weak and improper a peace. . . . What she exacts, and from herself first, he thought harshly, is only an impossible purity. Most of us make every sort of squalid compromise to keep—oh, not necessarily our own happiness, but the happiness of some creature we know to be weak. Or we lie, and go on lying, until our lives are rotten with the lie. And we give it a fine name. We call it tolerance, or common sense, or being civilised. Cousin Marie is not in that way civilised, she is a savage; but a savage so terribly innocent, so vulnerable, that—that I am ashamed. . . .

"So you imagine, do you, that I wanted the disgrace of a trial?" she demanded.

"Yesterday," he said slowly, "I thought you did."

"You were wrong: I wanted justice."

Monnerie thought: In all justice there is this fearful, this agonising contradiction. Staring at her, he said,

"Suppose you had known, before it happened, that François was going to give Robert away, what would you have done?"

In a curiously soft voice, she answered, "I should have killed him. And then myself."

"But why yourself?" He could not keep the irony out of his voice. "Since you would only have been doing justice?"

Her hands flew up. "Why, Jean, you know very well. Don't pretend to be stupid. It would have been right— even if it couldn't in the end save Robert, it would still have been right to kill—" she hesitated less than a moment—"our poor François. But it would have been unbearable, and I couldn't have done it unless I paid for it with my own life. . . . Why are you smiling?"

"Am I smiling?" he asked. "I'm sorry. . . . Yes, I suppose that's one way of comforting yourself."

Her eyes gleamed. "Comfort? Is that what you call it?"

"Why not?" Now he knew he was smiling—and that it was not a pleasant smile. "Don't we always name things to please ourselves? How much happier we feel about a murder when we call it justice!"

Impulsively, Cousin Marie touched his face in a light, almost timid caress. "Dear Jean, you know I'm not cruel. All my life I shall cry for François—only a little less than for Robert. But I am glad he is dead. There are too many evasions. There are too many people hurrying to excuse our traitors—especially the ones who were prudent enough to be only a little treacherous. It's frightful. It's like a poison you don't see in yourself, but it goes on working while you run about, sleep, eat, dance—and one day, when you have to make an effort, you find you can't, you're rotten all through. That's what is happening now. And it's not the old who will suffer for it. It's the young—who are being poisoned by our lies and our cowardice and dishonesty. . . . You know I'm right!"

He had moved away from her. "Yes, yes, I know."

"But, thank God, François came to himself."

He had his back to her now, and did not see the triumph in her face. He heard it in her light voice.

"What do you mean?"

"Thank God he had the grace to punish himself. Yes, I do mean grace. Oh, and the courage." She went on more gently, "I'm sure you were responsible for it. You must have talked courage into him."

Monnerie did not move. He asked calmly, "If that were true doesn't it make me a murderer?"

"Oh, no, no! It means that all the Monneries who were only simple and decent spoke to our poor Babba through you, and he listened to them. That's all."

He turned round. The look of incredulity and agony on his face disappeared at once, wiped out. But it startled her as much as if he had burst into tears. She hurried to comfort him.

"My poor Jean, don't blame yourself. Don't blame yourself for anything in this. You did all you could for François —all his life. I never saw any boy, any young man, so patient, so endlessly kind and gentle with a younger brother as you were with Babba. I can still see you, the two of you, walking out there—" she sent a swift glance over her shoulder at the garden—"talking, talking, and Babba laughing. If ever a child were lucky, supremely lucky, in his brother, it was François. He——"

Jean's hand on her arm stopped her. "Let's talk about him later," he murmured, "I have too much to do now."

Her voice changed; it became warm and full. "There's only one thing I must say—how thankful I am that you have Elizabeth. You need her and you need your happiness more now than ever. I daresay some of our neighbours will feel that the marriage ought to be put off for a month or two. Two deaths in the family. But I'm too old to care what people think, and I want to see you and Elizabeth happy together."

Jean's smile was an affair of the eyelids only. "You're sure she's going to be happy?"

"Of course! My dear boy, you've been altogether too

patient with her. You ought to have pressed the marriage on her a year, two years ago."

"No," he said with energy. "It would have been useless, she was too——" he moved his hands—"too young and restless, too unbroken. She had to be let run alone for a time."

"Nonsense! You know better than that. Nothing, let me tell you, bores a young woman so much as patience, you should have married her and started your family. If you'll allow me to say so—the sooner after you're married the better. Not——" she smiled—"that you're likely to bore her—but it's quite time." She hesitated and said, "This house could do with children."

"Not so very long since, it had one," he said inaudibly.

Cousin Marie ignored his grief—if it was only grief. "It's had a good many generations of children," she said calmly, "it will have more, they'll use François's things, and Robert's and yours, and it won't occur to them to ask: Who used this bed, this riding-whip, this book, before I had it?" She brushed his cheek with her fingers. "Elizabeth is an exceptionally lucky young woman. And she knows it."

The glance he turned her was good-humoured as well as mocking. "I'm not very sure of that."

She threw her hands up. "My dear Jean, a young woman without a penny to her name!"

"Yet really you're very fond of her," he mocked.

"Of course. But there it is—facts are facts." In the same brisk voice, she went on, "Elizabeth is a charming wilful well-meaning warm-blooded young woman. She'll make you an excellent wife, and a good——"

She stopped short, because Adam Hartley had pushed open the door. He looked past her at Jean, taking care to let nothing of his anxiety show in his face. With what might have been relief, Jean said,

"Ah—there you are. Come in."

Wine-glasses and the bottle of *pineau* he had brought out for Lardeau were on the table. Without asking Adam whether he wanted it, he filled a glass, gave it to him, and poured another for himself.

In her most nonchalant voice, Cousin Marie said, "Good morning, Captain Hartley. Are you leaving us before lunch or after?"

"After—if you'll let me stay until then," he said.

"Of course. Are you going far?"

"Today? No. I want to be in Marseilles on Friday, where I have a client. . . ." Her indifference and inattention were so plain that he checked himself and said, "I hope you'll forgive me for having been in your way here."

"You were no more in the way than I expected," she answered, calmly.

She was so completely and sublimely unaware of her insolence that Adam smiled.

In the same voice she went on, "I'm very glad that what you'll take away with you is only the memory of an act of —what shall I say?—of restitution. . . . I'm not excusing François. I'm only saying that, in the end, he behaved as he ought."

He found it hard to forgive her this. "It was a very heavy punishment for an irresponsible young man," he said quietly.

Cousin Marie had got up. She lifted her chin: the light, filtered through the sun blinds, fell on her face, searing its dry effaced beauty. "How absurd! Even a child is responsible, for his will—for his soul, if you'll let me use the word. To believe anything else makes life meaningless and human beings the most perverse of all perverse little animals."

The single kindness I can do Jean, he thought, is to refrain from arguing. At this moment his dislike of her was too great. . . . Is she insensitive?—intelligent women so often are. Or is it only the nonchalance and abominable self-sufficiency of the high priest cutting throats to the glory of his god? . . . He felt an uncontrollable wish to hurt, even—if he could—humiliate her.

"That's very exalted," he said drily. "I still think he might have been allowed to redeem himself. Dead, everything he did is irreparable."

Her fine eyebrows flew up, her hands, her light voice. "So you really think he could have repaired what he did? How like you! Perhaps he could have brought my son back to life?" She put her head back to look at him with derision. "No doubt there are moments when mercy is the right thing. But when a disease is infecting a whole nation, mercy is no cure."

"I don't believe in keeping alive hatreds," he said.

"And I," she retorted, "don't believe in keeping alive cowards and traitors. It is the difference between us."

"Over which there is no arguing." He looked at her with fury. "I shouldn't dream of arguing with you."

A joyfully mocking smile, cruel, almost young, came on her face. "It would be no use. . . . And another thing— if you can understand it—" she shrugged her shoulders, as much as to say: One can't ask too much of a foreigner— "there was a good little François, good, brave—too brave to live disgraced. And we might never have known him—but for yesterday's act of justice!"

The fixed glance Jean had been keeping on her face wavered, suddenly, to show the whites of his eyes. The glass he was holding slipped from his fingers and rolled across the table to the floor. He steadied himself at once. Making no move to pick up the broken glass he drawled,

"And François might still be alive."

"My poor Jean," Cousin Marie said gently.

He did not speak; she looked at him tenderly for a moment, then moved to go. He opened the door for her, closed it noiselessly, and leaned against it.

"My God, what you've been let in for," he said, very drily. "Nonsense."

The cruelty of talking to him about Elizabeth, at this moment, revolted Adam. To do it at all he could only do it shortly and brutally. But there was another thing he

must do first. And since, once he had spoken about Elizabeth, no further talk would be possible, he must get this other
over now. As if François's body, which made so little mark
under the sheet of his bed, had to be stepped across first.

"I have something I must talk to you about," he said.
"But—before I begin on it, there's something else."

"Yes?"

"I want to tell you that I regret, I regret very bitterly that
I told you I'd seen your brother in Orléans. If I'd held my
tongue, none of this would have happened."

Jean's air of indulgence took him aback.

"You weren't responsible. Or, if you like, all you did was
to flick a switch with your thumb and set the thing going.
But it was waiting there, ready to start—and once started
——" he moved his hand in a circle, rapidly.

"I could have kept my thumb off it," Adam said savagely.

"Nonsense, you weren't to blame. You wanted—as you
said—to get at the truth. That's all. Very natural."

"No. That wasn't all I wanted. As much as that, I wanted
someone to be punished. If I'd known what was going to
happen—who would be punished—I'd have cut my tongue
out. But that's not an excuse."

Jean smiled very slightly. "My dear fellow, you're too
scrupulous."

Adam did not speak. In the dead hours of the early
morning, before light, he had lain awake wondering what
difference, after all, there was between him and the people
who had hounded the mother of the *drôlesse*. True, he had
had no lust for personal vengeance. . . . But *is* that true? he
asked himself coolly. . . . It had surely been there in him?
Of course it had—respectably disguised as a wish for truth.
For an impersonal justice, comfortably and decently ad-
ministered out of his sight. . . . There was even a moment,
round about three o'clock, when he had the idea that, compared with himself, the guards in a concentration camp were
innocent. . . . They have no imagination; they have been

told to behave as they are behaving. It is a job like any other job which brings you in the money to feed a woman and children, why should they take on themselves to disobey the orders of their betters? . . . Daylight restored his sense of proportion and his wits. But by no means his peace of mind.

"You're very generous," he said. "I'm not asking you to forgive me my share of the responsibility—however small you think my share is. I don't expect you to forgive me." Nor for what's still to come. . . . He had to make an immense effort to keep his head above a rush of humiliation, grief, anger—and caught himself wishing he had never set foot in the house, never seen Elizabeth. In the same moment his need of her mocked him.

Jean shrugged his shoulders.

"Don't worry. It's not of any importance. My uncle had said quite enough to rouse Cousin Marie. She would never have given up until she got something out of François. Without you, he might have lied himself out of the worst. That's all. . . . Cousin Marie shocks you, doesn't she?" he added in an ironical voice.

"No," Adam said. "I can understand her being implacable—and insisting on a trial. What I don't understand is that she's glad the boy has been wiped out."

He stiffened himself to meet Jean's heavy stare.

"You're—forgive me, my dear fellow—outside this."

"I daresay."

"Why should she let him off? To do the same thing in the next war. . . . He's safe from that—safe. . . ." His voice dropped; he passed his hand over his face. "I blame myself, you know. If I'd been harder with him as a child. That difference of twelve years. . . . I had the responsibility of a father without his insight and experience."

Adam said carefully, "You can feel proud of him. I don't believe he really preferred suicide to prison—whatever Madame Regnier says. So it proves a cold courage—or a very great affection for you——"

There was a silence. Jean said,

"You're right. He didn't kill himself. I gave him enough of Uncle Daniel's barbitone to push him clean out."

Adam's first, his only, instinct was to hide his feeling of horror.

"I hadn't guessed."

Still with the same expressionless stare, Jean said, "You thought I wasn't capable of such cruelty—is that it?" In a softer voice he added, "I gave him two glasses of wine, one of them had the drug in it, and took him up to bed. I held him in my arms until he died. He wasn't alone."

Oh my God, Adam said to himself. . . . To show pity would be grotesque, unforgivable.

"Why did you do it?"

Monnerie had moved and begun to walk, with his long uneven stride, between table and window. He turned.

"Nothing else would have saved him from himself. Why do you ask?" His eyelids flickered. "You're horrified," he said coldly.

"No."

"Your face gives you away."

Adam shook his head. "I'm sorry."

Jean was silent, then spoke with an oddly impersonal bitterness. "You're lucky in England—that you're not riddled with hatreds. You weren't occupied. Wait until you've been faced by treachery in your own family. When you are—I don't say *if*—when you are, you'll find yourself doing a great many things you now think impossible and horrible." He smiled. "You may begin to wonder whether you are, after all, God's dear English. And that will make you much easier to get on with."

Stung into brutal frankness, Adam said,

"No. I'd sooner see us sunk and everything I value down the nick than have us go in for—for calculated murders. And if I had to execute my own brother. . . . No. I couldn't do it." He hesitated. "Let's leave it that I haven't the necessary moral hardness."

"Wait," Monnerie jeered.

No doubt there are springs of cruelty in us, Adam thought, and they could overflow. . . . But he did not believe it. He believed that the common English are always likely to astonish themselves and their betters by their patience, and patient indifference to the teachings of the cynical and the bloody-minded.

"No," he said again. "I have a horror of executions."

In a curiously sorrowful voice Jean said,

"Yet you were a soldier. And if you could have saved Robert's life by shooting François before he had given him away you would have done it."

"Yes. I suppose so. Yes. But not in cold blood—to punish."

"Not even to stop him carrying his rottenness about with him everywhere?"

"No."

In all the stages of reason and logic there are counter-reasons, a counter-logic. You can easily justify murder by reason—nothing easier. The self-corrupted intellectuals of a dozen countries make a profitable business of it in the service of one bloody creed or another. . . .

The fold at the corner of Monnerie's eyes held an eternity of smiling contempt.

"I'm sure that's what you call the logic of the heart," he murmured.

He passed his hand over his face in a gesture which was becoming familiar. "Surely even you can understand that it was an act of war," he said rapidly; "it's only an accident that it happened yesterday and not six years ago, or six years from now, when we may be at war again? . . . Think!"

"I have no right to blame you," Adam said. He had a revulsion of his whole being, and thought bitterly: I'm talking like a scoundrel.

Monnerie's mouth twitched. "Yes—you're a modest practical fellow—you'll always be satisfied with a half-reason and a half-innocence." His smile broadened. "God's English . . . all your crimes have been committed with your eyes shut. When you covet something, your neighbor's ox or his ass or his wife, you don't snatch it, you back into it. On the Last Day you'll be found backing into the kingdom of heaven, or I'm a saint."

Adam said drily, "It will be to find the French already established there—by some intelligent dodge." (. . . finger rubbing the flat grimy thumb—"*J'connais un truc . . .*") He caught himself back. "My dear Jean, forgive me—I'm talking nonsense."

Monnerie's face became forbiddingly void. He took a coin out of his pocket, spun it, looked absently to see how it had fallen, and put it back.

"The moment you are driven to choose between killing and a comfortable respectable cowardice. . . . *If thine eye offend thee,* and all that. . . . François was more to me than my eyes, and he was rotten—he had rotted beyond cure. . . . I tell you, if he had to be plucked out I'd sooner do it myself than try to shift the responsibility on to a policeman."

Adam hesitated. Say everything or nothing, he thought. In a curt voice he said,

"How can you be sure he was rotten? He was very young."

"You didn't see him crawling—begging to be let off— begging me to help him escape. I helped him."

Before the sardonically self-possessed agony on his face, Adam looked away. Nothing he could say was better than futile or irrelevant. Jean went on calmly,

"You have some sort of sense on your side. A soldier at least risks his life. But last night what did I, I, risk? Damnation. My chance of—no, my happiness."

He moved off blundering—like an overburdened carthorse, thought Adam—towards an open window. Stepping out into the thick grass, he walked a short way, then stood, in the terrible sun, looking absently about him, his glance moving from the blanched cloudless sky to the vacantly smiling Loire.

Adam watched him and tried to force his mind back to his own desperate enough problem. But the other man's powerful body standing there in the sun blocked the way, leaving him no room to think. In the silence he heard a cricket, drunk with the heat, shrilling on and on in the field at the side of the house. My God, he asked himself, is it really only twenty-four hours since I watched François dawdling about out there? . . . His deepest instincts, every nerve in his mind and body, rejected what Monnerie had done. With a deliberate refusal to think further, he said: The truth is, it's against nature—and that's the very devil. . . .

Jean had come back into the room. Halting just inside the door he said,

"You look as I always remembered you—nothing for nothing, and as stubborn as a mule. Or a judge."

"Don't imagine I'm judging you," Adam said brusquely. "I'm not such a fool—nor hypocritical enough."

"Wait to judge me until I come to you and begin explaining that I'm really quite innocent," Jean said with a sharp smile.

Adam said nothing for a moment. "Madame Regnier doesn't know, doesn't suspect?"

"No."

He hesitated. "Nor Elizabeth? No, of course not," he answered himself.

Almost coldly he wondered about the effect on her if she knew. It would break the last nerve holding her to him, he thought. He felt the blood rise at the back of his head.

Jean was shaken by a laugh very like a painful catch of the breath. "It's extraordinary—in the last few hours I seem to have used up all confidence in my own judgements. I spent an hour this morning wondering whether to tell her. Probably I ought to—but I don't *know*. A boring state of mind, let me tell you."

"I can't think of anything worse you could do," Adam

said harshly. "You have no right to lay such a burden on her. For God's sake!"

Monnerie's voice became almost jeering. "You think it would be unkind?"

"Yes. I do."

A silence.

"What was it you wanted to talk about?" Jean asked.

A torturing indecision paralysed Adam's mind. Hardly knowing what he was doing he walked over to the window and stood looking out, at nothing. . . . No, I can't tell him now. . . . What had been only difficult and painful had become impossible. I must wait, he thought dully.

He turned and met Jean's ironic stare. "It wasn't important. I won't bother you with it now."

Jean sat down. He lifted his head to be able to keep his eyes fixed on Adam; a ray of light falling on his face gave it a curiously naked look, naked of everything except a malicious curiosity and power. "It's our last chance to talk."

"No," Adam said calmly. "I shall be in France for at least a month. I shall come back this way. I won't stay here, but I'll see you."

"Has it to do with yourself—me? Anyone here?"

"To do with myself. . . . It can wait."

The gleam of anger in Monnerie's eyes vanished again at once.

"You're too modest," he said.

"Forgive me for that—if you can't for anything else," Adam said gently.

Jean passed a hand over his face. "I'm sorry. I'm not thinking clearly."

An intolerable weight of self-contempt fell on Adam. "It's not likely that you could," he said, "now. You ought to——" He broke off sharply as Elizabeth came in.

For a moment it seemed to him that sanity and forgiveness had come into the room with her.

CHAPTER 19

"THEY WANT YOU ON THE TELEPHONE," SHE told Jean, "the police."

"Right."

He went out with great strides, as if he were pressed for time.

Elizabeth watched him go. As the door closed she turned to Adam and said quietly,

"Cousin Marie says you are leaving this afternoon."

"Yes."

He lifted on his finger the hair falling into her eyes—this was one of her rough days. For a moment she rested her head on his shoulder; she lifted it again almost at once, and looked at him in the eyes.

"Then what is going to become of us? Of me, Adam?"

He realised for the first time, but in a confused way, what he was going to make her suffer. "Things will be all right," he said with an effort.

She stepped back, shaking her head. "No!" She tried to speak lightly. "Until last night everything seemed possible. As if all I need do—to deserve to be happy—was to be a little more careful or considerate or more serious. Now"—she smiled at him, with a pitiful air of gaiety—"now I can't do anything. And you're going away. . . ."

She stopped, and went on in a humble voice. "I love you."

He felt an agony of love for her, and contempt for himself—for his loss of self-control. Taking her in his arms, he moved his mouth down over her throat; he came on a pulse beating there like a second smaller heart, and pressed his lips on it, cruelly. Elizabeth touched his face, then put her arms around his neck and drew his head closer to her thin shoulder.

"How heavy you are," she said softly. "My child, my poor little child."

"I love you so much," he said inaudibly.

She did not try to keep out of her voice the immense, nearly terrified joy she felt. "It's almost wicked to be so happy, when Jean . . . He adored François."

For a second he felt something like anger with her for choosing the words that most quickly and most mercilessly separated them. For less than another second he listened to her heart beating below his cheek, then drew back and stood looking down at her. He had no idea that the smile at the back of his eyes was derisive, the derisive northern smile he hated in other men: his contempt for himself blinded him: he did not see her, and her bewilderment and shame—the shame of a disgraced child.

"Forgive me. I'm a selfish brute."

"What is it? What have I done?" she asked in a low voice.

"Nothing, you've done nothing. The wrong is entirely mine, my darling. I ought to have told you at once, before touching you. . . . I wanted it too much," he said with rage.

She was watching him with the courage of her fears. "What do you mean—what ought you to have told me?"

"We can't force this on Jean now," he said. He frowned, trying to hit on words that would convince without wounding her. "I've injured him deeply enough already. Even without that, to take the last thing he has from him—at this moment—with François dead. And dead in the way it happened." If I could tell her the whole truth, would it make it easier? Probably. . . . He said roughly, "And partly my fault."

"Your fault?" she said, bewildered. "But what did you do? You tried to help——"

He interrupted her. "Have you forgotten how much of it rests on me—on my stupidity? My complacent stupidity. I gave the boy away. A silly little treachery."

Elizabeth said fiercely, "That's not true. You're neither stupid nor complacent. You're tormenting yourself. Why are you doing it? Why are you telling lies?"

His glance fell on her hand: there were scratches on the brown skin, and small purple stains. She had been picking the black currants, he thought. He had an impulse to kiss it, and looked away, afraid of losing what self-control and decency he had left.

"Yes, I torment myself," he muttered.

"But why, Adam, why?"

She laid her hand on his arm. He moved so brusquely that she was hardly able to keep back a cry of dismay. She was in despair. Only a minute since he had been treating her as if she were a woman, and as if he loved her. Now, though she had only to lift her hand to lay it on him, he had gone impossibly far away. There was nothing she could do—except speak the truth. And that, she thought with a light bitterness, was all she could do in any case. Since she had no tricks. She said quietly,

"If you leave me, I shall die. . . . No, that's silly, and not true. But it will be the worst thing that could happen to me, far worse than dying."

How to make her see that he was asking her for nothing more than an impossible patience, an impossible—what was it?—tact? cunning? dissimulation?

"My love, my little love—little idiot—I'm not leaving you, I'm coming back for you. I'll take you away with me then. You have only to be patient—terribly patient——"

"No."

"Don't look at me like that—as if you weren't even listening. Listen. You must listen. You must see that to take you away now, to tell Jean now, would be indecent, it would be adding a second treachery to the first." His voice hardened in spite of himself. "I can't do it."

"And the treachery to me?" she said, looking at him.

This stung him. After a moment he said,

"To ask you to wait—to say that we must both wait—is that so terrible?"

"And when you come back—will it have ceased to be treachery?"

He made a movement towards her, half tenderness, half despair. Stepping back, she cried,

"If you go away and leave me here now it is the end, it's finished, everything is finished. . . . You're very sensible, very straightforward, very kind—and you're talking like a fool. How can I stay here and wait for you? Think. To go on living in this house, with them both, with Jean, with Cousin Marie, saying nothing, *nothing*. How can I? Tell me how, tell me what to do. Shall I ask Jean to put the marriage off again? Or let them go on preparing for it? Think, think." She made an effort to speak quietly, and said, "No, it's impossible."

Adam did not move: his pity for her, his anger—against himself, against the whole dark business—suffocated him.

"You could wait a month."

"Impossible."

"Why is it impossible?"

She smiled, a pitifully malicious smile. "I've told **you** why. . . . Oh, and for another reason." Her lips trembled slightly. "After you went away the first time I could sometimes, for a moment, see you, your face as you turned to look at me when I came into the attic, your hands. But tomorrow if I try to think of you I shall only see you turning your back on me. I couldn't bear that, I'd rather not think about you at all."

"You're being unreasonable."

"If you like," she answered.

"And the cruelty to Jean?" he said harshly. "The in-excusable unnecessary cruelty——"

She interrupted him.

"Besides, you won't come back. Once out of this house, out of this atmosphere of—of tension and hate, you'll see clearly all the reasons why it would be too unkind, too difficult, too painful to come back. And in the end, you won't come. . . ." She lifted her hands in the gesture which always made him think, ridiculously, of a very young bird learning the use of its wings for the first time. "Do you know what? You're punishing yourself through me—because it vexes you to behave badly to Jean. You—you egoist!"

"That's not true."

She looked away from him. "To wait," she said under her breath. "At any other time I could have waited for you for years—all my life. . . . But you ought not to ask me to wait now—in this house, on these terms." She gave him a clear look, without a trace of reproach. "How can I—I—turn my back on Jean, even on Cousin Marie—when I'm not sure any longer that you love me?"

Adam seized her wrist, and to silence her put his hand over her mouth for a moment.

"No," he said, with rage. "You're talking like a child. But you're not a child, you're the most balanced, the sanest young creature I know. And you know I love you. You know perfectly well, you understand perfectly well, why it's un-reasonable—unreasonably cruel, impossible—to crush Jean with this now. Don't you?"

"Such long words," she said, with the same smile. "As if it had anything to do with what's unreasonable. It's to do with me—with my being left here—to tell lies—or to behave decently, as you would say. . . ."

"Elizabeth——"

"You're hurting my wrist," she said, in what was suddenly a poor little voice.

He dropped it. Before he could answer her, the door opened, and Monnerie came in. He looked at Adam.

"That telephone call was about you," he said curtly. "In Tours they think that the policeman who came out here this morning, friend Lardeau, should have questioned you. I'm afraid you can't leave us—the inspector is coming out this evening; he wants you to wait here."

"But I know nothing," Adam said.

Monnerie gave him a coldly mocking glance. "Very well. You won't mind telling him that?"

"I shall tell him exactly that."

Startling them both, Elizabeth said in a rough voice,

"Why can't they leave us alone, the police? There's no sense in bringing Adam into it—no sense in anything. . . . I can't stand it any more."

She made a gesture of fury, clenching her hands. In a torn sleeveless shirt, her hair in her eyes, she was a disreputable enough figure, but neither man felt like smiling. Jean looked at her with that reserve of his which was so near sensuality.

"What is it you can't stand, my dear child?"

"Being called a child. Being treated as if I were a child." She had turned crimson; she might be on the edge of tears, but she laughed. "I can be patient—I have all the patience in the world. And I can stand anything except insincerity. Except the insincere kindness you use to a child because it's not wise enough to understand you, and can't help. And that I can't, can't, and never will stand."

She stopped, turned on her heel, and without a glance at Adam went out.

She ran upstairs to her bedroom, running furiously, and bolted the door. For some minutes, minutes that were completely lost and meaningless, she stood, not thinking, not even feeling. At last she moved, stretching her arms out, and folding them over her thin body—over nothing. I'm quite alone, she thought almost calmly—and quite worthless to anyone. Her head turned a little; she felt giddy, as if she herself were turning round a circle which had no way out. She had been pushed aside—excluded from a secret that only men, she thought mockingly, have the wits to understand. Mockery, bewilderment, grief. . . . Something in her collapsed suddenly, leaving her with no defense against her desolate feeling of humiliation. But her pride was the same size as her humiliation, exactly. I didn't beg him to take me, she thought: how thankful I am, oh, how thankful. I have nothing to cry about, I didn't do anything disgraceful. Why should I cry?

She laughed; and then, to cry, made all the gestures of her childhood, beating the back of a chair with both fists, screwing up her eyes, while the tears poured over her cheeks.

CHAPTER 20

Late in the evening the wind shifted to the west. As she crossed the hall the girl heard Adam talking in the drawingroom, to Jean. She stood listening to his voice: colder, and as it were less dark than Jean's, less vibrant, it had a note in it which was neither searching nor self-assured, but in some way both. Her lips trembled, and she did not trust herself to go in.

Instead, she went out of the house at the back and walked to the edge of the river. There should have been a moon, but the sky was covered with clouds. It was dark. Although the rain still held off, the trees were making that sound of distant waves, breaking, falling back, rushing on again, which promises rain, and the wind had freshened: nearer the coast it might be raining already.

She felt the air on her cheek as if another, smooth, warm, gentle, were pressing against hers. Under her hand on the low wall the stones kept a little heat from the long burning day. The cicadas were silent; but the willows, the dry grass, the reeds, muttered to themselves. . . . After a time she heard footsteps coming slowly across the lawn from the house, and her heart jumped like a fish thrown down on the bank. Alas for the heart's intuitions—when she turned, it was only Cousin Marie. In a momentary thinning of the clouds an ambiguous light fell on her face, giving it the gleam of marble, every mark of use and exhaustion sunk as deep in it as the veins.

"You're not cold?" she asked Elizabeth, looking at the girl's bare arms.

"No. . . . Is everything all right now at the Gachons?"

Cousin Marie did not answer at once. She stood looking at the dark surface of the river, so quiet on summer nights that the movement of an unseen bird in the reeds made the sound of tearing linen. Tired as she was, she held herself perfectly upright. Her black dress, buttoned to the neck, and the black scarf she had fastened round her head, covered her as if she had drawn round her a fold of the darkness itself. In the silence another shadow joined her, that of a young woman she knew better, far better, than she knew the girl whose hand rested near hers on the wall: however wide, nearly impassable, the distance dividing us from our younger self, it is infinitely narrower than the gulf between the living young and the old. That is impassable at any price.

She had not been at Daniel Monnerie's funeral in the afternoon. In no circumstances would she have gone, but she had the excuse that she had been summoned to the house where the young wife of one of Jean's labourers, Madeleine Gachon, was dying in childbirth—her first child. When she got to the house the young woman had just died: it had not been possible to save both child and mother, and since the child, a boy, was unusually strong and well made, the doctor and the young woman's mother, both of them, had chosen him. . . . She told Elizabeth briefly and without warmth.

"But her husband?" asked Elizabeth.

"Luckily he was away. . . . He'll come back tonight or tomorrow and find he has a fine son. . . . He's young, he'll marry again—probably soon." She added, "He's quite the best of the young workers—he has the knack of it, from his father and grandfather."

"I hope he won't thank you all for leaving him with a child and no wife," the girl cried. "I think it was absolutely wrong."

"I daresay," Cousin Marie said with indifference. "But it's you who are wrong. When Madeleine was carrying her child she was important because of it. And they tried hard to save her. . . . It's a risk, you know, having a child—and once you accept that risk. . . . No, no, they were right. When you're married and have children yourself you won't think any more; you'll feel it."

Fond as she was of Elizabeth, she reflected, coldly, that it was impossible, completely and forever impossible, to talk to her so long as any answers you got came only from the deaf blind energy of her young life raging in her. . . . The young shadow on her other side started and smiled. You, too, it said unkindly. Yes, she answered, of course, I, too—but I have forgotten.

"It was hardly worth her marrying," said Elizabeth angrily. Madeleine Gachon was her age: she had a vision of her lying bloodless and extenuated on the bed, her life slipping from her. Furious with pity, she told her: If I had been there I would have fought for you.

"You're talking like a child, and a spoiled child," Cousin Marie said, with contempt. "No woman who gets the chance to pass life on—even at the price of her own—has the right to turn aside. Well, perhaps she has the right—" she shrugged her shoulders—"but it's a worthless right. What can the right to remain barren ever be worth? Certainly no woman in our family can have it." She added calmly, "When you and Jean marry you won't want to argue about it."

They were silent for a moment. "How can you be so sure we shall be happy?" Elizabeth said.

Cousin Marie moved her shoulders lightly. "Even when

a marriage is, in a certain sense, a failure. . . . You know, I never wanted to marry Guy Regnier. He always bored me. And he had a habit of touching his tie with one finger which drove me wild. He was a fool, too, and wilfully unkind. . . . But I had Robert—so to think of it as a failure is idiotic." In a gayer voice, amused and mischievous—she was perhaps not talking to Elizabeth now—she said, "Whatever it is for a man, marriage, for a woman, is either the children or a state—a more or less comfortable state."

Elizabeth spoke with a timidity very unlike her. "Cousin Marie, I don't love Jean. Oh, as a brother, yes—as—" she bit her lip—"as a comrade, if you won't laugh at that."

"I shouldn't dream of laughing. But what nonsense! It's not a bad thing to imagine you're marrying a kind brother. It may make the reality more amusing."

"And if it doesn't turn out like that? If Jean himself is disappointed——?"

"Why should he be?" Cousin Marie said, with a smile. Glancing from the corners of her eyes, she thought she had guessed what was wrong, and said more warmly, "My dear child, you mustn't let yourself feel hurt because Jean had had no time for you these last days. It's only women who remember to put aside their griefs long enough to prevent a husband or only a lover from feeling himself ignored, or in the way——"

"I don't feel anything like that about Jean," the girl interrupted quickly.

"Men are so often preoccupied—" a certain amused scorn came into her voice—"and the way to behave then is to wait. You must never resent it—that's only ill-bred, unforgivably ill-bred. You wait, you smile, you find something to occupy yourself with, and when your turn to be needed comes round again, you are still all smiles." Her own smile at this moment gleamed briefly in the darkness. "The sooner you are married the better. Earlier than September—why not? Life isn't the complicated business the young like to think it is. It's much simpler and harder, and any happiness you find in it comes from outside, from the things you don't control or work for—a view from your window, a fine day, an unexpected undeserved kindness. So far as happiness goes, that's all there is!"

With despair, Elizabeth thought: What use is it to try to talk to someone so old and sensible?

"Perhaps—" she stopped, and went on in an uncertain voice—"perhaps you would always have felt that only an idiot can think about some one person all the time, every moment, so that you seem to be carrying the thought about in your body—like a fever——"

Cousin Marie's smile became ironic. "Only a complete idiot."

After a minute Elizabeth said, "I'm sure you're right."

"But of course, of course I'm right!" Cousin Marie cried. With more kindness she said, "You know, Elizabeth, how much I hoped for you to marry Robert. I'm just as content when I think that it is you who will live in this house and take care of it and Jean, and put children to bed in its rooms. I can't think of anything in the world you could do that would be more use, or better, or more rewarding. Can you?"

"No."

"You really feel that?"

"Oh, yes, yes," the girl said wildly. She struck the wall with her fists, "yes, yes, a hundred times yes. But don't go on talking about it. Let me alone. I'm not like you, I don't enjoy probing into myself to see what is going on. You're too inquisitive, too sensible, too old."

Cousin Marie looked at her with deep bitter displeasure.

"We'll forget this ridiculous scene. It was my fault for talking to you as if you were able to understand. . . . I take all the blame."

"I beg your pardon, Cousin Marie," Elizabeth said under

her breath. "Forgive me—I was abominable—forgive me."

Her remorse—the remorse of a good child—softened Cousin Marie. She put her hand out and touched Elizabeth, realising the coldness of her own fingers from the warmth and involuntary shrinking away of the girl's hand. "Don't be anxious—about anything. You're doing the right thing. I promise you. You can be content with yourself, and happy."

"Yes."

Cousin Marie withdrew her hand. The girl was harmless now, all her claws drawn back. Neither her claws nor her young fierceness were any use to her in this house. And no doubt what she wanted was not peace, not security, but to be shaken and hurt. Perhaps it was her right? The right of her smooth sunburned body, strong throat, and smiling magnificent mouth. I should tell her to run away, she thought sharply. Run away, fall and cut your hands, cry, cry, but live. . . . Are you out of your mind? she mocked herself. She must stay here, her duty is here. Let her do it. . . .

A bird started suddenly under the bank, scuffled madly for a moment, fell quiet. Between two mountains of cloud the colour of dark steel a valley had opened, filled with a fine dust of light, across which floated vaporous shadows, changing, thinning out, losing themselves finally in the ragged edges of cloud. The wind brought with it from the mouth of the river a tang of seaweed and from nearer at hand the scent of mignonette and fennel.

Elizabeth's voice was still a little uncertain, as if, to reach the older woman, it had had to cross a stretch of rough country.

"Just think—the Loire has been running away through this valley for centuries. And it will go on until the end of the world. Heaven knows how many women have stood just here to look at it. . . . No, I can't think about it. I hate to remember that it will still be here when I'm dead and can't see it—the river shaking the reeds, the moor-hens. And the other women. . . . D'you suppose they'll think about us?"

"Quite as often as you'll think about me when you come here."

"Of course I shall think about you!" But never, she told herself with a bitter calm, the calm touched at the lowest point of a failure, never of the one man I loved with all my heart. . . . She was not unhappy. She had never learned that bad habit: perhaps, too, in that same young heart, she did not believe that the failure was complete.

"Thank you," Cousin Marie said in a light voice. "I shall be a very modest unexacting shadow in your mind." In the close darkness she could smile without the fear of being seen and misunderstood by Elizabeth.

She heard a changed note in the river, a pulse beating at a great depth: some current, starting from the sea, had reached this point.

She shivered. "It's getting cold," she murmured, "we must go in."

CHAPTER 21

As she and the girl crossed the lawn,
they were being watched from the pitch darkness under the
archway of the inner courtyard.

They reminded Jean Monnerie of the figures in a tapestry
so old that the colours had almost disappeared, leaving
only blackened shadowy outlines against a confused background. He waited, out of sight, until they had gone into
the house, and until Cousin Marie closed the shutters, then
in his turn walked across the grass and stood in the same
spot by the wall.

He placed his hand where, he thought, Elizabeth had laid
hers. In spite of this gesture, half involuntary, he gave her
no more than a momentary tenderness. There was scarcely
any room for her in his mind: she was being pushed out
by the weight there of an anguish, a profound faceless
anguish, to which he was not yet ready to give its name.
Obscurely, very obscurely, he knew he was being edged towards the first steps of a journey. But where, but how, he had
no idea, except that it led into darkness, like a mole's;
and that like a mole he would come out again into the
light only after a long struggle underground. If ever. At this
moment he was an infinite way from imagining that there
could be daylight.

This stone, he thought, is still warm.

As he said it, he saw François again as a small boy, and he remembered watching him climb on to the wall at this point, and stand there crowing like a cockerel. He had forgotten the incident: it had waited in its husk until this moment; and suddenly the husk had split open in him, to reveal its single sharp pitiless seed.

He had an impulse, which he rejected, to get down and press his face against the stone. For the first time, the thought of going away, of an actual journey, came to the surface of his mind. But where, he asked himself coldly, could I go? . . . He thought in a dry way of service abroad, of the trouble worsening in Indo-China, of Father Baussan, who last night had confided in him that he was shortly going off to work in a leper colony in North Africa.

There was a shorter way than any of these, a much shorter journey—much easier. As though it had climbed, quickly, an immense distance, the thought of his death reached him at the same moment, with the same fugitive lightness, as a cold breath from the river. It was as welcome. To pay for a life with a life—how simple, how just.

All these thoughts and images slipped through his mind without his seizing one of them. He could more easily have closed his hands on the dark water flowing at his feet. He felt rather than thought them. More obscurely still, but with a terrible energy, he felt that whatever choice he made must be made with his whole force, engage the whole of his being. There must be a clear act of will. Simply to bolt, like an animal in a panic, or jump in the river only because it was there, waiting, a quick way out, would not do. Above all, it would not do for the patient anonymous men who generation after generation had given themselves in exchange for another shelving curve of the river bank, another strip of this indulgent generous soil, worked and reworked so long that every fold represented a child: nor for the women carrying down to a creek their baskets of washing; kneeling to polish the brick tiles of kitchens, the waxed arms of chairs, the ash-brown walnut of an old floor; stooping to draw water from the well, crumbling and lichenous, still in use in the inner yard—all so that the last Monnerie could stand here and argue with himself whether he had the duty, or the heart, to leave his sturdy vines and the decently raked paths of his garden. Ours is an age of exile, he thought, an age of murder and violence, but not all the exiles are men driven from their country. Some of them are self-exiled from their own past, from the mystery of a world they formed part of as I of this. . . . In the farther wall of the kitchen-garden were the outlines of an old fireplace and the smoke-blackened stones of the chimney: it was a wall of the house which had stood here before the present house was built on nearly the same foundations. He had the sudden piercing sense that, of all the past and present things on which he would be turning his back, this, this invisible but still living, still triumphing, earlier house was the one he would be most ashamed to leave. To betray.

The scent of mignonette came to him from the darkness. It reminded him of the scent, fainter, more elusive, but unforgettable, which rises at night above the vines in flower.

Now he could hear the sea in the Loire, very clearly.

CHAPTER 22

THE RAIN HELD OFF FOR THREE DAYS: THERE were clouds, and the high wind from the sea, but still no rain. It did not come until Friday; then it began just at the moment when François Monnerie was being let down into the Monnerie grave opened for Daniel—a few light strokes on the leaves, then a warm gentle shower, falling everywhere at once; ample enough to save the vines. A look of relief and satisfaction spread over every face in the group of people, neighbors and villagers, standing behind the family: in a few it had to make its way through a polite air of piety or grief, but it triumphed innocently even there— in a fold at the corner of the eyes, in a blackened sinewy hand held out instinctively to feel the drops.

From his station, behind the family but in front of neighbors, Adam Hartley could share the relief. He caught odds and ends of muttered talk.

"It had to come—and you see it didn't need prayers. . . ."

"Monnerie will be thankful. Yes, yes, of course, why not? He's human. And last year they did badly."

"Ah, he's hard, a sound decent man, but a stone. He feels nothing. Look at him now, I ask you. . . ."

"Marie Regnier—oh, a master woman. Him you can move the odd inch, but not her, never her. Not one inch. . . ."

Earlier he had overheard two women discussing avidly whether "it" had, after all, really been suicide, and not simply the foolish mistake made by a rather drunk young man, as the police believed. Or said they believed. "Nowadays, when everything is politics . . ."

Without moving his head he could see Elizabeth and Madame Regnier. The older woman's face was shut against all glances, inquisitive or friendly. . . . Would she, if she knew the truth, look any different? Probably not. She is simpler, he thought, than Jean. . . . The tears she had not been able to keep back disfigured Elizabeth; she looked older, and her eyes stared through their thick lashes with curious fixity. He felt something between pity and a mortal irritation. For three days, since the morning when he tried to convince her that Jean must be given time to get over—what a phrase!—François's death, she had been able to avoid him: he saw her at meals, she smiled, and that was all. He realised that he was running his head against a wall, the wall of her smiling obstinacy and—a contradiction, but the truth—her young modest pride. His helplessness, the intolerable ambiguity of his position, maddened him. . . . If I could only tell her, plainly and brutally, why I can't run a knife into Jean at this moment. And exactly what my interference set going. . . . He had his sense of responsibility well under control now; never, it would never keep him awake again. But the ugly experience had changed him. With a good deal else, he had learned that he was not awkward, he was only, when it suited him, deliberately blind and maladroit. . . . To keep himself decently still, he clenched the fingers of one hand over his thumb until they became cramped. I must see her again, he thought: I must talk to her. But how?

For the moment it had become morally, even physically, impossible to think about her any longer. He pushed her to the back of his mind.

No need to look at Monnerie to know that his face was

still, as it had been during the long walk from the house
to the village, intimidatingly cold and uncharitable. Adam
thought: If he can convince his conscience, or his mind,
that he was justified in cutting out of his family a rotten
growth—what a mercy! . . . He tried for a moment to
convince himself. The seductive voice of reason: why not
take a knife to any part which is incurably diseased? . . .
A second voice, as deep and instinctive as the labouring of
his heart, answered him that what Jean had done was an
error, irremediable. Perhaps irredeemable—at any price.
He thought: Jean, God help him, is being forced to listen
to the same two voices. He guessed weakly at the agony
of this endless dialogue, going on and on in Jean Monnerie,
in a solitude as nearly visible as that surrounding him now,
at the edge of his brother's grave.

No, he thought, it's impossible, there is no answer.

In the forced immobility of his body, his mind went on
putting the question to which there is no answer. A simple
murder, the sort which jumps like a knife out of jealousy or
hate or some other fault of nature, is innocent by the side of
the butcheries carried out coldly in the name of brother-
hood, peace, a glorious future and the rest of it. Murderers
of the simpler kind are innocently guilty and we hang them.
The second kind insist, with a boring smugness, on their
innocence. They kill nobly. They do not kill, they purge.
They kill in the name of the future, the infinitely far-off
infinitely splendid end of history, when peace, friendship,
happiness, the loyalty of wives to husbands, sons to fathers,
will come back into fashion, women will no longer feel
moved to urge their husbands' executioners to do their job
quickly, and all those uncounted millions of guilty men and
women, guilty of having wanted to be free and happy in their
lifetime, will be—not excused, not made innocent, but
obliterated, forgotten, even their graves. . . . Almost all
human beings, he thought, are simple. What they need
most is food, but what is important to them is to have a

place in the order of things, and to feel in their bones that they have it. Then, only then, their lives, like their deaths, have a meaning. And if you destroy in them their attachment to a field, to things as plain and even ugly as this church, the pointed roof of its porch, its staring-faced Virgin black with age in her hideous satin mantle, and the market leaning against one wall, then the heart goes out of their lives, the place meant for natural pieties and commands remains empty—until it is filled by an ideological piety trained to kill (purge, liquidate) with a cynicism and efficiency not yet reached in war. Not even modern war. Besides, you can hope for a war to end. But to have no hope except in the end of history! . . .

The thin bitter scent of box distracted him from these icy and uncomfortable thoughts. It swept him back, the clouds of rain following him, as far as the wind-eroded graveyard on the side of a northern hill and the child shivering there between two black-clothed women: he went with it submissively, like the child himself, only too glad to be distracted. No logic, no theorising brought him any nearer knowing how a brave honest generous and intelligent man reaches a point where it seems right, taking justice into his hands, to kill his brother.

Better give up reasoning about it, he thought drily.

Abruptly, his glance was caught by old Amélie. She was standing a little behind and apart from the family, close to a yew-tree, just at this moment she put her hand out and touched one of its leaves. She stroked it lightly, with a bent cracked finger, as if she were touching the fur of a little animal: a smile moved across the furrowed wrinkles of her cheeks and touched the dry puckered lips, a smile of irony and resignation, as if she were stretching her hand towards this green leaf from the other side of her life. The silence was suddenly full of this smile, this work-scalded finger caressing the leaf of a tree older and longer-lived than itself. For less than an instant he was certain that the stubborn-

ness, the never-failing patience and endurance of such as
old Amélie, were what gave human life its only sense, its
only justification in face of the abysmal absurdity of man's
place in the universe. They did not weigh heavier than
François's short life and his little moment of treachery.
Did not cancel his brother's irremediable act. But they took
this act up into themselves, and closed over it as the immense sky closed this valley, its river, its centennial trees.
Closed over it, and drew its bitterness from it.

He felt a brief, very brief excitement. It left him as
suddenly and derisively as the feeling of certainty that had
roused it; both were perhaps illusory, shadows detaching
themselves on the edge of perpetual shadow. . . . Heavily
shod feet scraped on the gravel; a musty breath rose from
clothes much too warm for the day. All was over. People
were leaving, after waiting respectfully for a minute to let
the family go first.

Mme. Regnier did not move until they were alone. Then,
with a not very kind glance, she said,

"Come, Elizabeth, we'll go. That's enough."

Later, Father Baussan came out to the house. Adam
saw him walking in the garden with Jean, gesticulating,
talking with even more energy than usual. Stooping over
him, Jean listened with an ironical and in some strange way
avid smile.

CHAPTER 23

NEAR MIDNIGHT, ADAM WAITED IN THE drawingroom for Monnerie to come back. He had been waiting since the end of the dinner he and Jean had eaten alone. Served by an Amélie in whom grief had extinguished, for the moment, her curiosity and mute resentments, they ate in complete silence until at the end Jean muttered something about work he had to do and took himself off.

The house was quiet, or as quiet as a house full of self-willed old furniture ever is. Sunk in the night and the comely fecund valley, why should it not be quiet and reassured, certain at least of living as long as it was needed? A window, open behind its shutters, let in the night, its scents of thyme and laurel, its sounds, reeds moving in the current, flying bats, owls protesting against the indecent moonlight, the whisper, silk brushing against silk, of the rain. . . . A faintly salt breath reached Adam from the river he could not see. No need for him to see it, he could close his eyes and evoke distinctly the wide tranquil-seeming water between its sandy islands and the firm line of its banks: it ran in him deeply—not at so great a depth as that thin cold northern beck where, on long summer days, a child launched his swiftly sunk paper boats, but near it.

I shall never see it again, he thought. The shock of this less than conscious thought ran from his mind through his nerves: half-suffocated, he stood up, to be able to breathe. . . . Don't I want to come back? . . .

He became aware in himself of an impulse struggling murderously with another. Relief and anguish. The relief of getting out of this house where everything he had done had been either an error or a betrayal. And Elizabeth. . . ? If I had to leave her here, he thought: her lightly sensuous gaiety, courage, smiling candour. The thought scalded him like an acid dropped on his flesh. What would become of her? What could she do with herself? . . . He knew the answer. There was something hard, resistant, and before all modest in her: the very core of her youth.

She would recover, he thought. So should I, but I should be finished. A fine figure of a man dead from the well-fed well-wined well-exercised skin inwards. . . .

He heard Jean Monnerie's quick but deliberate steps in the hall.

Monnerie made no excuses. "Ah, there you are. I thought you might have gone to bed."

"No, I waited to see you. I want to get away early in the morning."

"I have a lot to thank you for."

Although he knew that the irony was unintentional, Adam could not soften the edge of his voice.

"You have indeed."

"Not least for staying on in the teeth of Cousin Marie's invitations to you to leave," Monnerie said. "You've helped me—a great deal." A mocking stare widened his eyes, giving him a look of heartlessness. "Your obvious common sense certainly helped the police to decide that it was an accident— or at any rate that there was nothing to prove it wasn't." He added soberly, "I never thanked you either for lying to the inspector on Tuesday evening. I expected you to, of course. But I hadn't realised until then how damnably inconsiderate it had been to embarrass you with the truth. I've behaved badly."

"You're being absurd," Adam said. "I don't like policemen."

"I see. . . . You have scruples about executions, but none about leaving murderers at large."

"As you like."

There was a pause, then Monnerie said calmly,

"I've just been going through François's things. It's astonishing how little, apart from his clothes, he left. A few books. Almost no letters. The collection of birds' eggs he made when he was a little boy. Some bits and pieces of no value. . . . Surprising. He left very little more behind him than a child does."

"We shall none of us leave the accumulations our parents and grandparents did. Thank God."

"No. But some of us leave other things. Robert left us, his mother and me, enough anger to kill François. . . . I wonder a little if *he* will go on working. Probably not. We've heard nothing yet from any of the obscure little collaborators we shot and hanged."

"Unless you stop this you'll run into trouble," Adam said sharply.

"I robbed him of his life," Monnerie retorted, "the least I can do is to lend him a little of mine."

He was sitting with an elbow on the table, his head propped by a fist. Fatigue made him seem younger; there were fewer lines on his face, it had become smooth and lean, as Adam remembered it in the war.

"Don't try to do it," he said, "it's useless and dangerous." Let the dead stay quietly on their own side of that cold ditch.

Monnerie looked at him with a slight smile. "An extraordinary thing—when I was looking at the birds' eggs I thought he'd come into the room. I was so sure that I turned around. . . . There was nothing, of course—a sort of shadow on the window-seat. One summer we used to sit there—he was eight or nine—to talk. He was furiously lively, everything interested him, he was as quick as a little hare, so that I'd forget when I was explaining something that he was only a baby. Then he'd laugh and slap himself on the knee, a trick he'd caught from one of the men, and say: Help, I'm drowning! . . . It must have been that summer he took into his head not to go to sleep unless I sat there . . ." He paused, and said, "Do we ever know what we're doing?"

"Never." *I didn't intend this,* Adam thought wearily. . . . In spite of himself, he had felt less responsible since he knew the truth. What is an indiscretion compared with murder? . . . This hypocrisy revolted him.

"I was never surer I was right—" Monnerie was talking to himself. "Do you know that extreme lucidity when you are sure, instantly sure, what you must do—and afterwards it turns out to have been an illusion? Perhaps those flashes of absolute certainty and wisdom are always a trick of the devil—eh?"

"God knows," Adam said. "We do what we have to."

"The point is that I've silenced him. Cut him off not only from the sun and all that, but from answering me back."

"For God's sake, don't go on making up his answers for him. It's worse than useless."

"I daresay," Monnerie said, with an effect of indifference. He went on rapidly, "He had every right to blame me for not teaching him that nothing is simpler than running risks with your life."

"Don't credit yourself with so much influence," Adam said drily. "You did influence him—of course. So did his uncle's selfishness and scepticism and charm. But you exaggerate. He had something in his nature, a flaw of some kind—forgive me—vanity—the need to impress people. Something more than just the uncertainty of a young man."

"I daresay. But I could have been wiser with him."

"Every mother or father in the world thinks that. Every time their child hurts them by being himself."

"You're being kind," Monnerie said, with irony.

Before opening his mouth Adam felt the futility of anything he could say. "No. I'm only trying to stop your heading back into the past at every turn. It's useless. You go back as a different man, with entirely different thoughts——"

As if he were saying: It's a fine day, Monnerie said, "Yes, I go back as a man who has killed his brother." He smiled. "Don't you see it, you fool? I have to settle accounts not, not, with a young man crawling on the floor begging to be let off, but with that child who came in just now when I was tearing up an old exercise-book and wondering what to do with a case of birds' eggs and an old penknife. Couldn't you have done anything else? he asks me. . . . Well, could I?"

Adam said gently, "You asked too much of yourself. You haven't Madame Regnier's single-mindedness."

"And how," retorted Monnerie, "except by asking too much—of ourselves and others—could we have got through the years after 1940? . . . I asked too much of myself when I let Elizabeth risk what would have happened to her in the hands of obscene brutes. Theirs or ours, by the way." He glanced curiously at his hands. "And now, tell me—am I going to hold my tongue, and marry her? . . . Use her gaiety and simplicity as a bandage. . . ."

He stopped abruptly. Staring at the blankly shuttered window, what he saw was the girl crossing the lawn in brilliant sunlight, her arms bare; the light caught the fine down on skin as smooth as a brown pebble. She had been hurrying, and her thin body with its small breasts was damp with sweat: he knew that if he bent over it he would smell the water of the creek where she had been bathing. She belongs to me, she belongs to this house, he thought. It needs her as I need her, for its happiness . . . *No,* he said to himself, no—it disgusts me.

"If I can't ask her to marry the man I've become, the man who killed his brother, I ought to clear out of her way."

Adam said nothing. But it was only because he lacked at this moment the indecent courage to say: Then leave her to me. . . . Something else was at work in him. His capacity for moving about in another person's mind was nearly always a nuisance. He did not want to know that Monnerie was tortured. He did not want to know what to say to him that might help him. He knew both. And because to help was against his own interests, he was being driven that way.

"Can't you think of anyone but yourself?" he said drily.

Monnerie lifted his hands. "A marriage where you start with secrets. . . ." he said rapidly. "I don't mean trivialities, an infidelity. Not that I go after women, I haven't time."

Nothing like that would happen, he thought, or matter very much if it did. There are secrets you keep simply for comfort. But to hold your tongue about an event involving the whole of your life, to its strongest roots. . . . There would be an immovable stone across the current flowing between us, an estrangement at such a depth that—no! If this fool doesn't know that marriage is something other than being in love: a continuity—the chance to hand on more than a weight of vines, more than an old house, more than the pleasure of breathing, in sunlight and mist, the air from the Loire; even more than all these, a smile, habits— flowing above oblivion—I can't tell him.

"It surprises me that you haven't the courage to live with her and keep your griefs to yourself," Adam said.

Monnerie stared. "You're cleverer and more generous than I thought," he said, with something like curiosity.

Suddenly exasperated, Adam said,

"I'm talking sense. You could be happy."

Was he surprised that Monnerie laughed—a short jeering brutal sound? "Sensible? Yes, you're sensible, my dear fellow. You're vilely sensible. You're like everyone else. You'd tell as many lies as you had to, not one more or less, and tell yourself at the same time that it was worth it, we have the right to be happy, we all need happiness, so many square meals a day of greasy happiness, so many—" he swallowed a sentence too gross even for his contempt and disgust. "I beg your pardon," he said, with the flicker of an insolent unfriendly smile, "take no notice of me, I'm an unpleasant brute."

He stood up and walked to a window. Pulling a shutter back, he pressed his forehead to the glass separating him from the blackness outside.

Refusing to let himself think, Adam watched him. "What are you going to do?"

Monnerie turned his head. "Do you remember saying that we smiled alike—all of us, Daniel, François? Well, just now I caught sight of François out there—smiling. And it struck me that that's the only continuity there is— the way a family has of smiling, or walking more heavily on one foot than the other, or—no, especially a smile."

"The longer you go on like this, the less use you are—to Elizabeth—anyone," Adam said.

"Keep your pity to yourself, my friend," Monnerie answered in a low voice. "I don't want it. I don't rate it. I'm only my doubts, my vile thoughts and gestures—and my cruelty." He went on with less bitterness. "You know, there are still things I have to clear up with him. You haven't forgotten what he looked like—no, of course you haven't. That incredible liveliness and gaiety. He looked frail but he wasn't, he was tireless. What's so strange is that his face when he was dead was as severe as Daniel's, all the eagerness and grace wiped out—hard, unforgiving. . . . But I was right. I had every right."

Adam was silent.

In the same voice, of a man meditating aloud, Monnerie said,

"The truth is, you have to pay something for using these

rights. I can't stay on here, as if nothing had happened, living a comfortable decent life."

Adam gave way to a cruel impulse. "Why not? Since you know you were doing the right thing."

The calmness of Monnerie's smile disconcerted him. "Why not? Because I don't feel it. You're sure, you, that an act of justice is murder. You may be right. But I can't take your word for it. I have to satisfy myself what it was I did. *What did I do?*"—he moved his head restlessly—"justice or a shocking cruelty? Something I have to swallow as horrible but right? Or a crime I ought to—to expiate?" He smiled again. "It could be both, of course. The graves of a hero and a little coward look exactly alike."

He's clean out of my reach, thought Adam. He felt the same despair and impotent anger he would have felt if he had been watching the other man clinging by one hand to the edge of a raft. One by one the fingers of his hand were uncurling, deliberately.

"Listen to me," he said roughly, "the war—the resistance —everything made it impossible, absolutely impossible, for you not to do what you did."

Monnerie shook his head.

"No. You are wrong. Until the moment I did it, it was still possible for me—" he hesitated for less than a second— "for me to see through his rottenness to his innocence, and go on from that." He went back to the window for a moment. Turning round, he said in a savagely deep voice, "I'm not free. I've trapped myself. . . . I must get away," he added quietly. "I can't think here."

If he means what he's saying . . . Adam thought. He steadied his mind. *No!* . . . "You can't just bolt," he said flatly.

"Can't I?" Monnerie came to him quickly and took him by the shoulders, pressing his hands down on them. His face was alive with an affectionate malice and a sort of know-ingness. His eyes, only his eyes, smiled. "Do me a kindness."

"What is it?"

"Lend me your car to drive to Tours. I can take a train there. I'll leave the car in the Citroen garage—Pichard— and you can pick it up when you like."

The shocking joy Adam felt confused him. He let it take possession of him for a moment. This is what I'm like, what I am, he thought with contempt.

"How long have you been planning this?"

"Since Tuesday night. No, early Wednesday morning— when I was helping François to take his clothes off. . . . I had to lift him into bed. . . . No, no, I'm not pretending that I knew then I should have to go. But I knew something . . . Since then this place has been turning its back on me. As it did just now when I was in his room and thought I heard him come in. I spoke to him, and he took no notice— of course not, he couldn't see me. I wasn't there—only his murderer was there." He stopped, looked absently at nothing, and said, "You see? I'm being kicked out."

"You told me you could never live anywhere but here," Adam said in a low voice.

That's true, thought Monnerie. I haven't the time left to fill any other place with the memories saturating this: I shall always be the child of this house, my senses invaded at any moment by its voices, the smell of its old wood, the freshness of its newly washed tiles, the breath from the river—even to the noise of the crickets. Absent, I shan't cease to be the cell where it stores its honey.

"Wherever I go I shall be here," he said lightly. "It's a habit."

"Pure mysticism," Adam muttered. "Or, if you prefer it, pure nonsense."

Monnerie shrugged his shoulders. "As you like." He gave Adam a coldly inquisitive stare. "Why don't you stay a week or two in the village? *The Golden Lion* has no ameni- ties, bare scrubbed boards in your room, but you'll eat well.

As they say here, a light head and a gay stomach. . . . It
would help Elizabeth."

Adam ignored this. "And Madame Regnier? What are you
going to do about her? Let her get up in the morning and
find you've bolted? Don't you owe her more than that?"

The humiliating thought struck him that Monnerie knew
very well what he owed Cousin Marie and her impossible love
of justice. His stupidity vexed him.

Monnerie did not answer. Suddenly and very distinctly,
he had seen Cousin Marie standing in front of an open linen
cupboard; the shelves carried piles of fine white sheets,
stacked closely, below labels noting the year when they
were bought; there must be at least twenty dozen sheets;
she unfolded one after another, examined it, and when she
found a weak place her cry of alarm was louder than if she
had found herself on a sinking raft. . . . It is she, he thought,
who has held us together all these years. Has kept the house
in order, the silver polished for use, larder and store-cupboards
filled with their jars of honey, walnuts, pâtés, ready to be
handed on. She who has seen to it that, at least in one house
in France, the notion of life everlasting has a taste, a scent,
a weight.

"Let her think I'm off my head," he said, "it doesn't
matter. I'll write to her in a day or two."

With a rush of self-contempt, Adam said,

"I wish in God's name I'd never come back to this house."

There was a silence. Monnerie's face changed subtly. Without losing its calm it grew heavier and more impassive, as if
the life in the flesh were being drawn back. Lifting his head
to stare at Adam, he said,

"Yes, it would have been better. You wouldn't have seen
Elizabeth again—and that would have saved you a lot of
trouble and embarrassment."

The hostility of his casually spoken words was inescapable.
Adam thought: Well, here we are. He felt cool, cool enough,
but the taste of treachery came back. He said gently,

"So you think I've fallen in love with her."

"Haven't you?"

He had an impulse to tell Monnerie the truth as brusquely as possible. Get rid of it into him. His pity for the other man—or only his nerves shrinking from the sight of cruelty —hardened his throat.

"Yes. I have. I'm sorry about it, but there it is."

Monnerie's eyes were half hidden by the heaviness and the thick fold at the base of his eyelids; his head and shoulders hung forward as if dragged by their own weight. "It might be better for her if she had fallen for you—she would have had an easier life."

"Easier, yes," Adam said.

He hesitated. He had begun to feel something that was almost the pleasure of being in control of the conversation: a diplomat with a declaration of war in his pocket, to be used or not, as things turn out.

Monnerie smiled.

"You could have taken her away with you to your safe solid life. You'd quarrel, of course, you've been brought up in two entirely different worlds, but it wouldn't matter— there would be no murderous secrets lying between you that you couldn't talk or quarrel about. . . . On the whole —a pity."

Adam felt a sudden distaste for being jockeyed into confessing himself. Clumsy and undignified. What the devil has dignity to do with it? he thought, with the same exasperation.

"Do you want to talk about her now?" he asked slowly.

"Why not?"

"I imagined you had enough on your mind."

"You imagined—?" Monnerie said, ironically. "My dear fellow, I know you have more imagination than you ever use, but——"

"Wait a minute," Adam said.

His ears sharpened by the tension, he had caught a sound

outside the room, in the hall: a bat, or a stair creaking. He turned his head to be able to see the door.

Elizabeth came in quickly. She looked smaller and very thin in her pyjamas and washed-out cotton dressing-gown, but a measure of order and good sense came in with her. Everything that had been irrational and monstrous in the atmosphere fled from it, and with a sigh of relief the room went back to its life of an old shabby farm-manor without pretensions to tragedy. I could never, thought Adam, tire of eyes and a mouth which nothing can distort beyond what is natural and decent. . . . He noticed her bare feet: small and highly arched, but not slender.

Monnerie spoke first. "My dear child, what are you doing out of bed?" He paused, and went on smoothly, "You wanted, of course, to see Adam again before he goes——"

"No—" she shook her head—"it was you I wanted to see."

She stammered a little over the lie. Adam kept back an unseemly impulse to smile. She must have noticed it: turning to Jean, she went on quickly,

"No, that's not true. But I've changed my mind. I was going to say this to you tomorrow, when Adam had gone. I'll say it now." She laid her hand on his arm for a moment. "Jean, let's go away—let's leave this house. . . . No, please listen. Too much is being sacrificed to it. I'm not a Monnerie and I don't see why you need spend the whole of your life here, working yourself to death, saving, thinking of nothing but how to get this right and that right. . . . This house—" her voice rose—"I tell you, it's not a house, it's a burden you carry about. Do you ever hear Cousin Marie say anything except: *The best thing for the family will be. . . ?* Never: *the happiest thing . . .* Never!"

Her courage and her anger failed her together. She waited, offering him a candid smile.

Monnerie did not smile. Looking down at her without a sign of emotion, he asked,

"Do you really want to go away?"

"Yes. No. No. I want to help you, but you don't let me. I would do anything—and you go on treating me like an irresponsible young girl."

When did she decide this? Adam asked himself. This instant, when she came in and saw him standing there, and felt, as she must feel, the energy under his brusqueness, carelessness, smiling mockery? Or yesterday, or three days ago? He had the grotesque idea that he had been expecting it, and in the same breath he knew that now he was finished.

Monnerie had not moved.

"You're so gay and clear, my girl—my child—and you have so much courage—fortunately without knowing it. I don't want to spoil that."

"Even if I were all you think," she said in her light voice, "it would be wrong to try to protect me. I want to be used, I don't want to be spared. You make me ashamed when you treat me as if I should break down under a test."

"Who knows?" Monnerie said. "It broke François."

Adam said sharply, "Don't." He meant: Don't tell her, you fool.

Elizabeth glanced at him with what seemed indifference, but he saw that her hands were shaking, and felt a selfish pleasure.

"Our poor little Babba," she murmured. "What do you mean?"

"He was a spoiled shabby creature," said Monnerie in a biting voice. "If we'd been living in normal times he'd have got through by pleasing everyone, flattering people, telling them little lies. Reality—the unlucky fact that nowadays you have to choose—was too much for him. In the end it broke him."

Horrified by his voice, she said, "No. I was sorry for him."

He smiled. "You think I was too hard on him."

"What I think—" she closed her eyes, to avoid seeing his smile—"I think that if Cousin Marie had been willing to let him off, you would have been less severe yourself. . . . I ought not to say this—but she was crueller to François than Robert would have been. That's true, isn't it?"

Monnerie watched her with the same hard unwavering stare. "Maybe. Maybe Robert would have forgiven him. Good. But does that give you, me, anyone, the right to forgive his murderer for him?"

"I don't know," she stammered, "but——"

"But you think we were cruel," he interrupted.

"Cousin Marie was cruel . . . and I hate cruelty." She thought with remorse of Cousin Marie's griefs. "Oh, I don't know anything. . . . We can forgive everybody else in the world for being cruel, but not ourselves——"

Monnerie lifted his arms in a gesture of indifference and lassitude. "Perhaps you are right."

Elizabeth did not speak. Watching her, Adam saw that she was using all her strength in the effort to behave well and sensibly. He felt an agony of compassion and love—and bitterness.

"Perhaps I am only an inexperienced little fool," she said under her breath.

Monnerie took hold of her by the arms, as if he were going to draw her close to him. He did not do that: he held her between his powerful hands, looking at her attentively, a disturbingly erotic attention.

"Suppose I told you that I was responsible for François's death? . . . No, don't speak. Listen. Suppose the poor boy pleaded with me, and I was so brutally severe that I made him despair. Yes, despair. He was convinced that the only thing left for him to do was to get rid of himself. Because he was contemptible. Because I had rejected him——"

"Leave it at that," Adam broke in, "for God's sake, leave it. You have no right. . . ."

Elizabeth took no notice of him. Looking Jean in the face, she said quietly,

"It's not true."

"But if it were? What would you say?"

She lifted her hands to her head in a gesture of bewilderment. Still holding her, he made her sit down in a corner of the sofa with him. With an instinctive movement to detach herself, she folded her legs under her, so that she was kneeling. Monnerie let himself go, resting on her. He closed his eyes, and his head dropped on her shoulder, in the small hollow between it and her throat.

"Don't move," he said simply. "I need you. I won't ask you any more questions, I've asked myself too many since François died—there must come a time when I needn't go on with them. When I shall come out of the nightmare and find that I'm in this room, on this sofa I know the shape of as well as I know you and your arms and throat—" he moved his hand over them. "Let me stay close to you for a moment."

Adam thought suddenly: He's in hell—and all the same he's playing with us. He felt a spasm of hatred and some other, more decent, emotion.

Elizabeth held herself upright, with a fixed smile, like a child carrying a parcel too heavy for it. She said calmly,

"For as long as you like."

"We're closer to each other than two people ever were," Monnerie said.

Adam could not endure the scene. He started to walk out of the room. Abruptly, as if he had been waiting for him to move, Monnerie released the girl and sat up. Startled by his roughness, she looked at him with widely open eyes. She did not speak.

Smiling almost imperceptibly, he said in a bland voice,

"Now I'm going to tell you why you came down here, my child. You came because you wanted to look at our dear Adam again, if it were only for a minute. One minute. You were going to make that minute last you for the rest of your life. . . . You love him as absurdly as that."

Elizabeth stood up. Without awkwardness, without any show of pity, she answered,

"Yes, I do—quite as much as that."

She did not look at Adam as she spoke, and he did not go to her. He could afford to wait.

"And you'd decided to give him up?" Monnerie said, with an air of amusement. "Wonderful. What have I done to deserve so much abominable nobility round me? The loyal friend, the high-minded loyal young woman." His smile broadened. "You bore me with your loyalty. My dear Elizabeth, you——"

Adam cut him short. "No reason why you should use your tongue on Elizabeth. Talk to me."

"To you? Why to you?" Monnerie retorted. "Would you understand anything I said?"

They looked at each other across the table for a moment: their enmity had caught up a thread of sexual excitement—which excluded the girl, as if trying to reach a more obscure instinct. Out of a grief just as obscure, Adam gave way.

"We used to be able to understand each other," he said gently.

There was a pause before Monnerie said,

"That's true. If it weren't I shouldn't like and dislike you so much."

Elizabeth cried suddenly, "Jean—no, I can't leave you."

"Can't you?" he drawled. "Why not?"

"You're unhappy."

For what seemed at least a minute he kept his ironical stare on her face lifted to his. She endured it without turning away. At last he said,

"Yes, I'm unhappy. But you ought to be told why. . . . François didn't poison himself. He would never have done it—he was a wretched little coward. I killed him myself."

With a flash of something like horror, Adam thought: I was wrong. He's played his highest card. . . . Elizabeth's eyes, dilated and brilliant, had not flinched. The brief look of fear and revulsion in them gave way at once before a blazing tenderness. She took a step forward.

"I won't give you up."

The fall of Jean's eyelids gave his face an air of extreme pleasure, entirely physical. He lifted them again and asked, "Could you stand it?"

"Of course. . . . I'll help you in every way I can—with the house—with everything. We—we'll be happy."

The change in his face made her draw back.

"You really think I could marry you?" he said, smiling. "Marry, and turn Babba's room into a nursery for my son. . . . Trust myself to bring up another child. . . . Horrible. The idea of a servant, a sentimental little servant. Absurd and disgusting."

Elizabeth turned very pale. "Why are you trying to humiliate me?"

"Because you really do disgust me. All this eagerness to sleep with a murderer, and let him give you your children——"

"Need you do this?" Adam interrupted.

Ignoring him, the girl asked, "Why did you tell me about François?"

Monnerie was still smiling. "Because I knew what would happen. After all, I know you better than anyone, better than he does"—he jerked his head sideways at Adam—"and I knew, I was sure, that I only had to say to you: I'm lost, I've killed the only other human being in my world, and if you leave me I shall be alone, absolutely alone . . . I had only to tell you that, and you would offer to stay. You belong to that race of little savages who remain loyal for life to what is soiled, lost, done for—only because it is soiled, because it's done for. I betted on it—and of course I took the trick. . . ." With a quick movement, he took both her hands in his. "Your hands, Elizabeth," he said softly, "your small hard hands, would have closed round this—" dropping them, he touched himself with one finger—"this poor lost brute and held him up as long as you had the strength. . . . You're strong, it would have been a long time."

"But"—she hesitated very briefly—"you didn't want me?"

"No. I don't."

She made an obvious effort to steady her voice. "Then why need you have taken so much trouble to humiliate me?"

"Don't make a mistake," Adam said. "He was cutting you loose. So that you shouldn't feel any regrets. Any guilt."

Jean rolled an eye at him. "Romantic! I meant exactly what I said. If it humiliates Elizabeth, I'm sorry. The truth is, she—you, too—are living in a world where I can't breathe any longer. The idea of it, of going through all the gestures of living in it—no, I'm beyond that. If giving myself the pleasure of telling the truth is any help to her, or you—well, a reason the more for telling it."

"There was no need to do it," Elizabeth said quietly, "I'm not a little fool. I should have been staying of my own will. And in time I should have made us both happy— since that's the only way I can live." A trace of fear came into her voice. "If you want me——"

He shook with a nearly silent laughter. "Do I have to say it all again?"

Adam interrupted him, sharply. "No. You've said enough. . . . Thanks."

Monnerie turned on him an appraising stare. "You'll make her an excellent husband—not more than casually unfaithful. Perhaps not even that. . . . She'll be glad to get away, you know, even to your dull cold island." In a warmer voice he added, "Do me the kindness to take her away as soon as possible. The sooner this place is rid of you both the better."

Elizabeth moved suddenly. "You'll be all right? You won't —you won't harm yourself?"

He glanced at her without kindness. "Are you afraid I might kill myself? Nonsense. People kill themselves when they have nothing in their heads—or only some silly lie. Don't worry. I have no intention of letting myself off so cheaply. . . ." A look of derision crossed his face. "I might have killed myself after killing François. Quite easy—and I should have been able to say: Look at me, my dear friends, look, I'm paying for this terrible crime with my own life. Doesn't that make me innocent again? . . . It would have been in the best, the most exalted tradition—and a grotesque cheat! You say: I'll pay with my life, and then you slip over a fast one by paying with nothing but your two-bits'-worth of death. What's that if it isn't cheating?"

He walked across the room and stood with his back to one of the shuttered windows, his eyes under their heavy lids searching the room for anything it concealed in the way of an answer.

"I'm trapped," he said in a low voice. "Whatever I do, I'm trapped. If I can believe I had the right to kill him I can't live comfortably with my righteousness. And if I can't believe it . . ." He paused and went on in a stronger voice, the more impressive because it was toneless. "D'you suppose I haven't thought of trying to buy myself off? There are things I could do, I could go off next week with Father Baussan to his leper colony—you'd call that an expiation, wouldn't you? . . . But it would be useless!"

"Why?" Adam asked.

"It would be an escape—an evasion. You can't atone for a murder—if it was only murder—by goodness, by charity——" He became almost inaudible. "Another thing —Father Baussan is going among his lepers for love, for the love and serenity he draws from the cross he'll put up over his dead, no different from the crosses in any village cemetery. But I—what should I be going for? Even if I were to be offered *that* love, that serenity, I couldn't accept it. Never, unless—unless . . ." he let the phrase drag off into silence. "No. No, my God, I must find something else. A life where I shall count for very little. I could be a navvy—" he stretched his muscular arms—"or get jobs here and there in other people's vineyards, or a factory, or——"

Elizabeth ran to him and seized his hands.

"Let me stay!"

He freed himself, and pushed her away, gently enough.

"I told you. The thought of living with you disgusts me. When I want a young woman—for the briefest and most non-committal of uses—there are plenty of them about. Didn't I make it clear?"

She drew back, and looked at him with the hint, only the hint of a fine smile. She was defending him, Adam saw, from her pity—quite as much as defending herself from him.

"Yes, you made it clear," she said. She turned and walked across the room to Adam. "I should like you to touch me," she said lightly, "I want to be sure there are still ordinary things in the world. Things in their proper places. Simple —dull. A house with attics where children can play. Has your house a good attic?"

His fingers came on a trace of tears on her eyelids, but she was not crying. At this moment he felt nothing for her except the responsibility and the, as it were, habit of tenderness he had felt for young inexperienced soldiers under his command. She pressed against him a hot and shaking body. He had an impulse to carry her upstairs to her room and watch her fall asleep.

"If an attic will make you happy——"

"With you, I don't care whether I'm happy or not," she interrupted. "It couldn't matter less."

In an even voice Monnerie said,

"Well, are you or aren't you going to let me borrow your car?"

Adam took his arms from Elizabeth. He turned. "Oh, you can have it. Anything you like. But I wish to God you'd think again. You're not in a state to make decisions."

Monnerie smiled. "You mean I'm going cracked."

"You're overstrained."

"It's just possible," agreed Monnerie. His smile became sarcastic.

Adam had ceased to care whether he exasperated the other man or only roused his mockery.

"Do you mean to come back here?"

"Of course."

"When?"

"After you've taken Elizabeth to England," Monnerie said in a rapid voice.

"You're lying. What you mean is you're not coming back at all."

"How d'you know what I mean or don't mean?" He smiled, but he was contemptuous. "You know less about me than that chair." Without intending it, he had pointed to the round-backed leather chair in which François had tried to hide himself from them.

Adam said coldly, "What d'you know about yourself? This may be another of those moments when you know— know for certain—what you ought to do. And it could be another illusion!"

He knew as he was speaking that he had gone too far. Monnerie took a step, abrupt and deliberate, towards him. He stopped, his heavy body a block of anger: the lines on his forehead and between his eyebrows, the line scored from his powerful nostrils to the ends of his mouth, deepened as if a nail had been used on them.

"Is it an illusion that I killed him? I—I?" He pressed both hands, fingers widely apart, on his chest. "It's the one thing I can be certain of. I shan't be certain of anything else as long as I live—I shan't be certain whether I could have done anything else, whether I ought to repent, whether I can be forgiven, absolved—or how I can be forgiven, by whom or by what. It's what I have to find out . . . why I have to go on living. To live—" the words poured from him, half under his breath, a lava of grief—"to live in uncertainty, to live in hell."

His anger vanished as suddenly as it had started up.

"My dear chap," he said quickly, wearily, "I didn't *punish* him, it wasn't punishment—it was surgical, an act of . . ." he stopped, frowning. He shook his head. "No," he said absently. "But perhaps at the end I shall know the answers. A treat to come."

"You're torturing yourself to no purpose," Adam said. . . . The world is full of people who can ignore their hearts in the complete certainty of never hearing from them. But if you are not one of these animals it is fatal to push yourself to the limits of your will. . . . "You made a habit, in '43, of taking the more criminal of our jobs on yourself. Remember? Well—you're paying for the habit."

Monnerie looked at him with a friendly mockery. "That was at the time I was forming the habit of being fond of you. . . . I still am—and I hope devoutly that I shan't see you again."

"I'm sorry," Adam began. He felt a spurt of anger. "We were both in it—" and your Cousin Marie fully as much, he thought—"but I'm getting off without a scratch."

Monnerie made an impatient face. "For God's sake get it into your head that only one person is responsible—me." He smiled slightly. "You," he said. "The English captain."

"What did you say?"

"Nothing—I'm talking nonsense. . . ." He yawned suddenly. "Haven't we said everything we have to say?"

"Yes," Adam said, "Except—forgive me but I hope you'll come back here. You ought not to let this place go. All the vines you've replanted."

"Remind me—why don't you?—that too many people depend on me here, that I can't leave them to save their own tripes, I can't desert—can't throw everything back on Cousin Marie's shoulders, she's my God had enough. . . ." He stopped, and went on quietly. "I'll try to get back. I don't know yet what I can do. It must wait."

Adam thought: He will never be able to accept what he did. If he were less lucid he could forget it by throwing himself into some violent or dangerous life. Or, with the help of a little bad faith—nothing serious, nothing more than the habitual self-deception of a bad writer—he could build up between him and it a faked serenity. . . . Jean Monnerie's lucidity was driving him out to *think* his act. To wrestle with his angel—or devil. The only victory he could hope for—derisory at that, a single thread separating him from the abyss of absurdity and horror—was to arrive, at some moment, for a moment, at the point of being able to realise it completely, in complete lucidity. Victory would be nothing but this moment of lucidity—and indistinguishable from defeat. Exactly as the death a soldier accepts deliberately is, in the end, indistinguishable from the death, hurried, forced on him, of a coward. Indistinguishable—except to the man living secretly, hidden from every eye, out of reach of any voice or hand, living and secretly fighting until the last unnoticed flicker of consciousness.

He felt a useless anguish. "Forgive me for having come here," he said drily.

The familiar mockery sprang in Monnerie's eyes. "My dear fellow, I'm still trying to borrow your car."

"It's in the yard—take it. Keep it if you like, I can get another."

"Thanks, I won't do that," answered Monnerie. "I'll leave it at Pichard's." He seemed to hesitate, then walked quickly across the room, stopped, and looked from Adam to the girl with the same mocking inquisitive glance. "Surely you ought to see me off?" he said to her.

"No," Elizabeth said.

"Why not?"

"I don't know what would be the proper way to say goodbye to you. I would rather you left me here."

"You're smiling," Monnerie said gently.

"Would you rather I cried?"

"No, I like it. Thanks. Goodbye, my darling."

"Goodbye."

He went out.

Adam followed him across the hall and into the courtyard. The rain had stopped now; the air was fresh, still

cool, warmth hovering in it somewhere not far off, an up-
and-down wing-beat; just below the horizon, the light was
already at work, spreading outwards, turning what was left
of yesterday's clouds to a luminous fleece; the branches of
a tree full of birds swayed and shook them off to fly straight
up like the drops of a fountain. Adam started the car and
ran it out backwards between two carts. He showed Monnerie
this and that about it, warning him of its trick of stopping
for no reason in traffic. Then he stepped out, and Monnerie
got in.

"I know these Citroens," he murmured. He slipped it
into gear, turned to look at Adam, and said gently,

"Goodbye, my dear fellow, I shan't see you again."

"Why not?"

"I don't want to. You or Elizabeth. . . . I shan't forget
you."

He felt stretch in him, between himself and them, a desert
of indifference.

"Let me drive you into Tours," Adam said impulsively.

"I'd rather you didn't."

"Very well."

"Thank you," Monnerie said again. "And for all you're
going to do for me tomorrow—today. And good luck. But
you were born lucky."

He turned his head as Elizabeth, her dressing-gown flying
out, ran out of the house and across the courtyard to the car.

"I changed my mind," she said.

"You must be careful," Monnerie said. "It's becoming a
habit."

"You think I'm heartless. I'm not, I shall think about
you—not all the time, not every day—but often. But—but
come back here, so that I can think about you easily. Will
you?"

"Be sure I'll do my best for you," he murmured.

He smiled—like his brother and like Daniel Monnerie,
with the same warmth, brilliance, and exasperating assur-

ance. It came in him, Adam thought, from a profound resilience and gaiety—compatible with an anguish just as profound and lasting. No—not compatible. Incompatible and irreconcilable, always. They existed together—as, at the same depth of his life, the deepest, existed together his cruelty to François and his brotherly love. Incompatible, irreconcilable, and co-existent until his death. At least until his death.

For as long as he could hear the car, Adam listened. In the silence of the half-awake countryside he seemed to hear it for a long time, several minutes.

He turned to Elizabeth. She was holding her dressing-gown together below her throat, and he noticed the knuckles of her hands forced against the skin. She made a grimace which might be either a smile or the beginning of tears. He expected her to break down. But she drew a long breath, stretching her arms. Her voice was a cry of joy.

"What a marvellous day!"

He touched her; her shoulder-blade under his hand was the edge of a little knife. "Come," he said, "you must have a few hours' sleep."

"You, too."

His arm round her shoulders, he drew her into the house. Her body moved him only to tenderness—because it had been used to the limit of its energy; and she had not broken down.

CHAPTER 24

Cousin Marie was standing at the foot of the stairs. Except that her face was uncovered and clear, she might, in her dark shapeless bed-gown, have been either of the anonymous figures in grey time-eaten wood placed inside the porch of the village church. She was holding the candle she must have lit in her shuttered bedroom and blown out on the staircase: a thin black thread of smoke, drawn to one side in the air from the door, was rising from the wick.

Placing the candlestick on a chest, she asked calmly,

"What are you doing here at this hour, Elizabeth?"

"Nothing. Nothing I can't tell you about," the girl said quickly.

Cousin Marie's voice and derisively lifted eyebrows were less intimidating than her eyes. "You reassure me." She turned her shoulder on the girl. "Captain Hartley, what is going on here? I heard a car."

"It's all right," Adam said gently.

"Be good enough to tell me what has happened. I'll judge for myself."

He hesitated. A pleasant job I've been handed! he thought drily. "Let us go into the drawingroom."

Without a word Cousin Marie walked quickly past him into the room: as she passed him, he noticed that her face had the pallor and smooth false transparence of fine wax.

"Won't you go up to bed and leave this to me?" he said to Elizabeth.

"No, of course not," she answered, in a light voice.

He followed her into the drawingroom. "May I open the shutters?" he asked. He began to fold them back at once, without waiting for Cousin Marie to refuse him permission. In the last minute the light had grown stronger; already it was striking through the tops of the trees, and from the other side of the river came a high distant voice, some boy out early.

"Now," Cousin Marie said impatiently. "Tell me, please."

Looking at her, he began slowly, "Jean has gone away——"

She cut him short. "What d'you say? Where has he gone? Did you know he was going?"

"Not until an hour ago."

He watched her covertly for signs of anger or shock. Her face showed neither, only a polite surprise. In a smooth voice she asked,

"But why has he gone away now—and without telling me?"

Out of pity for her Adam spoke brusquely. "I daresay he was afraid you would try to stop him."

The look of sceptical amusement she brought on her face was admirably offensive. "You must be making a mistake. Perhaps you didn't understand all he said to you. Do you know where he has gone? For how long?"

"I'm afraid I don't. He'll write to you, I suppose, in a day or two."

Her glance said that he was really behaving too much like a fool. "Of course."

Irritated in spite of himself, he said,

"He's been under a very heavy strain—heavier, perhaps, than you have allowed for."

He expected to be slapped down. It didn't happen. Instead, she fixed on him gleaming, widely open eyes, the only source of life in her face, and asked,

"He's gone because François killed himself here?"

"Yes."

In a detached tone she said, "He blames me for it."

"No, that's not true," Adam said, with energy. "He has never said that, nor anything like it."

Cousin Marie laughed, a laugh she kept as low, nearly inaudible, as she could: it must have hurt her; she lifted both hands to her throat.

"As if he would tell you," she cried.

Adam thought: After all, she's an old woman, not able to interfere any more; she has to accept what she's told. "I'm sure he hasn't gone for long," he said gently.

Only because, at this second, with a still supple movement, she straightened her narrow back, did he and the girl notice that she had sunk a little. She shrugged her shoulders.

"It's quite unimportant—I managed alone during the war, when things were really difficult. I can manage again now. If, or when, he chooses to come back, he'll find everything in order."

Adam took care to keep out of his voice the admiration, as well as the pity he felt for her. "I can't tell you at all clearly why he has gone—except that he wanted to get away from this house. It's natural he should, you know. You mustn't blame him. Or—blame him, if you like—but only because he has gone off in this abrupt way."

He had made a mistake. Lifting her eyebrows, she said,

"Don't try to explain Jean to me, Captain Hartley. It's only ridiculous."

"Yes, of course," he said gently. "I beg your pardon."

She turned to Elizabeth. "But I don't understand what you are doing downstairs. Unless Jean sent for you?"

Elizabeth shook her head. A smile at once joyous and diffident crossed her face; she lifted her hands. "No. I came. I would rather tell you this tomorrow—later today, I mean. But it doesn't matter."

"Tell me what?"

"That I'm not going to marry Jean——"

The other woman's arms moved as though she were letting something drop between them. "Yes, yes, I understand you." She sent a mocking glance from the girl's face to Adam's. "You're going to tell me now that you have no better manners than to want to run away from us with a stranger we know nothing about—except that he has a habit of forcing himself on people. Well, really, my girl!"

"I shall be happy to tell you about myself," Adam said. "You needn't be afraid for Elizabeth." He added, with a little malice, "I'm not badly off, you can trust her to me."

"Cousin Marie, don't be so hurt," Elizabeth said. She added quickly, "Don't laugh like that. Let me tell you myself—everything. And let me talk to you before I go as we always have talked—as if you were my mother." She took an impulsive step towards Cousin Marie. "After all, you've been my mother for years."

Cousin Marie lifted a long fine hand, to ward her off. A charming smile, not quite unkind, softened her face. "It gives me no pleasure to have a daughter so little able to behave herself. . . . And now, my child, I should be grateful if you would run away—you'd better go back to bed." She turned this smile—gesture of a puppet only able to move its head—on Adam. "Do you mind, Captain Hartley? I should really like to be left alone."

She did not watch them go. Glancing over his shoulder, Adam carried away with him what was to be his sharpest memory of her: implacable, wilfully insouciant, mouth curved in a frigid gaiety such as old women love to arrange on a dead face. . . .

The air entering from the porch was already warm. He moved to put his arms round Elizabeth. For less than a moment she leaned against him; then stepped back, looking at him with a smile, brilliant and very slightly malicious.

"Don't try to comfort me. I must go—the next time you see me I shall be dressed and combed. . . . And let's leave as quickly as we can. If I'm to be treated as a badly brought-up young woman, I might as well behave like one. You won't see me crying—if I cry. I promise you, my darling."

She ran up the stairs, taking them two at a time. In the instant of vanishing into the corridor to her room she turned and waved her hand.

Wait, he thought, wait until I have her in the house she'll speak of as "my house." My room, my chairs, the lilacs in my garden. The web spinning itself between her and all these everyday objects—he knew exactly how politely and indulgently she would treat them—would close her against the past, against Jean Monnerie himself, more surely than anything. He had a moment of hard exultance. And close on its heels another when, without caring, he knew that his triumph was precarious—something in her would remain, all his life, unknown and foreign. In the last few minutes he had recognised in her very clearly the temper, the race, and the past of Cousin Marie herself.

He was perfectly happy—one of those moments, extremely rare, which equal a lifetime of disappointment and useless effort.

Smiling absently, he went upstairs to his room. No point in going to bed—he was neither tired nor sleepy. While he packed, he would be able to look at the Loire; at the light mist, no more opaque than a child's breath on a glass, rising from the valley; and the coming, rapid and inevitable, of light: a clear joyous witty light.

CHAPTER 25

ALONE, COUSIN MARIE STOOD FOR A MINUTE stock still. Then, without knowing why she did it—moved partly by an obscure instinct, and partly because they should not in the order of things have been opened until in two or three hours' time old Amélie shuffled in list slippers across the floor, grumbling under her breath as the acid in her joints nipped her, to open them—she closed the shutters. The room, which had been filled by a grey light, darkened again, the shadows pressed together in the corners between tall-boys and heavy cupboards, floated like strands of dark seaweed from the cornice.

The shock of Jean's desertion of her was so deep that she felt nothing. She stood stiffly upright, like some strong savage, wounded and held motionless by an instinct which is half pride and half the certainty that to move at all will be to drop. Without thinking about it she knew that she could not afford to feel. She could afford—yes, and take a bitter pleasure in it—not to be reconciled to her son's death: could afford, as that clumsy mannerless fool Father Baussan said, to scold God about it—because in the end even un-natural death is natural. . . . But Jean—for whom, of all of them, she had done most and had loved, because he was older than the others when she got him, with the turbulent uncritical love she would have given a young brother. . . . It was as if he had looked at her, at her years of serving him, and said: After all, you mean nothing to me, I'm off.

This, this unnatural indifference, which could as easily be contempt, she could *not* afford to look at. Not yet. Later, she might have to; might have to decide how much was her fault, what she had done and in what failed. Later, later, she told herself harshly. For the moment she had all she could do to accept calmly that she was alone.

Night after night I shall sit here, she thought slowly: in the endlessly long nights of winter, and the short, too short for rest, summer nights, and in the unbearable rending sadness of spring and autumn—alone. Her throat contracted suddenly. But no—not alone.

She glanced involuntarily at the sofa. It was too easy to mould the shadows under its curved end into the likeness of a fine emaciated head, the mounds of deep eyelids piercing her with their blind stare from a face emptied of everything but a strict irony. Turning away, she looked round the room, able, only because she knew it so well, to see the wax-filled cracks in the panels, the outlines, in their dark recess, of old vases, a clock, the fragment of Italian marble. Round the long oval table, the chairs were set as for a family—François's chair, Jean's.

"Yes, you are all here," she said aloud, "and you, too, my son. . . ."

She drew a quick breath. In a low voice, half propitiating, half confident, the voice of a woman talking to her grown-up son, she said,

"But no, my darling, it's not true. I tell you, it's not true, you're wrong—the dead have not forgotten how to hate, not forgotten how they were killed, nor who killed them. It's not true that if you touched the hand of one of your torturers lying next to yours you wouldn't draw back, wouldn't care. It's not true that now you have everything in common with each other—and with us, nothing. . . . What? . . . Because I can feel the sun on my hands I'm less close to you than your dead enemy? No, no, I'm your mother, I remember you, every day of my life I remember you, as you were—and as when you were little. . . . Don't smile at me like that. . . . My darling, you oughtn't to accuse your mother, you know very well that it's not because I'm hard-hearted or cold that I wanted François to be punished. . . . I don't know what you mean by peace. If you mean leaving cowards and traitors at large—no!"

She turned sharply. A large moth, which had been sleeping in the fold of a curtain, fluttered down a little way, then up again, to cling, wings turned back and quivering on each other, to the edge of a shutter. What startled it? she wondered. Did I?

It was very seldom she thought about her husband, Robert's father: even in his lifetime, sleeping beside him, sitting through long meals with him, she had had the strength almost not to notice him—except when some little thing he did irritated her. He might have been no more than an acquaintance, not even a distant relative. . . . How extraordinary it is, she told him, that I remember nothing about you; I know that there really was a time when, because of you, I lived through an agony of bitterness and humiliation. But I don't feel it. And everything else I remember about you is ridiculous, some physical tic, not one single sensual memory, even though—I admit it—you were the only person with whom, in spite of myself, in spite of you, I felt what now it means nothing to call pleasure; nothing, nothing. . . . Her face for a moment became younger and maliciously amused. You can go, she told this poor shadow of a shadow, standing fingering its tie: you were never here, in this room. Why try to creep in now? Be off—*shoo* . . .

Easy to be rid of him, too easy, since except for the few weeks when he made her unhappy he had scarcely existed. But there were others—those she had no right to send away. This was their house as much as hers, more than hers. She could not turn her back. She was forced to live with them. And now that she could not count on Robert to take her part against them. . . .

How many times, how many nights, had she hesitated on the landing outside the door of a bedroom, listening. The child had his night-light, of course, but there were some nights when it did not reassure him, the feeble little flame threw grotesque shadows on the walls, the furniture in the room muttered, stretched itself and made its old joints crack, and then he sat up in bed, crying, until she heard and came to him. "Little stupid, my little idiot, what's the matter? See, I'm here. I haven't left you, you needn't be afraid. No, no, Babba, no. Be quiet. . . ." His desolate grief was more than she could bear. He stood beside the table, crying, telling her over and over that he had lost all his things, his clothes, everything. "No, it's not true," she told him, with anguish. And in the same choking breath thought: But of course he has nothing, how could he have kept anything, he's dead. . . . It was no use. She closed her ears against this voice, weightless and without an echo. "I won't remember you. I won't. I did all I could for you, I made no difference between you and Robert. But you. . . ."

This, she thought coldly, must be settled. Robert, my darling, tell him I was right to insist on punishing him, tell him. . . . Her son did not answer and made no sign that he approved.

It would never be settled—as long as she lived. She knew it.

Only one person would be, perhaps, of her hard mind. Only Daniel Monnerie. . . . In the blackest night she could find her way to that part of the embanked wall where, in the warmth and soft darkness of a June night, she had waited, waited, expecting him to join her. She must, she told herself—now, it was only words—she must have stood there longing, demanding, asking, as secretly as the Loire asks the sea to fill it. At last he had come to her from the house—and talked wilful nonsense. . . . It was then, after that night, that she drew round her, as defense and as the meaning of her life, the copper pans in Amélie's kitchen, the wide shallow earthen bowls on the shelves of the dairy, bunches of herbs drying in an attic, children's shirts, the piles of bleached linen. If she had got for herself peace and room to breathe, it was from these, only from these. And is it my fault, she thought with sudden passion, that one day all this was laid waste round me? . . . As she watched it, Daniel's face changed, its look of indifference and contempt weakening to pity.

"Keep your pity," she said quietly, "keep it, I don't want it, don't need it. Yes, yes, I'm alone now. But I'm content. I wanted the guilty to be punished. You have been punished—you and François. I have no one, but I have seen justice done: I have no one, but I have peace."

At once, as if only by speaking the words aloud she had made them come at least partly true, she felt lighter and easier. Outside, at the other side of the closed shutters, there was a rising chatter of birds, like country fiddles tuning up; a dog barked loudly; from somewhere along the bank of the river a man shouted and another answered, their voices thrown across and back like an echo—really an echo, since they were the Duvosquel father and son, she knew them, and they spoke in the same lazy good-humoured drawling voice.

But the whole of life is only a very little more than echoes, than an older face reflected in a young one. She reminded herself of this, moved her hands, smiled her light, dazzlingly light, smile. . . . And if now most of those I hear, and see, come from the other side of life, at least I shall not spend my evenings quite alone. . . .

For less than a moment she thought: What did any of them give me, except mockery, unfaithfulness, indifference, neglect? . . . Quicker than a knife a second thought slipped through the crack this opened. She threw her arms up. Too late. . . . Why had Jean gone off without speaking, without a word? . . . Oh, if he comes back, she thought, bitterly, in blind bitter grief, if he comes back, at least I can force him to talk, to explain . . . Or would he say nothing, and she, too old, or too intimidated to ask questions, sit facing him across a table, year after year, for years, talking only about the vines, village gossip, the heat, the rain?

"Marie Regnier!"

She called herself to order sharply. Didn't I tell you not to think about him and his unkindness? . . . A reply sprang in her clear from—from what? It suffocated her—forcing its way through layer on layer of reserves, pride, anger. . . . I don't want anything given to me. No gifts. No charity. In the past, yes—but not now. The kindness, the loyalty, the love, one succeeds in getting for oneself, are worth nothing. Nothing. Nothing is important except to become. To die filled with what one has become, what one *is*. . . . She thought: I shall die filled with this house, with the walls, the herbs, the mended linen, the waxed parquet of floors. Nothing else matters. This is the body of my life, the rest only its garments; this is its poverty, the rest is superfluous; this is the only loyalty, the only thing hard enough to last. There was a time when I imagined that I was marked out to have an interesting brilliant life, to be admired and talked of, I know now that what I was marked for is silence and obscurity, an obscure life in this house, unending work for which I have not been thanked, and shan't be. I want nothing else.

With piercing joy she thought: I shall founder in this house and this valley. For two thousand years men and women have used themselves on the valley, and who remembers them? Yet not one of them was wasted.

A phrase which had been sleeping hidden in a recess of her mind, like the big hawk-moth in the curtains, chose this moment to come out and show itself. It was one of Father Baussan's: she saw his immense blazing eyes, negroid

244 THE HIDDEN RIVER

nostrils and mouth, and crippled body. No, I shall never like him, she thought. But what had he said the last time he sat in this room, offending and boring her with his clumsiness? That love which expects to be returned is not love. . . . Something else—prayer is not prayer unless there is no answer, only silence. Like the silence in her after Robert had been killed. Abruptly she remembered—was it a prayer, or part of one of the endless conversations with her God carried on by the only saint she admired?—*Think, Lord, that we don't understand ourselves, and we don't know what we want, and we push out of our reach what we long for. . . .*

I ought to go back to bed, she thought. No, it's too late. . . . The sun, she knew, must already be up. She had only to fold back a shutter to let in a light more smooth and nonchalant than the Loire itself.

Jean is somewhere in the light with his thoughts, she said to herself . . . Go where you like, she told him, without irony; at every turning you will find yourself here. As I shall be here—in the harsh February winds and floods, in the burning clear light of days like today, and when the thin autumn mists come down, and at that turn of the year when, as you children used to say, you've only to reach a hand up, the stars are so close. I shall be here. Probably, if you return, I shall have nothing to say to you. All I had to say will already have been said.

She moved: but instead of going towards the door her body took her to one of the windows. She opened the shutter a few inches, then widely; then opened all of them, letting into the room the valley, the Loire itself, solitude, and the light.